OPEN SEASON

A BREED THRILLER

CAMERON CURTIS

To Rudyard Kipling and Danny Dravot

CONTENTS

MAPS

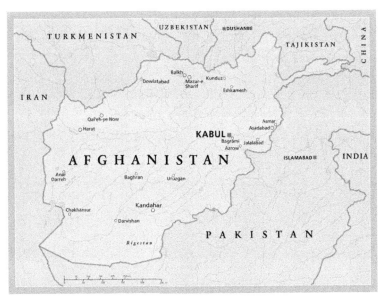

Afghanistan and Surrounding Region

Afghanistan Northeastern Provinces

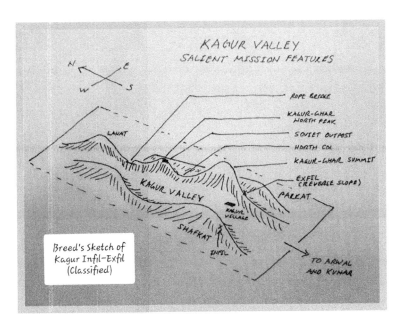

Kagur Valley

FOREWORD

I wanted to write a novel that was a war story, a thriller, and a love story. Most of all, the plot had to be a chase. What if Taliban hunted an American unit sent to rescue a captured officer and a woman soldier? An unrelenting hunt over an unforgiving obstacle course. The story had to be contemporary, hence the war in Afghanistan. Not the arid desert of the south. The high mountains of the northeast—the Hindu Kush.

Those mountains and the hardy mountain men who inhabit them have beaten would-be conquerors since Alexander the Great. He told his mother about that land. Easy to get in, not so easy to get out. The Afghans beat him. Then they beat the Moguls, the British (three times over), and the Soviets. Now they are fighting America and a multinational coalition to a standstill.

The action takes place where Afghanistan is bordered by Pakistan and China to the east, and Tajikistan to the north.

The three northeastern provinces of Afghanistan are Badakhshan, Nuristan, and Kunar. They are stacked one on top of the other with Kunar at the base. The capital, Kabul, lies a hundred miles west of Kunar. To the east, Kunar is bordered by Pakistan.

A reader of Rudyard Kipling's *The Man Who Would Be King* will be familiar with Kafiristan. Kafiristan did exist— it has been renamed Nuristan. It lies above Kunar.

Badakhshan is the northernmost of the three provinces. It is also the largest, butting up against Tajikistan to the north and Pakistan to the east. One other feature of Badakhshan is remarkable. Like a long panhandle, the Wakhan Corridor extends from Badakhshan, between Tajikistan and Pakistan, and reaches into China.

The harsh mountains of the Hindu Kush dominate these three provinces. Altitude varies from 3,000 to 25,000 feet. High mountain valleys, thousand-foot cliffs, hot days, and freezing nights. The Soviets learned armored forces could not secure that terrain. Only helicopters gave them an edge. An edge eliminated when America supplied the Mujahedeen with man-portable air defense missiles —MANPADs.

The terrain is so disorganized it defies description. In general, major rivers run north-south, but that is not always true. Major rivers are fed by numerous smaller ones and have multiple tributaries. Where the mountains run north-south, small rivers run east-west and feed larger rivers that flow north-south. Over the millennia, these rivers have cut the mountainsides into steep ridges.

Look at a map and search for Nangalam. You will find it on the Pech River, in Kunar. Over the years, American forces held Nangalam and used it as the hub of a network of forward operating bases and outposts in the Korengal and Waygal Valleys. In many ways, Nangalam is the base of a network of rivers and valleys extending north from Kunar.

The geographical features described are an accurate description of the northeast. In this wild country, I created my obstacle course. The land of *Open Season* is a closed abstraction, true to the spirit of Afghanistan, but designed to create a pressure-cooker battlefield. The terrain is so brutal the pace of a hunting party and their human quarry is measured in hours per mile rather than miles per hour.

The Kagur River is fictitious, as are the mountain and the valley for which it is named. It runs north-south through Badakhshan, straddling the boundary with Nuristan. The Arwal River is equally fictitious. In fact, it is the Kagur River, renamed as it continues further south into Kunar.

Surrounding the Kagur valley are three fictitious mountains of interest. Shafkat lies to the west, Kagur-Ghar to the east. North of Kagur-Ghar is Lanat. A fourth mountain, Parkat, lies east of Kagur-Ghar. The bridge from Kagur-Ghar to Lanat is my homage to Kipling and Danny Dravot.

The Kagur valley tapers as one approaches the origins of the river. In the northern reaches of Badakhshan, it provides access to Tajikistan, China, and Pakistan's Kashmir region.

Such is the obstacle course for *Open Season*. Battles around three mountains, long-range reconnaissance patrols to

Tajikistan and China, base camps hidden in northern Badakhshan. The Kagur and Arwal provide a highway from the north all the way to Nangalam.

Following the withdrawal of the Soviet Union, Afghanistan descended into a civil war. The area described was dominated by the Mujahedeen of the Northern Alliance. The remainder of Afghanistan was ruled by the Taliban. The character Zarek Najibullah is a Mujahedeen warlord. He has no love for the Taliban and Al-Qaeda.

The war in Afghanistan is America's longest war. There are many in America who would like to withdraw. There are also those who are passionately committed to maintaining a military presence. The politics of this dynamic provided motivation for the hunt. As America has drawn down its presence, other countries have taken on more of a role. These include Germany, Norway, Sweden, Hungary, and Turkey. These, and other countries, have not been named in *Open Season* because of my desire to maintain a tightly focused plot… not out of any lack of appreciation for those countries' considerable contributions.

I hope the reader will enjoy *Open Season* for what it is—a romantic adventure. One that could as easily have taken place in the era of The Great Game as during The War on Terror. The men and women who inhabit such tales are always the same. Characters of energy, courage, and intense passion. It is my hope that this will never change.

Cameron Curtis
May, 2021

1

EXECUTIVE PROTECTION

Bukidnon, Philippines
A Month Earlier

L ife is good.
  I open the front door of the plantation house
  and step onto the wide colonial veranda. The early
morning air is warm, with a hint of stifling heat and
humidity to come. I wear khaki trousers, Oakley desert
boots, and a white short-sleeved dress shirt. Over the dress
shirt, I wear a plate carrier. The level three body armor will
stop assault rifle bullets. My M4 carbine is slung over my
right shoulder. Four spare magazines are stuffed in the
vest's cargo pockets.

The warm breeze ruffles my hair and the collar of my
shirt. The air is laced with the sweet scent of pineapples.
Around the house, the crop stretches over hundreds of
acres. A quarter mile in the distance squat the greenhouses
and nurseries of Delos Foods. The administrative and operational buildings of a global food corporation.

"Hi, Mr Breed." Chrissie Garcia is the daughter of the Delos Foods' president and CEO. She's fifteen years old, a freshman at Brent International School, Manila. Home for Easter break. Her family stayed at the plantation over Christmas. Long enough for the kid to develop a crush on me. She's awkward and too shy to flirt, but the signs are all there. I treat her kindly.

"Hi, Chrissie. Ready to go?"

"I've been ready for hours. Here, I made you something for the trip." The girl hands me a big coffee thermos.

The container rattles. The sound of ice cubes. "What's this?"

"Iced tea," Chrissie smiles. She holds my eyes, tries to convey sentiment with the gesture.

"Thanks, Chrissie. I appreciate it."

The voice that interrupts us is confident and hearty. "Breed. All set?"

Juan "Johnny" Garcia, president and CEO of Delos Philippines. Average height and build, impeccably groomed. Khaki trousers and a white dress shirt, open at the collar. A man in control.

"Good to go, Mr Garcia."

"We fly out of Manila at three o'clock," Garcia says. He gives me a sharp look. "I don't trust these island connector flights to get us there on time."

I say nothing. The CEO should have left the island yesterday. Like most top executives, his job came first.

"Two weeks in LA," he says. "Chrissie shouldn't have to spend Easter vacation alone on this island."

Garcia doesn't want his daughter on the island at all. Threats have been made against expatriate executives and their families.

Three white Suburban SUVs are parked in the gravel

drive. The five other men in the Long Rifle Consultants Inc. detail prepare to mount their vehicles. Although dressed casually, all are unmistakably ex-military. They carry sidearms in open holsters, and M4 carbines slung low across their plate carriers.

I step off the porch and walk Garcia and his daughter to the middle Suburban. "Hop in," I tell them. "We'll roll in five minutes."

Chrissie gets in the back seat and Garcia piles in after her. I grasp the handle of the heavy bulletproof door, and make sure all his body parts are inside the vehicle. Principals have had bones crushed by careless bodyguards. The hinges have been reinforced to carry the armor's extra weight. I slam the door.

Kevin Carmichael gets behind the wheel. Parks his M4 between his left leg and the door. The SUV is armored, but it's a good habit. In a normal vehicle, the rifle provides a bit more protection against bullets. For me, there is a more important consideration—if I open the door, the rifle leaves the vehicle with me. I pile into the front passenger seat and park my M4 the same way. Set Chrissie's thermos of iced tea on the molding next to the bucket seat.

My short-range squad radio is in the left chest pocket of my plate carrier. I wear an earpiece and clip a small microphone to my lapel. I key the mike. "One-Five Delos from Delos Actual."

"One-Five Delos," Terry Posobiec responds. Poso is my number two security consultant. Like myself, he was once a member of 1st Special Forces Operational Detachment Delta, the army's elite counter-terrorist unit. He sits in the front passenger seat of the lead Suburban. "Go ahead, Actual."

"Are you good to go?"

"Affirmative."

Carmichael starts the Suburban's engine. Switches on the air conditioning.

"One-Niner Delos from Delos Actual."

"One-Niner Delos. Go ahead, Actual." Larry Keefe sits in the third SUV, our rear guard.

"Are *you* good to go."

"Affirmative."

I've gone through the radio protocol to test our comms. Time to contact our Philippine Army escort.

"Tiger Two, this is Delos Actual."

"Go ahead, Delos Actual."

It's First Lieutenant Reggie Bandonil, commander of the army company assigned to protect the Delos plantation. Today, one of his platoons will provide escort for our trip to the airport.

"Interrogative," I say. "Are you ready to meet on the highway?"

"Affirmative," Bandonil responds with a crisp tone. "Halt at the intersection, then follow our lead elements."

"Roger that, Tiger Two. Delos Actual out."

Bandonil, a graduate of the Philippine Military Academy, is a consummate professional. In command of the Delos detachment for the past year, he is gnashing his teeth. Bandonil has been saddled with poorly trained conscripts and old Humvees with inadequate armor. I have seen his men welding steel plates onto the sides of their vehicles.

I have a good relationship with Bandonil. The lieutenant and I have stayed up late at night discussing ways to shore up his company. Elite units of the Philippine Army and Marines get the best officers and men, the best equipment. An understrength company patrolling a pineapple plantation does not qualify.

"Okay, Poso," I say. "Let's hit the road."

Dieter Henke, driver of the lead SUV, pulls out of the driveway. Carmichael follows him, and Keefe slides into the number three slot. It's a two-hour drive from the Delos plantation to Laguindingan International Airport, or CGY. A quick hop to Manila, and the Garcias will board an international flight to Los Angeles.

Our little convoy leaves the plantation behind and drives to the main highway leading to Cagayan De Oro. Mindanao is a vast plateau, with mountainous country in the middle. The lush green slopes of Mount Kitanglad fill our rearview mirrors.

"Army's up ahead," Poso calls.

I squint. Four olive drab Humvees wait on the shoulder of the highway. Two on either side of the intersection. Bandonil will be in the second Humvee on the left. "Tiger Two, this is Delos Actual. Lead the way."

The two lead Humvees pull out, and Henke follows them. Once our SUVs are on the highway, the two trailing Humvees pull into the column behind Keefe.

Bandonil's Humvees are understrength and under-armed. A US Army platoon would have five Humvees, not four. The Humvees would carry Browning fifty-caliber machine guns on pintle mounts. The American platoon would have at least one Mark 19 automatic 40 mm grenade launcher. A machine gun that empties a drum magazine of grenades in a matter of seconds. The American platoon's firepower would dominate the field for a half-mile radius around the convoy.

The Philippine Army platoon's firepower is a disgrace. Only Bandonil's Humvee has a fifty caliber. The platoon has no automatic grenade launcher.

"They never make me feel as safe as you guys do," Johnny says.

"That's kind of you, Mr Garcia," I tell him. "They're not bad. And they follow pragmatic rules of engagement."

The Philippines has had a problem with its Muslim population since 1521. The famous explorer Ferdinand Magellan never actually circumnavigated the earth. He stopped for fresh water in the Philippines, and a local chief lopped his head off. More recently, Muslim militants in Mindanao conducted bombings, took over whole cities, and massacred Christian hostages. The president put the whole island under martial law. Heavy artillery and air strikes were used to annihilate insurgent positions.

It's easy to see how an international food company might get nervous. It's no fun trying to operate a business in a war zone. Hiring private security consultants protects their staff and keeps their executive insurance premiums down.

Highway is a generous term to describe this two-lane road. Traffic is moderate. Cars and light trucks. Traffic tends to move at the speed of the slowest vehicle on the road. You have to wait till there is no traffic coming the other way before you pass. If your vehicle is underpowered, or carrying four tons of extra armor and bulletproof glass, passing can make for entertaining moments. The good news is civilian vehicles make way for Bandonil's Humvees.

"Heads up, eyes open," I say into the mike. "We're approaching another town."

Stretches between towns are low-threat zones. You're doing fifty or sixty miles an hour on a well-maintained two-lane road. You're a fast-moving target. Towns are high-threat areas because you slow down. Insurgents hide among the local population. Rooftops are natural elevated positions from which they mount ambushes.

But—attacking inside a town risks civilian casualties. Unless the town is home to a Christian population, insurgents don't want civilians hurt. That means the riskiest areas are approaches to and exits from towns. Because vehicles are either slowing, or have yet to speed up. Because the civilian population is not at peak density.

Poso's voice crackles in my ear. "Actual. Kid on a bike, two o'clock."

My eyes swivel to the clock reference. A little girl, maybe twelve years old, sits on a bicycle. One leg on a pedal, the other providing support, she waits by the side of the road. Watches the convoy pass.

"Got her."

"Just watching the wheels," Poso says.

"Team, this is Actual. Kid on a bike, right side. Could be a spotter. Keefe, get your eyes on her."

I grip my M4 more tightly. It's locked and loaded. We pass the girl and slow as we enter the town.

Keefe is watching the girl in his rearview mirror.

"Actual." Keefe's voice is high. "Kid's got a phone. Repeat, kid's got a *phone*."

"Roger that." I flick the safety off my M4. "Team, this is Actual. You are cleared hot."

Garcia leans forward. "What's wrong, Breed?"

"Maybe nothing, Mr Garcia. Get Chrissie's head on the seat. Cover her with your body, like we showed you."

Bandonil should have heard the exchange.

"Tiger Two, this is Delos Actual."

"Go ahead, Delos Actual."

"There may have been a spotter back there."

"We saw her," Bandonil says. I can hear the strain in his voice.

My head is on a swivel, looking left and right, up and down. Rooftops, intersections. We're doing fifteen miles an hour, a sitting target. The road curves ahead of us. Soon, we'll be able to accelerate out of the town.

"Henke, Poso."

"Go ahead, Actual."

"Anything goes down, watch for escape routes. We are here to protect our principals, not fight insurgents."

"Copy."

I raise the muzzle of my M4, careful not to flag Carmichael. He has both hands on the wheel. As the driver, his job is to drive. We are sitting inside a tank, complete with bulletproof glass an inch and a half thick. Certified proof against bullets far more powerful than AK47 cartridges. Our own rifles are useless unless we open the windows or dismount. A last resort, but anything is possible.

There. An intersection, as we start to come free of the town's congestion. To our left, open fields. To the right, a gasoline station. At the end of a short street of cheap buildings and sari-sari stores. Set back twenty or thirty yards from the highway. A wide parking lot in front.

I watch a big five-ton truck pull away from the gas station. A surplus deuce-and-a-half, its flatbed loaded with sacks of cement. It rattles onto the road, gray dust shaking from the sacks. They are piled five high, supported by wooden rails.

An electric shiver races over my shoulders. "Tiger Two," I say.

Before I can get the warning out, the deuce-and-a-half surges into the middle of the intersection and stops in front of the lead Humvee. Too late, the army driver brakes. The Humvee crashes into the truck. Insurgents have hidden among the bags of cement. One of them raises an RPG to his shoulder and fires into the Humvee's windshield. A fireball engulfs the driver's compartment. The explosion blows the doors off and flings them twenty feet to either side. Screaming, soldiers tumble from the back of the vehicle. Flames consume their uniforms, lick their flesh. Other insurgents sit up, raise their automatic rifles, cut the troops down.

"Contact front," Poso snaps. "Shit."

Second in the column, Bandonil's Humvee rocks on its suspension. An orange ball of fire flares from its right side.

"Contact right," Poso says. "RPG."

"Tiger Two," I yell. Smoke billows from Bandonil's Humvee.

Behind us—another explosion.

I twist in my seat, look back to evaluate the situation. Bandonil's Humvee has been hit. So have the lead and trailing vehicles in the column. The point Humvee is jammed against the cement truck, engulfed in flames. Its occupants have been cremated.

A well-executed line ambush.

The insurgents have a security element in the cement truck, fixing our column in place. A second security element has destroyed our trailing Humvee. With our lead and trailing vehicles destroyed, we can neither drive forward nor reverse. We are stuck in the kill zone. Their assault element is dug into the shops on our right, thirty yards away. Lighting us up with automatic weapons.

Doctrine says we should plaster those buildings with grenades, assault into the ambush.

But—we have no grenade launchers.

A Mark 19 could annihilate the insurgent assault element with a single drum of grenades. I curse the Philippine Army, which left Bandonil inadequately equipped.

I look at the fields to our left. Our SUVs could make a run for it. But we would be sitting ducks for RPGs. The uparmored Suburbans are designed to be proof against automatic weapons, hand grenades, and small land mines. They are *not* proof against anti-tank rockets.

My radio crackles. "Delos Actual, this is Tiger Two."

Bandonil's alive. I can't believe it. His Humvee is still smoking. The hillbilly armor worked.

"Go ahead, Tiger Two."

"I have called for support. We must hold for thirty mikes."

He can't be serious. We're on the X. If we stay here, we die.

Muzzle flashes twinkle along the line of buildings to our right. Bullets smack into the bulletproof glass inches from my face. I'm conscious of a keening from the back seat. Garcia is covering Chrissie with his body. The girl is crying.

Philippine Army troops run between our vehicles, looking for cover. Where the fuck are they going. Trying to pile into a ditch on the other side of the highway. Eyes wide and staring, one guy freezes in front of us.

Like a thunderbolt, an RPG strikes between my Suburban and Poso's. A bloom of fire swallows the soldier whole, leaps across the hood, and breaks against our windshield. Poso's SUV is obscured by a fountain of asphalt and the concussion rocks our vehicle. There is a sound like rain pelting the Chevy.

More Philippine Army troops spill from Bandonil's damaged Humvee and the one behind Keefe. Most of them take cover on the left-hand side of their vehicles. Return fire with their M16s. The fifty-caliber on Bandonil's Humvee is out of action.

Carmichael sits next to me. He grips the wheel, knuckles white. The side of his face glistens with sweat. "What do you want to do, chief?" he asks.

We can't run to the fields on our left—we'll be picked off by RPGs. We can't fire through the bulletproof glass of our armored vehicles.

I key my radio. "Tiger Two," I say. "Get someone on your fifty. Put fire on that cement truck."

It'll take a brave man to stand behind that fifty caliber. Sparks flicker over Bandonil's Humvee. The bullet strikes are accompanied by the maddening clang of metal on metal. Gunfights are loud. They are louder inside a steel vehicle.

Rockets sizzling, more RPGs streak toward us. Deadly, but inaccurate. Some RPGs are fin-stabilized, *most* are not. Rockets that are *not* stabilized have slanted exhaust vents to impart a ballistic spin to the projectile. I've seen those rockets fly straight and true. I've also seen them corkscrew out of control or tumble in flight. Seen them pitch over ninety degrees and plunge into the ground.

One of the RPGs passes under Poso's Suburban and explodes. The blast lifts the four-ton vehicle a foot off the road on an orange pillow of flame. Great gouts of asphalt, dirt and rock shoot from under the SUV.

"Jesus Christ," Carmichael breathes.

"We're okay." Poso's voice trembles. The SUV's reinforced floor is proof against most mines. Tires have been modified with a run-flat system of rigid rubber and Kevlar inserts. "Actual, we can *not* sit here."

A figure crawls from Bandonil's Humvee and grabs the

fifty-caliber. It's the lieutenant. He racks the charging
handle, opens fire on the insurgents in the back of the truck.
Half-inch slugs rip the bags of cement apart. The insurgents
are torn to pieces in clouds of dust.

We have to protect Garcia and Chrissie, but—we are
out of options.

There is no time to think. People do not *rise* to the
occasion under stress. They *fall* to the level of their training. We have spent our lives training for moments like this.

"Pull off the road," I tell Carmichael. "Attack those
buildings. Right now."

Carmichael needs no urging. He throws the Suburban
into gear, pulls off the road, and floors the gas. The SUV
accelerates toward the muzzle flashes. The bulletproof
windshield stars with the impact of AK47 rounds. With
each smack, the windshield becomes more opaque.

An insurgent in jeans and a white cotton shirt raises an
RPG7 to his shoulder. His image is distorted by the spider
web of cracks in the bulletproof glass. He fires and the
rocket streaks toward us. I brace myself for the explosion
that will end my life. The projectile passes over our heads.
A trail of light gray smoke streams behind the orange flame
of the rocket.

Carmichael plows into the insurgent. Crushes him with
a four-ton battering ram. The man's broken body is flung
into the shopfront of the building behind him. A second
later, the SUV crashes through the front wall and windows.
More insurgents armed with AK47s are scattered by the
impact.

Leaders lead.

I trust Poso and Keefe to follow us. Throw open my
door, dismount right. Carmichael dismounts left.

"Stay inside," I tell Garcia.

Dazed by the impact, an insurgent crawls on his hands and knees. Searches the rubble for his rifle. I present my M4, shoot him in the side of the head. His skin splits around the bullet hole. Blood, bone, and chunks of meat burst from the other side.

Another man gets to one knee. Raises his rifle. I shoot him twice in the face. The bridge of his nose disappears into a black cavity. He pitches backward, sprawls in the debris.

On either side, I hear the sound of engines racing, the crash of Poso's and Keefe's Suburbans plowing into adjacent storefronts. Carmichael is delivering precise aimed fire. Killing insurgents struggling to extricate themselves from the rubble.

The sound of gunfire tells you a lot about the people doing the shooting. Left and right, I hear panicked AK47 fire on full auto. Answered by the deliberate crack of M4s.

The sound of AK47 fire dies away.

Double-taps from M4s. We are executing survivors.

"Actual, this is One-Niner."

"Go ahead, One-Niner."

"Clear, right."

"Copy. One-Five, sitrep."

"One-Five," Poso acknowledges. "Clear, left."

"Copy, One-Five."

I look back at the road. Bandonil's Humvee is sagging, its side blackened and scarred by the RPG explosion. The lieutenant is covering the cement truck with the fifty-caliber. His men are searching the deuce-and-a-half for insurgents who might still be alive.

Flames and greasy black smoke pour from the first and last Humvees in the column. Philippine Army troops stand helpless, unable to pull the dead from the burning vehicles.

The fires are too hot. Grotesque sticks of charcoal sit in the drivers' compartments.

Carmichael and I step back to our Suburban. The armored side panels and drive-flat tires have been riddled. The hood has been scorched and covered with muck—a rain of blood and human remains. Right in front of us—a Philippine Army soldier hit by an RPG.

Not the nicest thing for a fifteen-year-old girl to see on her way to Easter vacation.

Or smell. The copper scent of blood, the stench of guts and burned flesh.

I open the rear passenger door of the SUV. Garcia is still covering Chrissie with his body. The girl is whimpering. The executive straightens. Chrissie stares at me with frightened eyes.

Can't think what to say. Nothing can shield the girl from this carnage.

I reach into the front cab for the thermos. Unscrew the cap, tip the ice-cold liquid down my throat. Hand the drink to Chrissie with an encouraging smile.

"You make good tea, Chrissie," I say. "Have some."

2

THE CONTRACT

Clark Air Base, Philippines
Monday, 0800

The Clark Marriott services travelers flying in and out of Clark International Airport and Clark Air Base. The two facilities were once Clark Field, America's largest Air Force base outside the continental United States. When the US withdrew from the Philippines in 1991, the northern half of the facility was turned into an international airport. The southern half is an air base run by the Philippine Air Force. The US retained landing rights.

I flew into the civil airport the night before, found myself already checked into the hotel. The front desk gave me a message from Dan Mercer, founder and CEO of Long Rifle Consultants Inc.

The room smelled clean and fresh. I dropped my duffel on the carpet, stripped to my skivvies, and went straight to bed. I was to have breakfast at the hotel restaurant, bright and early. I would be met by a representative of Long Rifle.

The hotel is comfortable, air-conditioned. I step out of the elevator. Jeans, desert boots, and a loose cotton shirt. The restaurant is quiet, with a long bank of picture windows overlooking the lush fields and distant mountains of Luzon. Mount Pinatubo's perfect cone dominates the western view.

The waiter is smartly dressed in black pants, and a white jacket with gold buttons. He has the light, milk-chocolate complexion of Malays who migrated to the Philippines two thousand years ago. "Good morning, Sir. How many?"

"Two."

No idea who to look for. I assume they'll know me on sight.

The waiter sweeps his arm expansively, ushers me to a table by the windows. I sit down, ask for a pot of coffee and a pitcher of orange juice. It would be rude to order breakfast before my host arrives.

My mystery host.

Dan refused to say anything more than I was to be offered a new job. Should I accept, the remaining term of my current contract would be bought out. He implied I would find the offer rewarding.

I enjoy duty in Mindanao. The local insurgents are active enough to keep my skills sharp. Plantation life is great. Not sure I want my contract bought out. Another year jogging around the plantation, sipping ice-cold pineapple juice, would suit me fine.

The coffee hits the spot. Black, with the flavor of a sweet bark. I stare out the window at Mount Pinatubo. Ten miles west, across a vast table of green fields. Long dormant, the volcano erupted in 1991. Fifteen thousand US

Air Force personnel and their families were forced to evacuate.

I look past the buffet. An attractive woman is speaking to the waiter. He gestures, and she strides toward me.

Shit.

Anya Stein. Dressed in her signature black pantsuit, slim and bladed. Dress shoes with half an inch of heel, polished glossy black. Designer shades pushed onto her crown. She has Harvard Law written all over her. Not a Long Rifle rep. Stein is CIA.

"Breed," she says. "Don't get up."

Stein's hair is soft, dark brown, shoulder-length. Her complexion is as pale as a New England winter. She sits across from me.

"What are you doing here, Stein?"

The woman waves the waiter away. Pours herself a cup of coffee. "Is this good? God knows I need it."

"It's the best," I tell her. "Made from coffee grown in the mountains. A species imported by the Spanish, five hundred years ago. Moroccan."

Stein stirs sugar and cream into her coffee. Sips carefully. "It *is* good."

"Come on, Stein." I lean back and my chair creaks. I'm an average guy. Average height, average looks, husky build. Not an ounce of fat on my frame, and muscle weighs more than fat.

The woman stares at me, collects her thoughts.

"You're the reason I'm here."

"Obviously."

Stein is thirty-five, looks younger. Ambitious as hell, she fights fires. If anything goes wrong, they'll hang her out to dry. She hasn't been caught out yet.

"I could have phoned you last night," she says, "but I

wanted to speak in person. I let you sleep while I sat in a C-17."

Not a hair out of place. I could cut myself on the creases in her suit.

"It's important. I get it."

"You are about to receive a job offer."

Oddly phrased. Nothing about this rendezvous is normal. Dan should have presented the job. Instead, Stein sits in front of me, implying the offer will be presented by someone else.

"Am I."

"Yes. Dan Mercer was briefed twelve hours ago. Dan said, of course Long Rifle was interested, but you were currently on contract. The man who made the offer said he would make it to you in person. He was confident you would accept."

"ALRIGHT. HOW ARE YOU INVOLVED?"

Stein shrugs. "I put the idea in his head."

"You're here to see me before he does."

"Yes." Stein shifts in her chair.

"Crude, Stein." I finish my coffee, pour myself another cup. "Not up to your usual standards."

"It's a complicated situation." Stein frowns. "I had to improvise."

"Of course. Tell me."

"Have you heard of Robyn Trainor?"

"Yes, I have."

Sergeant Robyn Trainor was a US Army Cultural Relations Team specialist. An interpreter, attached to patrols and special missions in Afghanistan. Eighteen months ago, Mujahedeen captured her in an ambush. US forces worked hard to find her. Delta and DEVGRU, the army and navy special operations units, were placed on high alert for a rescue attempt. The Mujahedeen moved her around. No opportunity presented itself. After a year, prospects of a rescue dimmed.

Stein gives me a satisfied look. "We negotiated her release."

"Negotiated. How?"

"Certain overtures were made. For the last six months, Colonel Robert Grissom has been meeting with the Mujahedeen who took her. She was freed two days ago."

"Great. What do you need me for?"

"You know how complicated Afghan politics is. She was captured by a band of brigands led by Zarek Najibullah. You've heard of him."

"Yes. He wants us out of the country, but he's not a rabid fanatic. A practical man."

"Indeed. He's mostly interested in smuggling opium north into Russia. Weapons and explosives south. Grissom negotiated Trainor's release. They were making their way back along the Kagur Valley. A group of Taliban, led by Abdul-Ali Shahzad, ambushed them. Wiped out the escort and took Trainor and Grissom."

The plot is thickening. I can see the mess Grissom and Trainor have landed in. The Taliban are a loose alliance of insurgents, brigands, and drug runners. They are frequently at each other's throats, but they are united in a desire to evict Americans from Afghanistan. Najibullah and Shahzad compete for control of the lucrative smuggling routes in the north. Routes that run across the mountain valleys and peaks of the Hindu Kush. The borders between Afghanistan, Pakistan, Tajikistan and China are lines on a map. Meaningless to the Taliban and Pashtun villagers.

Shahzad is a nasty character. His Taliban are spread the length of the border with Pakistan, frequently with embedded Al Qaeda units.

I squint at Stein. "Why are *you* so interested in an army sergeant?"

Heaven knows I'm not. Not enough to leave my cushy gig in Mindanao.

Stein stares at the volcano. Mount Pinatubo's perfect cone. Its peaceful slopes conceal incomprehensible violence.

"Grissom wasn't negotiating Trainor's release."

"Go on."

"Grissom was using Trainor as a cover. For six months, he was in and out of the Hindu Kush, negotiating a peace deal with Zarek Najibullah."

"Wait a minute." I straighten in my chair. "I read the news. We've been negotiating with Shahzad and the Eastern Taliban, not Najibullah. The Shahzad talks fell through."

Stein turns to me. "That's correct. The United States wants out of Afghanistan, period. We have fewer than five thousand troops in-country. Not enough to win, but enough to make a vulnerable target. We want out, but don't want to leave Al Qaeda with a functional refuge. We want to leave a balance of power between the Afghan national government and the Mujahedeen that keeps Al Qaeda at bay. Shahzad's assurances were not convincing."

"Grissom was your fallback plan. You used him to open a back-channel to Najibullah."

"You got it," Stein says. "Trainor was our excuse."

I shake my head. "How do you know Zarek didn't kidnap her to lure *you* into a negotiation?"

"I don't... He's crafty," Stein muses. "Zarek, huh. You on a first name basis with the old pirate?"

"Delta spent years trying to kill those warlords. He was the one who always found a move we didn't expect."

"He *is* good. And he's avoided entanglements with Al Qaeda."

"You struck a deal. Zarek wouldn't have let Trainor go otherwise."

"Yes." Stein smiles. "At the precise moment talks with Shahzad broke down."

"I assume Shahzad knows."

"Of course. That's why he took them."

"You want to mount a rescue."

Stein looks cynical. "General William Anthony wants *you* to rescue them."

The day is full of surprises.

I have known Lieutenant General William Anthony for twenty years. He was my first CO after I passed selection. Anthony is a man's man and a warrior's warrior. I'll follow him anywhere. His career, moribund prior to 9/11, took off like a rocket when the United States went into Afghanistan.

"He doesn't know you're here, does he?"

Stein has always been Machiavellian. "No, he doesn't."

"I don't like sneaking around behind the General's back."

"The negotiations are my responsibility. I'm not sure General Anthony is on board."

Stein wants to be Director before she's forty.

"Why wouldn't he be?"

"There's a strong neoconservative faction that transcends party affiliation. A lot of folks don't want us out of the Middle East. They don't like that our troop strength has shrunk from a hundred and fifty thousand to five thousand. The writing's been on the wall for a long time."

"General Anthony is a soldier. He may not always agree with civilian authority, but he follows orders. A man of his stature has nothing to prove."

Stein looks skeptical. "We had a council of war yesterday, agreed on a rescue operation. He had a team in mind. I suggested they bring someone who knows the Kagur blindfolded. There was only one correct answer."

I can see where this is going. "Surely more than one."

"Back in the day, fewer than half a dozen operators knew the Kagur well. None of them are currently in Afghanistan. Only one was within an eight-hour flight of Bagram. General Anthony arrived at the correct choice."

"Me."

"I studied the files of every man who could do the job. You went on long-range patrols into Tajikistan and China. Twice."

"Yes. I went through the Kagur twice. It nearly killed *me* twice."

"Two three-month patrols. The first into Tajikistan. The second into Pakistan—and penetrated China. Played hide-and-seek with the Chicom and Taliban. The Wakhan Corridor and Kashmir. You mapped every Pashtun village, every Taliban base camp, every camel and donkey trail used to run drugs and guns."

Stein does her homework. Three-month patrols. Six weeks out and six weeks back. Through the Kagur valley, but not *in* the valley. Three months humping over the mountains on either side. Along slopes that are sheer cliffs, over goat trails that are nothing more than rugged carpets of rock. Hot days, freezing nights and altitude. Physical exertion ten thousand feet above sea level saps the strength of the fittest soldier.

"Anthony passed the test." Stein continues without missing a beat. "He is a hands-on leader. He knows his men like family. Keeps track of them after they leave his command. Had he proposed anyone but you, I would have seen the choice as a red flag."

"You're barking up the wrong tree, Stein. I'd trust General Anthony with my life."

"If I blow this peace deal, they'll hang me naked from the Washington Monument." Stein looks grim. "Anthony will buy out your current contract. Pay you a hundred thousand dollars for three days work. You won't be in command, but otherwise a full member of the team."

"That's all there is to it?"

"I hope so." Stein finishes her coffee. "I have a bad feeling about this, Breed. That's why I want you there."

"How have you kept the General from knowing you're here?"

"I'm on my way back to Washington. There's a C-17 waiting for you at Clark Air Base. As far as Anthony is concerned, you have not been briefed. Dan Mercer has done nothing more than give you travel arrangements. When you arrive at Bagram, you will receive the briefing again, and Anthony will make the offer."

"What makes you so sure I'll take it?"

Stein's eyes search mine. "Do you feel you made a difference in Afghanistan, Breed?"

"Every discrete action in which I participated, contributed." I shift in my chair. "But I don't think I influenced the larger picture."

"You're a patriot, Breed. If you bring Grissom out, you'll end America's longest war."

3

RETURN TO BAGRAM

Bagram
Monday, 0530

S tein didn't have to work hard to sell me the job. My gig in Mindanao is cushy, but I want to see Afghanistan again. Truth is, I wouldn't have left if I didn't have to. It was the best job in the world. I was an elite Delta Force operator, doing what I'd wanted to do my entire life. Why would I leave?

A pretty girl once asked me, "What is the worst thing about war?"

Without thinking, I answered, "It ends."

The girl didn't go out with me again. I was too honest. Combat is the one situation in which I am fully present to the moment. Over a decision made in an instant, life and death hang in the balance. There is nothing like it.

· · ·

THERE ARE two major cities in Afghanistan. Located in the northeast, Kabul is the capital city. It is nestled in an inverted V between the Hindu Kush mountains to the north, and the Koh-i-Baba mountains to the west. Kandahar, the second city, lies to the south. It is the gateway to Helmand province, vast poppy fields, and the arid desert areas of the southwest.

Every arable acre of Helmand is devoted to poppies. No other crop produces sufficient profit margin for farmers to survive. Opium from Helmand is trafficked west to Iran, and north to Russia through the high mountain passes.

When the United States invaded Afghanistan after 9/11, commanders divided the battlefield into a northern zone and a southern zone. America fought in both zones, but the major effort was always north and east of Kabul. The heaviest fighting, the most dramatic operations, were in the mountains of the Hindu Kush.

There are two major airfields in Afghanistan. Kandahar Air Field services the southern sector. Bagram Air Field, near Kabul, services the north.

I'm flying into Bagram.

It's an eight-hour flight from Clark Air Base to Bagram. Travelling east to west, you gain time zones. If I leave at 0900 Philippine time, I should get there 0530 Afghan time. The vast cargo bay of a C-17 Globemaster is familiar. A lap of luxury Stein has arranged. For years, I've flown in worse. I find some cargo containers lashed to the deck in the middle of the bay. Throw my duffle on top, climb on.

The loadmaster yells at me. "You gonna be okay there, bud?"

"You got a spare cargo strap?"

"Yeah." The loadmaster calls to one of his men. "Airman. Get this guy a cargo strap."

The airman throws me a webbed cargo strap and secures it around the container. There could be turbulence around the mountains as we approach Bagram.

"That sort you out?"

"Yeah, dude. Wake me when we get there."

"You got it."

I rummage in my duffel, pull out a bed bag and inflate it. Lay it on the container top, roll my jacket into a pillow, and pop an Ambien.

Sleep has been elusive since I left the army. Ambien helps, but it's addictive. I was getting over it in the Philippines. Learning to sleep unaided. Flying in a C-17 to Bagram is a good reason to climb off the wagon.

I stuff a pair of wax plugs in my ears and throw myself on the bag. Pull the cargo strap over my chest and under my arms. The takeoff sequence is a dream. In minutes, I'm watching the movie in my mind.

IT WAS TWO YEARS AGO.

The screaming wouldn't stop.

High-pitched screams of agony and terror.

The village was in southern Afghanistan. There were mountains to the east, of course, but the local high ground consisted of foothills. Not as difficult to navigate as the mountainous country to the north. This was poppy country, where Afghanistan's major crop was grown.

Two of our men had been taken the day before. They were being held in the village, which was Taliban-controlled. My spotter and I had been ordered by Lieutenant Koenig to infil and locate the prisoners. Evaluate the chances of an escape.

Our Rules of Engagement forbade engaging unless we could do so with a reasonable probability of rescue.

We all knew the chances of rescue were slim. A rescue force could go in with armor, or it could go in by air. Probably both. The Taliban would be waiting. In the worst case, the prisoners would be killed immediately, the rescue force would take heavy losses, and the death of civilians would be inevitable. More of our men might be taken prisoner.

Two of us went in. Me with an M42 sniper rifle, and my spotter with an M4 to provide security. We knew what the consequences would be if we were caught. I intended to kill myself before I let that happen.

We climbed a low hill eight hundred yards from the village. Built our firing position.

That was when we first heard the screams.

"What the fuck are they doing?" Moe Tarback asked.

I didn't answer. Set my M42 on its bipod, took out a beanbag, and shoved it under the toe of the rifle's butt. The M42 was a modified .308 Remington 700 with a heavy barrel. A classic hunting rifle, one of the most accurate sniper weapons available. My first rifle, when I was twelve years old, was a Remington 700.

Tarback lay behind his spotting scope, and took out his gear. Laser rangefinder, Kestrel anemometer, a notebook of firing solutions for the M42.

With the scope at 3.6x, I scanned the village. We had a good angle, I could see the square clearly. The screams continued, spaced with pauses as though the torturers were drawing out the exercise.

"I can't tell where the screaming is coming from," I said.

We were prepared to displace if we could find a better firing position. This hill was good. I couldn't see elevated positions closer to the village. It was hard to imagine a better angle.

"Neither can I." Tarback squinted through the spotter scope. He positioned himself behind me and to my right. He wanted to have as clear a view as possible of my bullet trace.

There were villagers going about their chores in the streets. Taliban were mixed among them. Everyone in Afghanistan has a rifle, whether it's an AK47 or an old Lee Enfield. Rifles are the soul of an Afghan.

"Horizontal range 786," Tarback said. He had taken a reading with the laser rangefinder and inclinometer. Double-checked with the spotter scope reticle. The horizontal range to a target is the distance from the shooter if one measures flat to the earth. When firing from an elevated position, the line-of-sight range is always longer than the horizontal range. The horizontal range is the correct range to use in the firing solution.

The rifle was zeroed at four hundred yards. I moved my hand to the elevation turret and dialed in the adjustment.

From his position behind me, Tarback counted the click-stops and checked my work.

The wind was blowing dust from the streets.

How convenient.

"Wind 10, right-to-left, full value. Deflect three-point-six."

"Roger that."

I made no adjustment to the turrets. I knew the windage, and I would shift my crosshairs by the appropriate hold-off. Wind speed and direction changed frequently. I could move faster by cuffing the adjustments rather than dialing them in.

Slaughterhouse screams.

We lay there for hours. The blood-curdling screams continued. Spaced-out, carefully paced.

Screaming uses energy. A man can't sustain full-throated screams for more than a few minutes. If torturers continue their work without pausing, their victim becomes exhausted and ceases to function. Some nerves continue to conduct pain stimuli. Others are dulled. The torturer can't tell the difference because the victim can no longer make noise.

The Afghans know this. Their women are skilled in the art of torture. They use knives, they take their time. While the women work, the men watch or stand guard. In this case, there were a lot of armed Taliban in the village. They expected rescue to come from the air.

Tarback was shaken. "God almighty," he said. "How long has this been going on?"

"Day and a half," I murmured.

The screams must have lowered in pitch over the course of the day. I didn't notice because the process was gradual. The winding down of a life, like the running down of a clock.

"There," Tarback said.

"I see them."

Two women in *burqas* were dragging a man from one of the houses. A naked carcass of raw, bloody meat. The thing's mouth opened, the sound beyond description. I saw white eyes, white teeth. Ragged skin, black with dried blood, peeled from red skeletal muscles, white ribs, and the pink-white abdominal wall. Translucent, enclosing dark, violet bowel. Afghans cheered.

Ropes were tied around the man's wrists. They had used those ropes to bind him inside the house. Now they were using them to drag him into the square.

A third woman dragged a second carcass from the house. This man was silent.

"Jesus Christ," Tarback breathed. He keyed his mike. "One-Five Actual from One-Five Bravo."

"Go ahead, One-Five Bravo." Koenig's voice.

"Two, repeat two POWs dragged into square. Their skin's been taken off."

"Say again, One-Five Bravo."

"You heard me." Tarback was about to vomit.

Koenig made his decision. "One-Five Bravo, do *not* engage."

I made mine. "Update firing solution."

"Wind 10, right-to-left, three-quarters," Tarback said. "Deflect two-point-seven."

I did a mental calculation, shifted my hold-off. Took up the slack in the two-stage trigger.

Wondered if I was making a mistake.

Koenig yelled into the mike. "Breed. Do *not* engage."

I reached the moment of my natural respiratory pause and broke the shot.

The carcass jerked, the screaming stopped.

A cry rose from the Taliban and the villagers. I cycled the bolt, chambered another round.

Koenig knew I would not stop. "Goddamn you, Breed."

Fired.

One of the women dragging the prisoners went down, I hit her center mass and watched the *burqa* crumple like a hollow suit of clothes.

Cycled the bolt a third time.

Fired.

The second woman's head jerked. No blood. The explosion of her head was contained by her clothing.

Men pointed at our position. At eight hundred yards, we must have looked like specks to them.

"One-Five Actual," Tarback called. "Request immediate exfil. We are moving to LZ now."

Fired again. A miss. The third woman ran.

Cycled.

Fired.

The round caught the woman in the back, between her shoulders. She pitched forward and lay motionless.

I drew back the bolt. The magazine was empty. I fished in my pocket, took out a loose round, and loaded the rifle manually.

Tarback packed the spotter scope. "Let's go, Breed."

I took aim and put the last round into the second carcass. To make sure the man was dead.

Tarback grabbed my back plate and hauled me to my feet.

We ran like the devil was at our heels.

Because he was.

LIEUTENANT GENERAL WILLIAM ANTHONY didn't rise to greet me when I entered his office twenty-four hours later. The great man's adjutant, Colonel Tristan, gave me a dirty look. Left us alone and closed the door. I felt like I was standing in the presence of Caesar. There was no soldier I admired more.

My salute could have cut paper.

The general acknowledged my salute but turned his attention back to the files on his desk. "Stand easy, Breed."

"Yes, Sir." I clasped my hands behind my back and shifted to parade rest.

"We go back a long way, don't we?"

"Yes, Sir."

"I was your first CO. You are, quite simply, the best."

"You trained me, Sir."

General Anthony met my eyes. "Don't be modest, Breed. You have an aptitude. All I did was develop it. I was a lieutenant colonel when you passed selection. Our careers have progressed together. Afghanistan, Iraq, back to Afghanistan. It's been a long war."

The statement didn't call for a response. I said nothing.

"We have to stop this incident from spinning out of control."

"Sir."

The general raised his hand. "Wait, Breed. Hear me out."

I bit my tongue.

"You shot three Afghan women and two American POWs."

I had no spit.

"Your report is clear. The women flayed the POWs and were dragging the naked remains through the streets. Lab work indicates one of the men was dead when you put a bullet in him. Maybe you couldn't tell from eight hundred yards. The other was still alive, but unlikely to survive. The facts of the case are not in dispute. Lieutenant Koenig... the Officer in Charge... and your spotter, tell the same story."

"General, I have stipulated the contents of the report are accurate."

"Koenig ordered you not to engage. You violated the Rules of Engagement. The comms were recorded."

"Yes, sir."

"Breed, the administration wants me to convene a general court-martial."

I felt light-headed.

The general paused. Set his jaw. "As the convening authority, I have negotiated a solution with the administration. No one wants the embarrassment. The public can't handle how dirty this war is. The army will allow you to resign with an honorable discharge and a full pension. The matter will be suppressed. It will never be spoken of again. It did not happen."

"An Afghan legend, Sir."

The general shook his head. "You're already a legend, Breed. This matter is time sensitive. You can take half an hour to think about it in my outer office. I must have an answer before you leave the building."

"You can have my answer right now, Sir."

"I thought so."

I saluted, turned to leave.

"Breed."

Hand on the doorknob, I stopped. Turned to look at the general.

"I would have done the same."

I nodded. Jerked the door open and stepped out of the army.

"BAGRAM. EVERYBODY OUT."

The loadmaster slams the flat of his hand against the side of the container. The boom rattles my brain. With a groan, I raise myself on one elbow.

I pack my shit and hop off the container. The loading ramp has been lowered, but it's still dark outside. I walk onto the tarmac.

"Breed."

Warren Koenig. Shit.

"Koenig."

I don't like Koenig. Never did. It isn't that he's an asshole, he's just... mediocre. Bell curves are ubiquitous in nature. You find them everywhere. Elite units are no different. Once you weed out ninety-seven percent of applicants through selection, the remaining three percent describe a bell curve. It's inevitable. Captain Warren Koenig was not an apex performer *among* apex performers. On an operation, a man like Koenig can get you killed.

"General Anthony sent me to meet you. He'll see you at 0700. There will be a team briefing at 0800."

"Suits me."

"Wear this." Koenig hands me a civilian contractor ID card, laminated, with a metal clip.

"Old photo."

"It was on file. Let's get you to quarters. You have some time to collect your gear."

Koenig leads me to a Humvee and we pile in.

"Breed, that situation with the women. The ones you shot."

I haven't spoken to Koenig since I left the army. I do not want to speak about that incident now. "What about it?"

Koenig starts the engine. "I was doing my job. I followed the Rules of Engagement."

"I followed my conscience. Forget it."

"Alright. Some things have to be said."

Bagram's airstrip is twelve thousand feet long, enough to land the largest American and Russian transport aircraft. Masses of support buildings, hangars, and housing facilities form a small city arranged next to the runway.

Koenig parks the Humvee next to a block of cheap housing. Four rows of close-set, bungalow-style huts. Pretty standard for Bagram. Quarters are luck of the draw.

"Team's hand-picked," Koenig says. "Brought in from all over. We're in here. Women's quarters, the row across the street."

I dismount the vehicle and sling the duffel over my shoulder. Koenig leads me into one of the huts. Eight rooms and a toilet facility. The three rooms nearest the door are unoccupied.

"Take your pick," Koenig says. "Most of this block is empty. Lots of space since the drawdown. More coming free every day."

I grunt. Pick the spare room closest to the entrance, set my duffel on the floor. There are four racks in the room, two sets of top and bottom bunks. The unoccupied living space is the first tangible evidence I've seen of the troop drawdown. I've never seen such luxury.

"Nice, huh." Koenig grins. "Each of the rooms is built for four. The troop drawdown has been so sharp, we each get a private room with space left over."

"I'll take it."

"Come on, I'll introduce you to the team."

The first room on the left is still dark. The man inside is asleep. Koenig throws the door open and bangs the wall with his fist. "Hubble, roll out. Briefing at 0800."

The room on the right is occupied by a young sergeant in digital fatigues. The pixelated camouflage pattern has been determined through testing to provide concealment in a wide variety of environments. He wears a studious look, and plastic birth control glasses. Nerdy army-issue BCGs guaranteed to repel the opposite sex. Secured by a thin black elastic attached to the temple tips.

A homemade bookshelf has been shoved up against one wall. Plywood boards, nailed together. The books are field manuals, texts on electronics, chemistry, and explosives. A cardboard carton on the floor is packed with technical magazines.

"Ballard is our eighteen-echo," Koenig says. "This is Breed. Civilian contractor."

Eighteen-echo. A special forces communications sergeant. It is his job to manage our radio lifeline to base.

Ballard and I shake hands. Koenig leads me to the next pair of rooms.

"I haven't agreed to anything yet."

Koenig permits himself a thin smile. "The general is persuasive."

"I haven't seen him in a while."

"Sergeant Lopez here is a hard-ass," Koenig says. "Eighteen-delta, our medic. Lopez, this is Breed. Civilian contractor."

Lopez is in his late twenties. He's wearing digital camouflage pants and jump boots. Bare-chested and sweating, he sits on the edge of his bunk doing bicep curls. He grunts an acknowledgment. His attention seems fixed on making the tattoos ripple on his biceps and forearms. A fierce hawk has been tattooed across his pecs.

One wall of the room is decorated with a huge poster of a silver-and-gray, 1965 Shelby Cobra. A showpiece in pristine condition. Parked in a suburban driveway. "Lopez likes his cars," Koenig says.

The captain turns. The doorway to the right is open. A Eurasian man is sitting on the edge of his bunk, cleaning an M110 semi-automatic sniper rifle. He wears shoulder-length black hair under a faded green baseball cap. A cigarette dangles from his lips. He takes a long drag, exhales as we poke our heads into his room.

"I heard of you, Breed."

"What you hear?"

The man is Japanese, or Korean, with European blood. He puts the rifle down, takes the cigarette out of his mouth, and rises to shake my hand. "I'm Takigawa," he says. "I hear you are a bad-ass hunter. A legend."

A firm grip. He's six-one, solid muscle.

Koenig says, "You'll work together. Takigawa is our eighteen-bravo, the best sniper we have in-country."

Takigawa shrugs. "Not much action anymore."

"Takigawa is holding your gear," Koenig says. "I'll leave you for now, be back in an hour."

Koenig turns on his heel and leaves.

Takigawa puts the cigarette between his lips and lifts a big cardboard carton from one end of the room. Hands it to me. Digital camouflage, boots, plate carrier, chest rig, pistol belt. He leans into a closet and grabs a second M110. Suppressed. Exactly like his own.

"Let's get this stuff to your room," he says. "Get you kitted out. Captain tells me they had your sizes on file. Hope you're still in shape."

A year spent jogging, and sipping pineapple juice.

I hope so too.

4

THE GENERAL

Bagram
Monday, 0700 Local Time

L ieutenant General William Anthony's command is in the same corner of Bagram it was the day I left the army. The number of troops in-country has been drawn down, but the general's HQ has grown. It's a secure compound. A fenced-off three-story building inside the wire that protects Bagram. There are two gates, one for VIPs, another for day staff. Koenig drives us to the VIP gate.

The MPs at the gate check Koenig's ID and my civilian contractor badge. They log us in, wave us through. Koenig parks the vehicle, and we march into the building.

I recognize the old HQ. A huge concrete office block has been grafted to it. "I don't get it," I say to Koenig. "They're drawing down the troops, and the HQ space has tripled in size."

"That's right," Koenig says. "As conventional troop

strength is drawn down, we expand unconventional forces and air power. Most of our operations these days are air strikes. Tactical aircraft or UAVs. This building is devoted to UAV command and control."

"I thought we direct UAVs from California and Texas."

"We can, but it's more convenient to do it from the same time zone."

An elevator whisks us to the general's command suite on the third floor.

The pretty first lieutenant in the antechamber is exactly what I expect from the general. Attractive and toned, she looks like a storehouse of vigor. She'll be promoted to O-3, Captain, spend six months in this billet, and move on to another command. Make way for the next bright O-2 looking to test herself against the general's rigid standard.

The woman checks me out. She obviously knows Koenig and is not impressed. She studies my fresh digital camouflage, notes the absence of unit patches and badges of rank. Healthy, vigorous women are outnumbered by men at Bagram. Without embarrassment, the O-2 checks out my rank on the Man Buffet. The general will have to watch this one.

"Captain Koenig," she says, "who is this gentleman?"

"He *was* Chief Warrant Officer Breed," Koenig informs her. "Now a civilian consultant."

The O-2 lifts her phone. "General, Mr Breed is here."

She replaces the phone in its cradle and rises to usher me into the office. Her dress uniform is hand-tailored. Expensive woman, a West Pointer. Class ring on her right hand. Polished heels. Her thighs and calves are cut like she spends four hours a day doing CrossFit. The general must be a masochist.

I enter the inner sanctum and the O-2 closes the door

behind me. The temptation to salute is overpowering. I remind myself I am no longer part of the green machine.

"Sit down, Breed." The general is exactly as I remember him. "It's been a while."

Digital camouflage, three stars. The Old Man is in his fifties, lean and hard. His face is craggy, like the mountains of the Hindu Kush. He's standing in front of a picture window that overlooks the airstrip and a good part of the base. Two A-10 Warthog close-support aircraft accelerate down the runway, lift into the sky, and bank toward the mountains.

I sit in one of the hard-backed chairs that face the general's desk. Anthony remains standing, hands on his hips. He picks up where we left off years ago. Without interruption. The difference is I'm no longer a W-5. I'm no longer in the army.

A file sits in the precise geometric center of the desktop. The general flips it open. Spreads two eight-by-ten photographs on his desk. One of a man in his forties wearing the uniform of a full colonel. The other of a pretty girl in her twenties, wearing digital camouflage, the three stripes of a buck sergeant. The man looks like a senior executive at a Fortune 500 corporation. The sergeant is a girl next door.

"Principal One is Colonel Robert Grissom. Principal Two is Sergeant Robyn Trainor."

General Anthony paces. Gives me the same briefing Stein gave me at Clark. I compare the two briefings. Test and probe for differences. There are none. The two stories are consistent.

"I need you to bring Grissom out of the Hindu Kush." The general steps back to the picture windows. The particular mountains he is staring at are the Koh-i-Baba, but I forgive him. "There's no one left who knows that country like you."

"That was years ago, General."

"No one else has been on the ground that far north."

Stein is worried about General Anthony's commitment. Let's test him further.

"General, I've spent the last year lying on a beach. I'm not in shape for those mountains."

"You'll be finished in two days. We'll buy out your current contract and pay you a hundred thousand for two days work. That's over two hundred thousand dollars. Then you can lie on a beach."

"I could take your money, General. But I'd be a liability."

General Anthony leans on his desk, looks me in the eye. "You'll take the job, Breed. Not for the money."

"With all respect, Sir. I'm not thrilled with a country that wanted to court-martial me for doing my job."

"You're a patriot, Breed. You won't hold the mistakes of the last administration against the country."

I AGREE TO THE MISSION. The general and Stein think they have my number, but they're only half right. The mountains beckon. Their harsh beauty, the hot days and freezing nights, the crisp air at ten or twelve thousand feet. The challenge of natural danger combined with a vicious enemy is irresistible.

General Anthony leads me out of his office, past the O-2 with the worked-out body. She looks ready to devour us both. We stride down the hall and step into a big conference room. The blinds have been drawn and a projection screen has been lit on one wall. Koenig, Takigawa, Lopez, Ballard, and Hubble are seated around a long table.

A sixth man occupies a corner seat. Unlike the rest of us, he wears dress blues, and the insignia of a bird colonel. On the table in front of him sit a black leather folio, a notebook, and a Montblanc pen.

"I believe you know my adjutant, Colonel Tristan," the general says.

How could I forget the colonel. He walked me to Personnel the day I was discharged. Looked at me like I was a bug. He wears jump wings and a green beret, but he is not a Tier 1 operator. He's a staff officer, lapping at the general's heels.

Six faces around a table. An opportunity to take a closer look at the team I'll be working with. My first impressions are usually accurate. I see no reason to change them. Only Hubble escaped scrutiny at the barracks.

The last time I saw Hubble, he was buried in his rack. I have a better view now. Big guy, at least six-two. Late twenties. A boyish face, hardened by the job.

"I assume you have all met Mr Breed," General Anthony says. "Captain Koenig, the floor is yours."

The image of a high-level super-planner is a myth. Most missions are planned by the men who have been assigned to execute them. If I'm here to test General Anthony's commitment, Koenig is the first red flag I've seen. Koenig told me the team was hand-picked. I don't know any of the other men personally, so I can't comment. But—having served with Koenig on several missions, I *do* know he is not top-shelf. The choice of Koenig as mission commander does not reflect well on Anthony.

Maps and photographs have been spread on the table. Koenig manipulates a remote control, and an image from

Magellan Voyager fills the screen. Voyager is a popular software tool. It combines satellite photo imagery with GPS and map technology. Creates realistic 3D images of the Earth's surface. It covers everything from urban areas to the north pole. The software is available commercially. The difference between the commercial and military versions lies in the resolution achieved and the frequency of update. The difference is top secret.

The general and I take seats.

"Thank you, Sir." Koenig darkens the room and flicks on a laser pointer. "This is the theatre of operations. The mountains of the Hindu Kush, in the far north of Afghanistan. Turkmenistan here, Pakistan to the east. Here, the Wakhan Corridor, like a finger of Afghanistan, pokes into China."

Horrible terrain. It looks like a child crumpled a sheet of paper, opened it, and threw it onto a table. The surface is a disorganized mass of mountains and valleys, anywhere from seven thousand to twenty thousand feet. Most of the country there runs between ten and eighteen thousand feet.

Koenig clicks the remote. The image zooms in on a detail of four mountains. The peaks straddle a narrow river valley.

"This is our target area. Four mountains, but only three concern us." He flicks the remote and names are superimposed on the image.

Three mountains. One in the southwest, lower left corner of the group, one immediately to the east, and one at the northeast, upper right corner.

"The mountain at the lower left is Shafkat. The one to its right is Kagur-Ghar. The river and the valley are named after it. The one north of Kagur-Ghar is Lanat. Meteorology forecasts favorable weather for at least the next seventy-two hours. We have three helos, including gunship support, dedicated to the mission.

"The target is in the village of Kagur at the base of Kagur-Ghar. The plan is simple. Our main force, consisting of myself, Lopez, Breed, and Takigawa will be inserted at the western slope of Shafkat. Hubble and Ballard will be inserted on the eastern slope of Kagur-Ghar.

"The main force will make its way around Shafkat and observe the village by day. Early the next morning, that force will assault the village and rescue Colonel Grissom and Sergeant Trainor. They will use this trail to ascend Kagur-Ghar and make their way to Landing Zone One. LZ One is on the southeast face of Kagur-Ghar. Hubble and Ballard will man a blocking position from which they will ambush any pursuers. They will then fall back on LZ One where the whole team will be exfil'd."

Koenig takes a sip from a glass of water. Clicks the remote control. The screen is filled with a satellite image of a Pashtun village. Terraced eight levels high, set against the west face of Kagur-Ghar. A rocky escarpment leads to the river. Goatherds are leading a small flock across a wooden bridge to graze them on Shafkat's slopes.

"This is the village of Kagur," Koenig continues. "In Badakhshan, north of the Nuristan provincial boundary. Satellite imagery suggests our principals are being held in this house. This is the largest of three bridges joining the east and west banks. There are two smaller ones. One a mile south, another a mile north. Goatherds use the bridges to graze both sides of the river."

Click.

The screen shows a magnified photograph of a house on the lowermost level. Two men standing outside have been circled. The image shows their AK47s, turbans, and chest rigs.

"These sentries stand outside the house at night. Sometimes during the day. There are other sentries at higher levels, but they move around. The ones at the ground level always cover this house."

"How old is that photograph?" I ask.

"No more than twenty-four hours."

"Any photographs of the principals themselves?"

"Two days ago, they were spotted on the march, heading toward this village. Satellite photographs showed they were forced into the house. Nothing since."

"Enemy strength?"

"There is the local population. They are sympathetic to Taliban. We are certain this group belongs to Abdul-Ali Shahzad. Twenty or thirty were spotted on the trail. Shahzad has two hundred this side of the border."

"Where are they?"

"Up to two days ago, they were at Kagur village. Yesterday they moved out, headed north. We lost contact."

"Why did they move out?"

"Not sure. Intel suggests Zarek Najibullah is approaching from the north. Najibullah and Shahzad are at war."

I lean back in my chair, process the information. Search for weakness.

"Go over the assault plan," Anthony says.

"Yes, Sir." Koenig thumbs the remote and the image on screen is replaced by the image of the village. "The assault team will observe the village from the east slope of Shafkat the first night. It will then descend and approach the village at 0400 hours. Two snipers, Breed and Takigawa, will shoot from this phase line on the west bank of the river. A range of two hundred yards. They will take out the sentries with suppressed M110s and subsonic loads.

"Lopez and myself will cross the bridge and assault the house. When we have freed Grissom and Trainor, we will all climb the steps to the second terrace. We will then follow this goat trail to the tree line. Koenig traces a path on the mountainside with the laser pointer. Once there, we will navigate Kagur-Ghar and pass through Hubble and Ballard to LZ One for exfil."

General Anthony surveys the room. "Challenge?"

I say, "This plan has us infilling tomorrow morning, attacking the morning after. Shahzad's main body could return in that time."

"Unlikely," Koenig says, "if Shahzad is looking to take on Najibullah."

"That's a guess."

"If he returns, we abort. Try something else."

"I don't know," Takigawa says. "It seems *inefficient* for the captain and Lopez to attack through us. Breed and I will be closer. We should go right in. The captain and Lopez can provide cover."

"You're not equipped for CQB," Koenig says. "Those M110s are too big for the job."

Close Quarters Battle is shorthand for old-fashioned door-kicking.

"What are you carrying?" I ask.

"HK416s."

"Good CQB weapon," I observe. "But there's no way to suppress five-five-six. It's a supersonic round."

"What do you suggest," Anthony asks.

"Captain Koenig is correct," I say. "The M110 is not suitable for CQB. Takigawa and I will go in with silenced Mark 23s. Pistols are much more effective indoors. The captain and Lopez should cover us. HK416s are tailor-made for suppressive fire."

"I agree," Takigawa says.

"We will maintain IR light discipline," I tell Takigawa. "At close quarters, our NODs should be sufficient."

Infrared technology is commercially available. It is possible the enemy will have the ability to detect IR radiation projected by night sights. I would rather be cautious and rely on passive photomultipliers in Night Optical Devices—NODs.

There is a long silence.

"Do we agree?" General Anthony says. "We infil tomorrow morning before first light. The following morning, Breed and Takigawa will silence the sentries and conduct the assault. Captain Koenig and Lopez will provide cover. Hubble and Ballard will man the blocking position."

There is no disagreement.

"Alright, gentlemen." The general gets to his feet. "Let's arm up."

Koenig looks at me. "Looks like you have time to get some sleep."

"I slept on the plane," I tell him. Turn to Takigawa. "Let's collect our weapons. I need to zero my rifle."

"I'll show you the range," Takigawa says.

I will never go on a mission with weapons I have not tested myself.

5

INFIL

Shafkat
Tuesday, 0300

Our Black Hawk helicopter makes less noise than an office fan.

Few people realize it, but each blade on a helicopter's rotor assembly is a wing. The loud clatter of a helicopter is caused by each blade passing through the turbulence of the one in front of it. This gives helicopters their characteristic "egg-beater" or "chopper" sound.

Extensive work in wind tunnels and materials technology created streamlined, swept rotors. The turbulence of each blade was halved. More innovation reduced the exposure of each blade to the vortex of the one before it. The result was a virtuous circle. Twenty-first-century rotors that operated in whisper mode with no reduction in lift.

The technology is top secret. Only two such helicopters have been assigned to the theatre. If one of them goes down, nano-thermite explosives built into the airframe will melt the machine to a puddle.

Back in the day, we would infil after a series of phony drops. Our helo would go to one place and hover, move to another place and hover, and repeat the process half a dozen times to confuse the enemy. On one of those head-fakes, we would either land, or fast-rope to earth.

Operating in whisper mode, we fly directly to our insertion point.

The pilots fly blacked out, scanning the instruments and terrain through their NODs. In the back, we sit with two door gunners and a crew chief. Each of us carries his personal weapon and sidearm. Load-bearing gear includes a plate carrier, chest rig with spare magazines, and grenades in the side pockets. A short-range squad radio is carried in an upper left chest pocket. Two or three spare magazines sit in our rucks, with stripper clips of extra ammunition to reload empty magazines. Top it off with two quarts of water each, MREs, spare batteries, and Claymore mines. Each man's total load, including half-shell helmet and NODs, is about sixty pounds.

Takigawa and I carry less ammunition than the others. We are armed with M110 semi-automatic sniper rifles in 7.62 mm, the NATO equivalent of the venerable .308 Winchester cartridge. This ammunition is bigger and heavier than the 5.56 mm ammunition of the HK416s carried by the others. Each M110 magazine holds twenty rounds, while each HK416 magazine holds thirty. My chest rig carries six mags, while the others carry eight. It's the price Takigawa and I pay for our specialist sniper roles.

Takigawa and I each carry an extra ten-round magazine. These mags hold special subsonic loads for use with the M110 suppressors. A suppressed subsonic bullet will be virtually flash-free and silent. The only noise will be the sound of the rifle's action cycling.

The crew chief raises his right hand, fingers spread. "Five minutes."

I look to the front, past the pilots. The black bulk of Shafkat is rushing toward us. I drop my NODs and switch on. Tug my gloves tighter on my hands.

"Two minutes."

Takigawa and I will fast-rope from the left hand side of the Black Hawk. Koenig and Lopez will exit from the right. Hubble and Ballard will stay aboard and infil on the far side of Kagur-Ghar, where they will move to their blocking position.

My earpiece crackles. "Thirty seconds out."

The windscreen of the helicopter is black, filled by the side of the mountain. Our insertion point is nothing more than a rocky ledge on the western slope of Shafkat. The pilot hovers, swings the tail boom around to adjust the alignment of the fuselage. The crew chief kicks the ropes over the side. One rope left, one right. The cables snake twenty feet to the ground, whipping in the rotor blast.

"Go," the crew chief says.

I grab the rope with both gloved hands. Swing my weight out over the void, brace my feet against the edge of the compartment floor. I take a deep breath, kick, and lock my ankles around the rope. I slide down like a fireman on a pole. I hit the ground and step aside. Drop to one knee and unlimber my rifle.

The rotor blast envelopes me in a maelstrom of dust, twigs, and pine needles. Anything that is not embedded in earth, or anchored to rock, takes flight and whirls around me in the dark.

A quick look back. Koenig is down. Kneeling, he

provides security on the other flank. Takigawa and Lopez fast-rope onto the shelf. We turn and watch the crew chief haul up the ropes.

The Black Hawk turns in place, pitches nose-low, and flies away.

Four men, alone on the mountain.

WE KNEEL, motionless, facing the four points of the compass. We hold our rifles ready, scan the terrain with our NODs. The dust settles on the rock shelf. Koenig faces the mountainside, stares at a wall of rocks and trees. Takigawa and Lopez each face a curve of the mountain, one south, one north.

I stare out at magnificent blackness. Before me is a shallow valley, a mile and a half beneath our ledge. Beyond, a range of mountains stretches south-by-west, leading to the distant Koh-i-Baba, seventeen thousand feet high. Kabul lies out there, somewhere in the dark. Cradled by the inverted V formed by the Koh-i-Baba and our own Hindu Kush.

The sky is clear. An infinity of stars, dazzling under night vision. I'm hypnotized by the horizon. I raise my NODs for a better view. We are so high, I can see the curve of the Earth. I exhale, watch my breath fog in the cold.

Fifteen minutes pass. I hear a snap of fingers and turn. Koenig motions me to take point.

Fair enough.

None of the others has been this far north. In fact, the last time I passed this way, my route covered the eastern flank of Kagur-Ghar. That was a more direct route north, following the Kagur River valley to where it dog-legged east into Pakistan and the Wakhan Corridor.

But—I had been this way before. I had reconnoitered the village of Kagur, and *that* made me the expert. You develop a sixth sense on the ground that you don't get from studying satellite photographs and contour maps. You learn the texture of the ground under your boots, the smell of the forest, the heat of the day and the chill of the night.

I get to my feet, sling my rifle across my chest, and lower my NODs. Set off into the darkness.

We need to hike three miles around the southern face of Shafkat. The bulk of the mountain screened our infil from eyes in the Kagur valley. The target village is on the other side of the river. I've chosen this route because it allows us to walk, Taliban-style, on the rocky slope itself. Properly executed, we'll reach our destination on the east face by dawn.

Improperly executed, one or more of us could break a leg or fall right off the damn mountain.

There's no point procrastinating. I step off the ledge and onto the slope. Test the footing with my boot. I take one step, then two. I've done this before. It gets easier.

Soon, I'm covering ground at a healthy pace, moving north-by-east, following the curve of Shafkat. My uniform steams from sweat wicking into the frigid air. I rest my right hand on the M110 slung across my chest. My left is free. I walk with a slight lean. Whenever my balance is in doubt, I reach out with my left hand and brace myself against the rock face.

Koenig follows me, then Takigawa. Lopez is last in line.

None of them have covered country like this before. They thought the slopes of the Korengal to the south were rough. Now they have something to write home about.

Half an hour into our march. Something is wrong. I

raise my right fist to halt the column. The mountainside in front of me has disappeared. NODs restrict your peripheral vision. I look left and right, up and down. At my feet, the mountainside slopes sharply into a deep ravine. It plunges a hundred and fifty feet before climbing the other side. It's like a piece of pie has been carved from the side of the mountain.

Koenig joins me, puts his hand on my shoulder. "What the fuck is it?"

"Ravine," I tell him.

The captain looks around me. "I can see that, goddamnit. What are we going to do about it?"

"Would you like to speak louder? I don't think they heard you in Kagur."

Koenig drops his voice to a hiss. "Don't fuck with me, Breed. We have three hours till dawn."

I'd factored ravines into my estimates when I planned the insertion. Forgot to tell Koenig. It's inevitable you will run into ravines, because they cannot always be discerned from satellite photographs and contour maps. Observed from above, they appear as black lines. Jagged shadows. When you run into them, you are brought to a halt because there is nothing in front of you but blackness.

"We have two choices, Captain."

"Get on with it."

"We can climb down and up the other side. Or, if the route is passable, we continue to follow the contour of the mountain. The ravine has to come to an end at some point on the face. Either way, we take a bit longer. Which would you like to try?"

"What do you recommend?"

"This chasm isn't particularly wide. It probably doesn't stretch too far into the face. I'd follow the contour of the mountain. If that route is impassable, we'll climb down, then back up."

"Okay, do it."

The route is passable.

Four times more, in the three miles we have to cover, we run into ravines. Each time, I follow the contour of the face. Each is a gamble, but I figure climbing down and back up is riskier. Koenig and the others have little experience in the mountains. Descending can be more dangerous than climbing, and there is no clear advantage with respect to effort.

Three hours later, off to the southeast, we find the mountain plunges into a narrow valley. A sinuous river, the Kagur, winds its way through the middle. Far in the distance, three lights twinkle. Goatherds. Lanterns in a shack, or small campfires.

I stretch my hand out, lean against a boulder. Wait for Koenig to catch me.

"What is it now?"

"That's the Kagur River. See that mountain across the way?"

Fifteen thousand feet high, snow-capped, the mountain dominates the terrain for miles. The summit is on the south peak, opposite our position. To the north, a long col, or saddle, stretches until it rises to a second peak of ten thousand feet. The north peak slopes onto a long ridge that plunges into a chasm. The pair of peaks and the north col look like the back of a sleeping dragon. Beyond, another tall mountain.

"Hard to miss," Koenig says.

"That's Kagur-Ghar. The summit is too hostile any time of year. Over there, at the end of the saddle, is the north peak. It's dark, but if you look with NODs, you can make out the village at the base of the south peak."

"Fuck me," Koenig mutters. "It makes you feel... small."

"Beautiful, isn't it? So beautiful it can kill you. Hubble and Ballard are on the other side right now, making their way to the blocking position."

"We're almost there."

"Yes, and we don't want to be exposed on this slope when daylight breaks."

The slope below is too rocky to support many trees. Here and there, copses decorate the face. Patches of bushes. Higher on the mountainside, three hundred feet above us, is a proper forest. A band of trees, two tree lines. The lower tree line below which trees struggle. A traditional tree line much higher, where the wind and cold prevent trees from growing at all.

"Guess we should make for the forest," Koenig says.

He's learning.

"Yes. We have time. We'll take it slow."

I shouldn't be such an asshole to Koenig. It's just that I never liked him.

Admit it, Breed. You love being out here, where Koenig doesn't know his ass from his elbow. Where... you're coming back into your own.

We've been on this rock less than four hours, and already it's like I never left Afghanistan. I'm moving on the slope like a mountain man. My hips and shoulders rock gently with the swaying of my fifty-pound ruck, six pounds of ballistic plate, and ten pounds of sniper rifle. All in rhythm with my gait over the sharp rocks and loose shale.

Koenig and the others are in better shape than I, but

they're sucking shit. I've been pre-adapted to the harsh environment.

Joy sings in my blood as I climb the slope to the trees. My legs burn, but I shrug off the fatigue. Koenig gasps behind me, falls behind with every stride. I'll be nicer to him, but not yet.

I don't bother to look at my watch. The night sky tells me what I need to know. We're heading straight north. The sky above Kagur-Ghar is lightening. The stars above are sharp and bright, those hanging over the snow-clad summit are dimming.

The spot I've picked on the tree line provides the view I expected. I step into a cozy nook behind a big pine tree and look into the black valley. Scan the shiny worm of the river, the little bridge, and the dark shapes of houses in the village.

I lower myself and sit on a soft carpet of pine needles. Drink in the smell of sap, and early morning frost. Stretch my legs out.

Koenig, Takigawa, and Lopez join me. I pull my gloves tighter. Clouds of steam surround our sweating bodies, but exposed metal is ice-cold. Grasp a rifle with your bare hands, and your skin will lock tight, as though bound with glue. I set the butt of the M110 on the ground and lean on it, careful not to touch the barrel with my cheek.

We've arrived on schedule.

Dawn is an hour away.

I LEAN against the pine and allow myself to sleep. Everyone will want to catch their first glimpse of the target by daylight. I'm in no hurry. It'll be another pile of rocks.

When I wake, I find an ocean of fog has rolled in and

filled the valley. It's so thick it's risen almost to our position
on Shafkat. Only a snick of Kagur-Ghar's north peak is
visible. A quarter of the south summit peeps above the
blanket.

The sun has risen and hangs over the saddle that joins
the two peaks. The saddle itself is obscured by fog, and the
sun shines through the mist like an orange orb suspended in
space. A circle of light you can stare at without hurting
your eyes. I've awakened to one of the most beautiful
sights God ever put on this earth.

It's cold. Frost covers the pine needles and forest floor.
My uniform, wet with sweat an hour ago, has frozen and
frosted over so it crackles when I move. The air is sweet
with the smell of the pines.

I unclip the NODs from my helmet and squeeze them
into a pouch on the left side of my plate carrier.

"It's beautiful," Takigawa says.

"Yes, it is."

I like Takigawa. A tough, hardened warrior, he's
blessed with an innate Japanese appreciation for beauty. I
imagine him making origami birds, killing time in the
barracks.

Koenig's squad radio crackles. "Five-Five Actual, this
is Five-Five Kilo."

"Go ahead, Five-Five Kilo."

Ballard's voice. "We are preparing to move to blocking
position."

The pair were landed on the east slope of Kagur-Ghar.
It made sense for them to wait for daylight before plunging
into the forest.

"Copy that," Koenig says. "You've got time."

"Actual. We have eyes on six Talis moving north-by-
east on Parkat."

The hairs stand up on the back of my neck.

"Have they spotted you?" Koenig sounds anxious.

"Negative, Actual. Looks like a patrol, moving away."

Koenig looks at me. I shrug.

"Advance to your blocking position," he tells Ballard.

"Five-Five Kilo, copy. Moving now."

I twist the cap off my canteen and drink deeply. When I'm done I open my pack and take out a pair of compact Leitz 16 x 35 binoculars. I loop their strap over my neck and settle back. Wait for the fog to clear.

THE SUN on my face wakes me. The fog has burned off, and we have a clear view of the village. Takigawa has taken out a powerful spotting scope and is studying the ground. To keep sunlight from glinting off the front element, he's deployed a honeycomb lens shade.

I ask him what he thinks.

"It's what we expected," Takigawa tells me. "Nice to see the village and battlefield for real."

He's right. All the maps and satellite imagery in the world can't beat eyes on the ground. I rise to my feet, grunt and stretch. Deploy my own lens shades, and lift the binoculars to my eyes. Glass the village.

It's not large, as Pashtun villages go. Maybe forty houses, distributed across nine levels and eight terraces. It climbs the mountainside, like those perch villages you find in the south of France or Italy. The houses are gray and brown, separated from the river by twenty yards of rocky escarpment. A wooden bridge has been flung across the river to provide villagers and goatherds access to the west bank.

Each level is between four and seven houses wide.

Stone steps rise along the sides of the village. Steep stair-cases like those found in Montmartre in Paris. These are narrow, two feet wide, with landings at each level. The houses are built on the terraces, with paths in front. Walking on a terrace, one can step off the path right onto the roof of the house on the level below.

Crucially, two long sets of steps, one on either side, lead up the side of the mountain and away from the village. These steps lead to goat trails. The goat trails are barely visible, but they each run another hundred and fifty feet to the tree line. There, they disappear into the forest.

"You know the sixty-four-thousand-dollar question, don't you."

Takigawa grins. "Are Grissom and Trainor held in the house we think."

"Exactly. The other day, satellite photos showed them entering together. We don't know if they have been moved."

I focus the binoculars on the lowest level. Third house from the left. I adjust the diopter.

"No guards," Takigawa observes.

On the satellite photos, we had seen what we thought to be sentries in front of the third house.

"Damn. No sign at all?"

"There are sentries on the riverbank. And another pair on the high terraces. General security. They aren't dedicated to any house in particular."

"We sit all day if we have to. If we don't see anything come nightfall, we'll have a decision to make."

Hours pass. Koenig and Lopez sleep. Takigawa and I take turns at the scopes.

"Breed."

I jerk myself alert. Raise the binoculars. A slight figure

in American digital camouflage has stepped from the third house and is walking toward the river. The figure's head is swathed in a dark headscarf and veil. It's a woman, carrying a plastic bucket with a wire handle.

"Trainor," Takigawa says.

"I'd bet on it."

A Talib carrying an AK47 follows the girl. She goes to the river, fills the bucket, and carries it to the house. The pair disappear inside.

"Confirmed." Takigawa lifts his eye from the spotting scope and leans back, propping himself on his elbow.

"I'll feel better if we can confirm Grissom is in the same house."

"We may not get that confirmation," Takigawa says.

"It would be nice if we did."

"He's got to take a leak sometime."

"So does she. The communal toilets are out back."

"Fuck."

We're not planning to descend the mountain before 0300 hours. I'll wait all day and night. Nice to rescue Trainor, but...

Grissom is the mission.

KOENIG SQUATS on his haunches next to me. "What's the story, Breed?"

I lie prone behind Takigawa's spotting scope. We've attached a clip-on photomultiplier tube to its front element. It's 2300 hours, and I'm still watching the house. Takigawa is preparing his M110. He's loaded a magazine with subsonic rounds and clipped an AN/PVS-30 photomultiplier to his 3.6x-18x daylight optic.

"The girl's in the third house from the left." I speak

without moving my eye from the scope. "We cannot confirm Grissom is in the same house."

"He's *got* to be in the same house."

"They could be holding him somewhere else, out of prudence. They could be holding him somewhere else to torture him. They could be holding him somewhere else to keep him from speaking with the girl. He could be dead and buried. There are any number of possibilities."

"What do you propose we do, Breed?" Koenig sounds ready to burst with frustration. "Wait another day?"

"That's your decision, Captain."

Takigawa sets his rifle aside, takes out his Mark 23 .45-caliber pistol. Clips on a silencer. The .45 ACP round is subsonic. The Mark 23 is silent except for the sound of its action. If you're prepared to operate with a single-action weapon, our pistols are equipped with slide-locks. Slide-locks prevent the actions from cycling altogether. The result—totally silent pistols that need to be cycled by hand.

"Goddamnit." Koenig rises, paces with his hands on his hips. "Why *not* wait another day?"

"We don't know what Shahzad's main body is doing. All we know is they moved north yesterday. They could show up on our doorstep at any time."

"We should abort."

"That's an option," I tell him. "But they might kill both Trainor and Grissom. Without our having made an effort. We might have saved at least one of them. General Anthony will have a lot to answer for."

A twinkle in his eye, Takigawa glances at me.

"Of course," I add, "you could call General Anthony. The buck stops with him."

I lift my eye from the spotting scope. Koenig is so

worked up, I do a double take. He is an average officer, but I have never seen such a case of decision-lock under stress.

"What do *you* recommend?" The captain is quivering.

I smile. "There remains a ninety percent probability Grissom and Trainor are being held in the same location. We should go in as planned."

6

THE RESCUE

Kagur-Ghar
Wednesday, 0400

W e descend Shafkat like death's shadow. Followed by Takigawa, Koenig, and Lopez, I lead the way. It's slow going. The difficult terrain looks ghastly in the glow of my NODs.

Takigawa and I carry M110s, slung across our chests. Our daylight 3.6x-18x scopes have been equipped with powerful photomultipliers. By starlight, at a thousand yards, we can drop a man with a single shot.

Behind us, Koenig and Lopez hold their HK416s low ready. Their job is to provide cover.

At eight thousand feet, there is no light pollution. I flip my NODs out of the way, and scan the terrain with naked eyes. The village is dark against the black bulk of the mountain.

I stop at the edge of the tree line. Drop to one knee, hand-signal the others to do the same.

Prone on the rocks, I unlimber the M110 and open its bipod. Takigawa lies to my right and does the same.

The night is still. The only sound is the whisper of water flowing under the little wooden bridge. Kagur village looks like a house of cards stacked against the side of the mountain. I pick out the façade of our target. It sits at the lowermost tier of buildings, in the center of the village. The front of the house is built from gray stones, each a foot across. They're piled high, stacked like pancakes and braced with heavy beams. The structure looks as formidable as a Scottish castle.

To our left, at the edge of the village, are the stone stairs that lead onto Kagur-Ghar. A goat trail rises toward the tree line. The mountainside is so steep, the steps and trails are cut in dizzy switchbacks.

I sweep my gaze back to the target. A sentry squats to one side of the big wooden door. His back and AK47 rest against the wall of the house. Ten feet away, a second man stands with his rifle over his shoulder. I signal Takigawa to take the standing man.

We turn on our AN/PVS-30 photomultipliers. At a hundred and fifty yards, I dial the scope to 5x and zoom in on the squatting figure. His chin has been lowered to his knees. He's asleep, trusting his friend to keep him safe. In the magic spell cast by the scope, the stone wall glows green. The man's turban is washed white.

I dial back to 3.6x magnification. A wider field of view, improved situational awareness. The rounds in my magazine are subsonic loads. They will drop faster than standard 7.62 ammunition, so I hold the crosshairs above my normal zero. My breathing normalizes, and I take up the slack in the trigger. At the moment of my natural respiratory pause, I break the shot.

There's a soft snap. The only sounds are the cycling of
the rifle's action, and a soft tinkle as the spent shell casing
rattles on stone. The muzzle flash is a brief flicker. Smaller
than the flick of a cigarette lighter, it dies in a heartbeat.

Simultaneously, Takigawa fires.

My bullet drills the crown of the squatting man's head.
He jerks, and a black flower blossoms against the wall
behind him. The standing man crumples like a sack of
grain.

Not a sound from the village. I sweep the scope over
the darkened houses. The structures climb higher and
higher on the mountain. Narrow footpaths crisscross the
slope. Each path is at the level of a doorway on one side
and a rooftop on the other. No other sentries reveal
themselves.

I turn off the photomultiplier, sling the rifle across my
back, and lower my NODs. Together, Takigawa and I draw
our Heckler & Koch Mark 23s, clip silencers onto their
muzzles, and get to our feet.

Koenig and Lopez step close.

Without a word, I turn and cross the bridge.

I STRIDE across the escarpment to the front of the house.

Long front windows have been shuttered. There is no
electricity in Badakhshan. Interiors are lit by open windows
during the day, lanterns at night. Not a glimmer of light
shows through cracks around the sills.

The door is Indian cedar, intricately carved by Pashtun
woodworkers. I can't see the hinges, the door must open
inwards. HK416s presented, Koenig and Lopez drop to
kneeling positions on the escarpment. Koenig nods to me.

No doorknob, no lock. It is a small village, and the

Wahabi penalty for theft is an effective deterrent. I push the
door open and enter the main room. Hold the Mark 23 at
compressed high ready. Two-handed grip, close to my
chest, thumbs parallel. Slightly hunched, I step forward.

There's a man lying on a mat at one side of the room.
He raises himself on one elbow and stares at me. Reaches
for an AK47 propped against the wall. I thrust the Mark
23 forward, thumbs pointed at him, and fire twice. In the
green light of the NODs, his face explodes in a black
stain.

NODs are terrible. They restrict your peripheral vision.
I swing my head and pistol right. There is a cold fireplace
against the other wall. Wooden shelves with household
supplies. Clear. Swing my head left. Another doorway,
wide open. No door, only a long curtain of woven cloth. In
the corner, a hole in the floor. An open staircase to the
house's lower chamber. Animals are kept there in the
winter.

I retract the Mark 23 to my chest, tuck my elbows.
Move toward the second room. I sense Takigawa moving in
behind me. The first man inside is always right, the second
man follows his lead. Takigawa will cover the hole in the
floor to make sure no one comes upstairs.

Gunfire erupts from outside. The sharp crack of
HK416s, the drumbeat of AK47s.

Fuck.

I sweep the curtain aside, thrust myself into the next
room. A wide bedroom, mud and stone walls. Shuttered
windows on my left. Glass. A luxury in the mountains.
Mats on the floor, boxes against the walls. A bearded man
in Pashtun clothing tries to rise from the floor, swinging a
rifle towards me. I present the Mark 23. Engage. Double-
tap, two in the chest. The man collapses, and I fire a third

shot into his head. The action cycles with a snap, the spent brass rattles on the floor.

More gunfire outside. Shouts.

Two figures sitting on mats, leaning against the wall. Sleeping?

I swing the NODs for a close look, cover them with the Mark 23.

"Let me see your hands."

"We can't." A girl's voice.

The figures stare at me. A man, and a strange, shrouded figure. Hands behind their backs, speaking English.

Grissom and Trainor.

"Breed." Takigawa remains in the main room, covering the stairs. "We have to get out of here."

I unclip the silencer, holster the Mark 23. Draw my knife from its scabbard, haul the man to his feet.

"You Grissom?"

"Yes. That's Sergeant Trainor."

I turn Grissom around, cut the leather cords that bind his hands. "Let's go," I tell him.

The colonel rushes to a large dark shape pushed against the far wall. A big wooden chest. Clothing has been piled on it. He grabs a field jacket and shrugs it on. Pulls a plate carrier over it.

I grab Trainor by the upper arm, yank her to her feet. Pull the headscarf from her head. Blond hair flares white in the NODs. I cut her bonds and sheath the knife.

Grissom throws her a field jacket, followed by a plate carrier.

"Grab that weapon." I point to the dead man's AK47. Unsling my M110.

The colonel holds the rifle low ready, fumbles with the safety. He's not familiar with the AK47.

Trainor pulls on her field jacket and fastens her plate carrier. Glares at me, snatches her headscarf from my grasp. "Breed," Takigawa barks. He brushes the curtain aside with one hand to clear the opening.

The sound of gunfire outside gets louder.

"Let's go." I push the girl into the living room. Grissom is already through. Takigawa has stepped to the front door. He's holstered his Mark 23 and unlimbered his rifle. Swapped the subsonic for a full mag of NATO ball. I do the same.

Takigawa drops to one knee and peeks around the front door. Raises his rifle and fires. The suppressor hides his muzzle flash, but I hear the distinctive supersonic crack of 7.62 mm rounds leaving the muzzle.

I look around the corner in the direction Takigawa is firing. My eyes sweep the village. The houses are dark, but muzzle flashes sparkle from rooftops and windows.

The Taliban aren't hitting anything. Takigawa's suppressor hides his muzzle flash and makes the sound of his gunshots difficult to locate. They guess he's at the target house, but can't be sure. He's switched his photomultiplier on. A soft green glow washes through the daylight scope, bathes the orbit of his right eye.

What are the Taliban shooting at?

My eyes sweep the riverbank, the bridge, the stone escarpment.

Nothing.

Koenig and Lopez are gone.

7

SAMS

Kagur-Ghar
Tuesday, 0430

K oenig and Lopez are gone.
I pan to the right, along the edge of the
village, the stone steps leading to our escape
route. High on the mountain, the goat trail.

There. Muzzle flashes flare from the top of the steps.
Koenig and Lopez have climbed to the terrace and are
laying a base of fire. Can't believe they got there so fast.

I push Trainor toward the stairs. The girl needs no
encouragement. She bolts and takes the steps two at a time,
fast as she can without falling. She hunches over, avoids
looking at the flashes that would destroy her night vision.
Arms outstretched, she stumbles repeatedly. Gets to her
feet, keeps climbing.

I slap Grissom's back, propel him after the girl. "Go."
Raise my rifle, engage a rooftop target. Fire. Watch the
Talib fall.

"Covering," Takigawa says.

I turn and follow Grissom. The stairs are easier for me with the NODs. Koenig and Lopez fire along the length of the terrace. They pin down the Taliban in the village. Trainor reaches the top, disappears into the darkness.

My thighs are burning with the effort of the climb. In the thin air, my breath comes in painful gasps.

A cry above me.

Grissom spins and crashes his shoulder against the steps. I lurch forward, grab him by the sleeve before he rolls off the side. No guard rail, the mountain plunges sixty feet to the escarpment. The colonel's rifle clatters into the darkness. Had he fallen backwards against me, he might have knocked us both off.

"I'm hit." Grissom's hands clutch the side of his head.

With the NODs, I examine the wound. It's like a patch of hair has been shaved from his scalp. Wet and black, blood glistens. White bone peeps from the wound. In shock, he stares at me.

"Breed!" It's Lopez. "Come on!"

Takigawa bumps into us from behind. "Go," he says. "I'll take care of him."

We reach the top. I can see the goat trail leading around the side of the mountain, toward the tree line. Trainor's wiry form scampers over the rocks. Pointed along the goat trail, she runs blind, no idea where she's going. I scramble after her.

Throw a glance over my shoulder. Takigawa grabs Grissom by his plate carrier. "You have to keep up," he says. "It's a quarter of a mile."

More like half a mile, but it wouldn't do to tell Grissom that. The colonel looks stronger on his feet. He nods and starts after me. I turn away, focus on the trail, and try to catch the girl.

"Trail" is a loose description of this path. The mountains of the Hindu Kush are full of tracks like this. Rough and uneven, studded with sharp rocks. I feel pointy stones through the soles of my boots. It's the easiest, most direct path from the terrace to the tree line. Worn by years of men and animals passing the same way. Two feet across at its widest, it plunges a hundred feet to the escarpment on my left. A boulder-strewn mountainside rises sharply to my right.

I move as quickly as I can, leaning slightly toward the cliff. If I stumble, the rock face will support my shoulder. I'm gaining on Trainor. She's tiring. The gradient and the thin air are getting to her.

Behind me, I hear Grissom and Takigawa gasping. The Delta's labored breathing sounds like a machine, a bellows sucking great gulps of air, fueling his straining muscles.

The colonel's breathing has turned into a high-pitched whine. Takigawa's breathing is regular and disciplined. Grissom's carries a hint of panic.

The crackle of rifle fire reaches a crescendo. At the bottom of the trail, Koenig and Lopez cut loose a volley of automatic fire. It's a reliable tactic, the only time Deltas use their rifles on full auto. In a tactical withdrawal, the last two men in the file cut loose a withering fusillade to cover the retreat.

Trainor and I reach the tree line at the same time. I don't quite tackle her, but I reach forward and grab her by the straps of her back plate. "Hold on," I gasp. "We'll regroup here."

No argument. The girl is exhausted. She collapses, head-down, on all fours. I turn back to the trail, unsling my

M110. Grissom and Takigawa are no more than thirty feet away. I tilt my head to the tactical radio tucked into my left chest pouch. Key the transmitter. "Five-Five Actual, this is Five-Five Sierra."

"Five-Five Actual," Koenig says. "Go ahead."

"In position to cover your withdrawal."

"Copy, Five-Five Sierra. Moving now."

I raise the M110 to my shoulder, brace myself against a tree. Raise my NODs and turn on the photomultiplier scope.

Takigawa and Grissom stumble into the tree line. Takigawa knows the way to the LZ. "Get going," I tell him. "Take them with you."

The three disappear into the forest. Below us, the sharp crack of HK416 gunfire dies completely. Through my scope, I watch Koenig and Lopez break contact and hurry to the goat trail.

The staccato drumbeat of AK47 fire continues from the village. The Talis don't know what they are shooting at. All they have to key on are the last muzzle flashes they saw from Koenig and Lopez. This is random, searching fire. Its sound rises and falls in waves as it sweeps over an area. Aimed fire sounds deliberate. Single shots or short bursts directed by an intelligence that wants to kill you.

Slowly, the AK47 fire dies. Taliban wearing man-jams, leather vests, and chest rigs packed with magazines run across the terrace. They converge on the goat trail.

I lay the sight on the first man to reach the trail. Exhale slowly, break the shot. There's a supersonic crack, but no muzzle flash. The action cycles, ejects the spent brass. The Talib crumples.

The next man hurdles his friend's body and runs onto the trail. He's wearing a vest with a double pack of AK47 magazines across his chest. They could deflect the round. I aim for his face and fire. The man's head snaps back and he drops his rifle.

The remaining Taliban press themselves against the rocks on the side of the terrace. They can guess where the sniper fire is coming from, and they hurl a torrent of automatic fire against my position. Aimed fire, now. Short bursts. Bullets snap overhead and whack into tree trunks.

Koenig and Lopez run past me.

I check the tritium dial on my watch. From this vantage point, I can hold off the Taliban. But—I want a ride off this mountain. Five minutes should do it. Hubble and Ballard are holding another defensive position half a click further along the trail.

Clutch the M110 to my chest. Displace, crawl to another tree fifteen feet away at the edge of the tree line. Prone, I cover another Talib running onto the trail. Fire. The man pitches forward onto his face. Shift my aim, shoot a Talib firing from the side of the terrace. He drops his rifle, falls sideways.

Displace. Crawl to another tree. More Taliban emerge from houses built higher on the mountain. They swarm the mountainside. No goat trails there, but these mountain men were born to climb. They walk on gradients that would freeze the blood of a lowlander.

They are executing a vertical envelopment. If they attack along the goat trail, I hold the high ground. If they approach from the mountainside, they attack from an elevated position. They want to do both at once.

I pick off one of the men on the mountainside. He screams and tumbles, arms and legs stretched out. He crashes into the rocky slope once, twice, then lands on the terrace a hundred and fifty feet below.

How many are there? Maybe thirty. The gunfire can be heard for miles. Alerted, Shahzad's main body can bring another hundred to the fight.

Despite the vertical envelopment, my position is superior to that held by Hubble and Ballard. I can improve our odds by thinning the Taliban ranks.

Muzzle flashes from the mountainside *and* the terrace. The Taliban are moving again. *Fast.* Across the mountainside, without the benefit of a path. And over the goat trail from below.

I shoot another Talib on the mountainside, then the lead man on the goat trail. Bullets from above and below splinter the tree trunks around me. Whacking sounds like giant hammers driving nails into the wood. Chips of bark rain down. Again, I displace. I never fire more than two shots from the same location.

They're getting close. I shift my fire. For every round I send along the trail, I fire two at the mountainside. An elevated position is the greater threat.

"Five-Five Charlie, this is Five-Five Sierra."

"Five-Five Charlie." Hubble's voice.

"Am withdrawing to your poz. Estimate thirty Taliban behind me. Say again, thirty. Twice fifteen."

"Roger that, Sierra."

I fire twice more, lower my NODs, run like the devil.

A trail. Inside the forest, I make out crushed vegetation where Koenig, Lopez, and the team have passed. I run full tilt, can't be bothered to look behind me.

"Five-Five Sierra."

Fuck protocol. "Go ahead," I gasp.

"That you, sounding like a herd of elephants?"

"Got maybe two hundred yards on them."

"Withdraw through us, Sierra."

Can't bother to answer. The trail curves, following the contour of the mountain. I run past the blocking position. Hubble and Ballard are invisible, tucked behind cover. They picked a key bend in the trail, where it shifts from an uphill slope to a level contour. When Taliban reach them, once again our men will be fighting from an elevated position.

I'm through the tree line, and onto the eastern slope of Kagur-Ghar.

The sky is lightening. I raise my NODs and stop for breath.

"Five-Five Actual, this is Five-Five Sierra."

"Go ahead, Sierra."

"You at LZ One?"

"Affirmative. Come on in."

I follow the tree line. There, I make out Koenig and Takigawa. Koenig is standing. Takigawa is on one knee, weapon raised to provide security. Grissom is leaning against a tree while Lopez tends his wound. Trainor kneels next to them.

Can't call this an LZ. Loggers pared back the tree line for fifteen yards from the edge. Our plan had been to use det cord to blast a proper landing zone. No time for that now. There's just enough space for a Black Hawk to land and extract us.

Behind me, I hear gunfire and the boom of explosions. Claymores, bound to trees, detonating. Scattering steel ball bearings over interlocking arcs. The blasts shred Taliban charging Hubble's position. Our men must be displacing, withdrawing to the LZ.

I make my way to Lopez and Grissom. "How is the colonel?"

"Round grazed him," Lopez grunts. "Skull may be fractured, and he has a concussion. He needs proper medical care."

Head shots don't always kill people. The toughness of the human skull will amaze you. The target must be hit "On The T." A bar between his eyebrows and a vertical support running down the line of his nose to his chin. Off the T, the hit is unlikely to be fatal. *Especially* if delivered with a small-caliber round.

Hubble and Ballard emerge from the tree line. They hug it, as I did, and run toward us. I drop to one knee and cover them with my M110.

The helos will approach from the west, follow the contour of Kagur-Ghar, and recover us. The first rays of the rising sun lend an orange glow to the fog that obscures the valleys. The mountains are snow-capped lumps of rock rising from a primordial soup.

Ballard unlimbers his high frequency ManPack. Its lightweight whip antenna folds like a walking stick for transportation. Deployed, it is five feet tall. He hands the handset to Koenig.

"Eagle One, this is Five-Five Actual."

"Go ahead, Five-Five Actual."

"We are at LZ. Say ETA."

"Five-Five Actual, we are three minutes out."

The exfil mission will have three helos. Two Apache gunships and a Black Hawk. The first Apache roars around the side of the mountain and passes overhead, its chin gun wagging. Slaved to the gunner's optic as he scans the tree line. The second flies two thousand feet higher, providing cover.

"Five-Five Actual, this is Eagle Two."

"Go ahead, Eagle Two," Koenig says.

"Are you in contact?"

"Affirmative, Eagle Two. We are taking fire. Have thirty, twice fifteen hostiles two hundred yards south along the tree line. Say again, two hundred yards south my poz."

"Copy that, Five-Five Actual. Two hundred yards south your poz."

"Give us a gun run. Keep it *south* of the LZ. You are cleared hot."

"Copy, cleared hot."

The Apache banks and pulls hard for a guns pass. In the distance, I watch the Black Hawk come into view.

A puff of smoke spurts from the tree line. Extends into a long contrail, reaches for the Apache.

"Eagle Two," Koenig yells. "RPG."

Frozen, the breath caught in my chest, I watch the contrail and the Apache converge. A red and black flash marks the impact. I squint as a black piece of metal breaks away from the helo. The tail boom and rotor drop like a rock. The pilot's cabin, weapons platforms, and engine housings continue onward. Without the horizontal stabilizer, the torque of the main rotor rips the fuselage apart. Pieces rain onto the mountainside.

Koenig is aghast. "Jesus Christ."

The second Apache dives on the clearing, chin gun blazing. It rakes the tree line.

Another puff of smoke.

"Eagle Three," Koenig calls. "RPG."

We watch the contrail reach for the Apache.

The pilot banks sharply, and... the missile *turns* to follow him. The contrail traces a wide, sweeping arc in the sky.

RPGs don't turn.

Intel suggested Taliban had begun to protect drug and

weapons caravans with surface-to-air missiles. We dismissed the possibility. We were wrong.

"Son of a bitch." The pilot reverses his bank, stands the gunship on its side. He pulls as hard as he can, breaks in the opposite direction. Fires countermeasures—decoy flares to confuse the SAM's seeker head. Pairs of flaming spheres pour from the tail of the Apache. Two... four... six flares. The decoys burn hotter than the helo's engines.

The contrail continues to curve, but the Apache turns inside it. The contrail disappears into the distance.

"Eagle One from Eagle Three."

"Go ahead, Eagle Three."

"Those are not, repeat *not*, RPGs. They're SAMs, guiding on infrared. Back off two miles."

"Roger that, two miles."

The Apache and Black Hawk begin a long orbit south-by-east.

"Five-five Actual, this is Eagle One."

"Go ahead, Eagle One."

"We are being called off. Make for Secondary LZ."

"They can't *leave* us," Trainor exclaims.

"Roger that, Eagle One." Koenig's voice is flat.

Helpless, we watch the helos depart to the south and disappear behind Kagur-Ghar.

"Alright," Koenig says. "Pack your shit. We have to stay ahead of those Hajjis."

We're fucked.

8

BROKEN ARROW

Kagur-Ghar
Tuesday, 0500

W*e're fucked.*
        "Alright, Breed." Koenig stares at me.
        "This is where you earn your pay. We need to
get to LZ Two by seventeen hundred hours. What's your
recommendation?"

Koenig has a talent for pissing me off. Our breach of
the target house went off without a hitch. I don't know what
happened outside, but he and Lopez were spotted. Had it
not been for that blunder, we'd have gotten away clean.

"LZ Two is on Lanat," I tell him. "Covering those four
miles in twelve hours is enough of a problem. We need to
shake the bad guys."

I jerk my chin toward Grissom, stare Koenig in the
eyes. "How do you expect to shake Taliban with Grissom
and Trainor along?"

Shadows flit behind the distant tree line.

Flashes of light. Bullets whack into tree trunks. Takigawa returns fire.

Koenig wrestles with an emotion halfway between frustration and fear. "You're the genius. You tell me."

Capitulation.

Eyes narrow, Trainor glares at us.

I turn to Hubble. "Where did you spot that Taliban patrol?"

"Humping toward Parkat twenty-four hours ago. They should be well on the other side of that mountain by now."

Further down-range, the way Talis move. But—they will rush back.

"Give me comms," I tell Koenig. "I want the long-range transmitter."

Koenig's squad radio is no more powerful than mine. We all carry FM band radios capable of communicating a mile. Useful to communicate between team members, but too weak to reach Bagram. Ballard carries the high frequency transmitter and separate satellite gear. Koenig nods to him.

Ballard gets Anthony's headquarters on the high frequency radio. An advanced 25-Watt ManPack with a range of four hundred miles, weighing six-and-a-half pounds. His choice is understandable. The sight of a comms sergeant holding up a satellite antennae tends to draw enemy fire. The HF whip is more discreet. He offers me the handset.

Fireflies light the tree line. A bullet clips my rucksack. Hubble raises his rifle and opens fire.

"Two-One Alpha, this is Five-Five Sierra."

"Go ahead, Five-Five Sierra."

"Troops in contact. Require immediate, repeat *imme-*

diate air strike, LZ One. Grid reference—Yankee Romeo 815 621. Broken arrow."

Broken arrow. The code for friendly aircraft in the vicinity to respond—because an American unit is about to be overrun.

"Five-Five Sierra, that is danger close. Confirm you are calling air strike, your poz."

The Taliban start toward us, firing from the hip. A bullet skips off a stone at Trainor's feet. She cringes.

"Confirmed. Burn this mountain down."

"Roger that, Five-Five Sierra."

"Sierra out."

I hand the handset back to Ballard. "Let's get moving north," I say. "Follow the contour of Kagur-Ghar, stay inside the tree line."

"What about the SAMs?" Trainor asks.

"We've never lost a fast-mover to SAMs. Lost a lot of helos."

Koenig shoulders his ruck, reasserts his authority. "Hubble, you're point. Takigawa, slack. I'll follow. Breed and Trainor behind me. Lopez, watch Grissom. Ballard, rear guard. Let's go."

"One more thing," I tell him.

"What the fuck, Breed."

Takigawa and Hubble continue to fire. Taliban throw themselves to the ground.

"We can *not* stay here." Takigawa says.

I reach into a side-pocket of my ruck, pull out an infrared strobe.

"It's getting too light for that," Koenig snaps.

"Maybe not," I say. "If it is, no harm done."

I set the strobe at the edge of the tree line. Where the forest is dark, but the strobe can be seen from the air.

"Let's move out," Koenig barks.

We set off at a fast pace. Koenig's team is hard and fit, but Grissom and Trainor are another matter.

Marching with a sixty-pound ruck is a familiar feeling. I've distributed the gear about my body. The heavy pack hangs from my shoulders on thick, padded straps. I feel the weight of its contents pressing against this side and that. The spare batteries for my radio and NODs, stripper clips of 7.62 mm ammunition to replenish the magazines I carry. Six in the belly-rig of my plate carrier, four in a side-pocket of the pack. Two quarts of water, plus the canteen on my pistol belt. I take the NODs from my half-shell helmet and store them in a pouch, left side of the plate carrier.

The burden sways gently with my body, and my gait adjusts to the movement. Hiking over rough country with heavy gear is like riding a bike. Do it enough, and your body develops a sense of balance. It's light enough to see now, though the shadows inside the tree line are deep. When we step onto bare slope, the glare to the east is blinding.

Trainor strides between me and Koenig. She moves over the rocky trails with the sure-footedness of a mountain goat. A lithe economy, as though she is used to hiking in these mountains. She wears standard-issue digital camouflage and level three body armor. The clothing she was captured in. No rifle, no helmet. Muslim fighters always make female captives wear headscarves. To humiliate them, and render them compliant with Sharia law. Like a cowboy's kerchief, she wears the headscarf loosely knotted at her throat.

She hasn't lost fitness during her eighteen months captivity. I have some sense for the capabilities of women in cultural liaison roles. They are no slouches, but Trainor seems a cut above, despite her small size. Five-seven, maybe a hundred and thirty pounds.

The colonel is going to be a problem. I think back to my conversations with Stein and Anthony. Grissom is the mission. Grissom is the peace deal.

Grissom is sucking shit through a straw.

He's a big guy, six feet tall. Military intelligence. Wounded, but looks strong enough to march on his own. Wobbly, but not because of his injury. He's having trouble negotiating the rocky terrain, the woods with gnarled tree limbs. The colonel has not developed the balance one acquires from long hours humping over rough country. That makes his stride inefficient. He will tire quickly.

Where did Trainor develop that balance? The facility of movement over mountains. What was her eighteen months in captivity like?

Five minutes have passed. Ballard's high-frequency radio crackles. "Five-Five Sierra, this is Dog One."

I stop, allow Lopez and Grissom to pass. Ballard holds the handset out to me. High above us, a dark speck. Occasionally, the speck glints in the dawn sunlight. "Go ahead, Dog One."

"Confirm grid reference unchanged."

"Confirmed, Dog One. Have deployed IR strobe, edge of forest."

We stop and look back. Taliban are crossing the LZ in a long file. Damn, I wish they were bunched up. I'll take what I can get.

"I see the strobe," the pilot calls. "Right on the grid."

"Roger that," I tell him. "Approach east to west. Say again, *east to west*. Guns and bombs on target. Give me everything you've got—on the strobe."

"Copy, east to west. On the strobe."

"They're crossing the LZ right now. You're cleared hot."

"Copy, cleared hot."

The speck grows in size as the aircraft dives on the mountain. It's a silver cross, a fuselage with straight, blunt wings. An A-10 Warthog loaded with bombs and napalm, armed with a 30 mm rotary cannon.

There's a whistling whine as the jet closes on the mountainside. The Taliban lift their faces to the sky, point at the angel of death. The Gatling gun spews fire, and the landing zone is obscured by flying rocks, splintered trees and body parts. Broken tree branches are indistinguishable from human arms and legs whirling through the air. Close in, you might hear the wet slap of bloody flesh falling to earth. Two five-hundred-pound bombs and two drop tanks filled with jellied gasoline detach from the plane's wings.

The mountain erupts with the explosion of the bombs. The rock shelf is blasted from the face of the mountain. Great gouts of rock, earth, and shattered trees spurt from the slope. An instant later, the napalm explodes, covering the mountainside with a strip of orange flame. Greasy black smoke boils into the sky.

The A-10 climbs away. From the forest, another SAM streaks skyward. The Taliban waited to give the missile's seeker head the best view of the jet's hot exhaust.

"SAM on your six."

A burst of decoy flares pop from the A-10's tail. The plane breaks hard left and the missile zeroes in on the brilliant orbs.

"Let's go," I snap. "We have to make time while they're sorting out that mess."

"Five-Five Sierra," my radio crackles. "How's that look?"

"Out-fucking-standing, Dog One. How about another guns pass?"

"Five-Five Sierra, roger that. There's more help behind me."

"Thank you, Dog One. Watch out for those SAMs."

"Too easy, Sierra. Good luck."

The A-10 strafes the landing zone again before it departs to the west. Another A-10 arrives and plasters the mountainside. The second A-10 loiters, makes three guns passes after expending its bomb load. For an hour, the Taliban crawl into holes and cower behind rocks.

No more SAMs are fired. The Talis are saving them for easy pickings. Rescue helicopters, or unsuspecting low-flying aircraft.

For that hour, we hike at a pace as close to running as Grissom and Trainor can manage. When I see Grissom is ready to collapse, I order the team to slow their pace.

Koenig wants to speak. The trail isn't wide enough for us to hike two abreast, so he lets Trainor pass, and walks ahead of me.

"Talk to me, Breed," he says. "There's a rope bridge between Kagur-Ghar and Lanat. How exposed are we?"

I choose my words carefully, speaking between breaths. "It's four miles from here to Lanat. We're beneath Kagur-Ghar's south peak—the summit. It has a long north col. A saddle. The north peak is lower, with an old Soviet outpost on top. A ridge stretches two miles from the north peak to a ravine that separates us from Lanat. There's the bridge."

"How long to the bridge?"

"At least eight hours."

"Eight hours!" Koenig spits. "For fuck's sake."

The rule of thumb for rough terrain is two hours a mile.

In these mountains, with an injured man in the party, such an estimate is optimistic.

I jerk my head over my shoulder at Grissom. The colonel is moving forward with a determined step, eyes focused on the trail. Lopez has wrapped a bandage tight around his head. The fabric is brown with blood.

"Eight hours," I say. "And another three to LZ Two, *after* we cross the bridge."

"How many Hajjis left?" Koenig stares at the oily black napalm smoke obscuring the mountainside. "The air strike couldn't have gotten all of them."

"Don't forget Shahzad's main body. There are no easy routes over the west face and north ridge. They can't flank us to the west. Odds are, they're right behind us."

"They'll catch us."

"We *have* to get to the bridge." I'm doing most of the talking. Explaining my thinking to Koenig is a waste of breath. "If we cross first, we'll blow it behind us."

The desperation of the plan is not lost on Koenig.

The captain glares at me. Without another word, he shoulders past Trainor and resumes his place in the file.

Trainor stumbles against the rock face as the captain brushes her. Throws out an arm to steady herself. Annoyed, she stares after him, then turns and looks back at me. For a moment, our eyes lock. The girl heard everything we said. She's alert, thinking hard. Unlike the colonel, who is fast becoming an automaton.

I jerk my chin at her. "Watch where you're going."

Trainor turns her attention back to the trail. I didn't mean to sound harsh, but we don't need her to sprain an ankle.

"You in charge of this mission, Breed?"

It's the first I've heard her speak. A hint of a South-western accent.

"No," I gasp. "Reckon I'm a *consultant*."

"A *consultant*." The girl stifles a laugh. "You've been here before."

"Save your breath," I tell her.

The sun has risen, low in the sky over the dark whale-back of Parkat. In its rays, the low fog shines like a silver ocean. I'm uneasy. Hubble and Ballard saw a Taliban patrol on that mountain. It is likely the mountain men are pacing us on that ridge. They are invisible against the black moun-tainside. *We* are exposed in the sunlight.

It's a devil's bargain. Inside the tree line, less exposed, our pace will be halved. On the rock slope, we move faster, naked for all to see. We have to move on the *edge* of the forest, use the trees to disrupt our silhouettes.

"You must love it in these mountains," Trainor says.

The girl won't quit. Well, if she can spare the breath, I can.

"How do you figure that?"

"Only reason anyone would come back… who didn't have to."

9

ON THE RUN

Kagur-Ghar
Tuesday, 0800

"Take five." Koenig raises his right hand.

I'm not sure it's wise to stop. The little rest you get from such a short break is never worth the loss of momentum. Your muscles cool down. There's time for lactic acid, once flushed by circulating blood, to pool in your tissue. All the more painful to stir to life once you begin to hike again.

No, Deltas on long-range patrols eat and drink on the move. We stop only to urinate or defecate into plastic bags, stored in our packs. Waste is disposed of in a manner that will not reveal the patrol's presence. I would hike sixteen hours over these mountains before stopping to sleep.

Koenig must be thinking of our charges. Unwilling to sit, I turn to Lopez and Grissom. The colonel sits with his back to a tree, and the sergeant is checking his wound.

I squat next to Grissom, rifle across my knees. "How are you doing, Colonel?"

"Fine." The exhaustion in the colonel's voice tells me he is anything but.

Lopez takes a flashlight from his pack. Shines it in Grissom's eyes. "Look left, Sir. Look right. Up. Down."

"I'm fine, Sergeant."

"I don't think so, Sir." Lopez pockets the flashlight. "You've got a concussion. I can't tell how bad it is, or whether it will get worse. Do you feel dizzy?"

"No."

"If you start to feel dizzy or disoriented, let me know. This is rough country. Ain't no shame in hanging onto someone."

"Our mission," Koenig says, "is to get you back safe. Did you strike a deal with Najibullah?"

I didn't notice the captain approach. He stands over us, hands on hips.

"Yes." Grissom shields his eyes from the glare of bright sunlight behind Koenig. "The peace deal, and the release of Sergeant Trainor."

Lopez and I exchange glances. The photosensitivity is a side-effect of the concussion. Grissom's pupils are not contracting when presented with bright light.

"Have you got the details of the peace deal in writing?" Koenig asks.

"No." Grissom taps the side of his head, the blood-stained bandage. "Najibullah was adamant that nothing be put in writing until everything was agreed with the highest authority. The details are all in here. Sergeant Trainor is also aware. Shahzad would never expect us to trust a girl."

Koenig snorts. "I've spent fifteen years trying to under-stand these people. Don't think I ever will."

"They want us off their land, Captain." Grissom closes his eyes and leans his head back against the tree trunk. "That's all they want."

"We'd better get going." Koenig turns and signals Hubble. "Let's roll."

I get to my feet and sling my rifle. Trainor stands ten feet away, staring at us.

Grissom's decision to brief Trainor on the peace deal strikes me as odd. On the one hand, it ensures that should he be killed, the deal will live on in Trainor's skull. On the other hand, in Shahzad's clutches, there was additional risk she might reveal what she knew.

"Wait one, Captain," I say.

"What is it now, Breed."

"We have Talis on our trail. We should try to delay them."

"How do you propose to do that?"

I CALL Hubble and Ballard over. "How many Claymores did you use at the blocking position?"

"Four," Hubble says. "All we had."

"Okay. The rest of us carry one each. We'll give them to Ballard. Fishing line out of our survival kits. He can plant them next to the trail every four hundred yards or so. Should keep the Talis guessing."

"The chances of their hitting one are low," Koenig says. "The chances of their hitting all four are nil."

"That's true," I say, "but if they hit one, it'll fuck them up. Keep them guessing."

"We should do it," Ballard says. "Not much extra work for me."

"Okay," Koenig agrees. "Make it fast."

Each of us hands Ballard a Claymore. A curved metal case packed with explosives and ball bearings. A separate kit that includes a battery and firing wire. We hand Ballard the Claymores and all the fishing line from our survival kits. He will use it to create makeshift tripwires. When one of the mines explodes, the ball bearings will be scattered through a sixty-degree arc.

"Let's go," I say.

We move out, in the same order as before. Ballard hangs back, searching for places where the Claymores and tripwires can be concealed. He lays the traps every quarter mile. If the Taliban trigger one, they will be much more careful where they step. The mines may force them off the trail.

"Aren't you the creative one," Trainor says.

"I think of things," I tell her. "Don't you?"

"Not like that. How long have you been a consultant?"

"A little over a year."

"For these guys?" The girl sounds skeptical.

"No, in the Philippines."

"Sounds like paradise. How long over here?"

"This is my second day."

Trainor stops and turns to me. "You're kidding me."

"I was in the army for a long time."

"They brought you in to run the show." Trainor turns back to the trail and keeps hiking.

"Don't say that too loud."

"Huh. Not like it's a secret." Trainor snorts.

I force myself to keep my head on a swivel. Scan the dark bulk of Parkat. The girl is a distraction. "What about you, smartass? What's your story?"

"What do you want to know?"

"Why'd you join the army?"

"Couldn't get a job. My parents made me promise I'd get a degree, so I picked something I was good at. Languages. Nobody would pay for a twenty-two-year-old kid who spoke Farsi. So I joined the army. Surprise. They gave me more training and shipped me here."

"Why Farsi?"

"My grandmother and mother were Iranian. Moved to Colorado after the fall of the Shah. When I was a kid, I loved the *Arabian Nights*. When I got older, I read a lot of Kipling. Everything to do with this part of the world. It was fun, exciting, romantic."

"Kipling wrote for boys."

"Did he? I love *The Man Who Would Be King*. And *Kim*. Kim was a spy."

I say nothing.

"I always liked doing boys' things," Trainor continues. I'm impressed by her wind. She synchronizes her speech to her breathing. Speaks just loud enough for me to hear. "Grew up on a ranch in Colorado. Learned to hunt, shoot, ride. Army basic training was easy for me. But nothing prepared me for what it's like over here."

"A lot of soldiers find that," I tell her. "Hunting isn't the same when the animal you're after shoots back."

Kaboom.

We all jerk. In unison, we look back along the trail. Far away, around the curve of the mountain, black smoke boils from the napalm fires. Closer, about three quarters of a mile away, a small puff of gray smoke. A Claymore.

I key my squad radio. "Good work, Kilo. One less to worry about."

"Your idea, Sierra. Let's hope it keeps the little pricks guessing."

"Was it your first mine or your last?"

Ballard has set only four.

"The first. But they will be more careful now."

We turn back to the trail and keep hiking.

"How do you think Colonel Grissom is doing?" Trainor asks me. There is genuine concern in her voice.

I'm terrible at cheerful bullshit. "Not good," I tell her. "He wasn't in shape for this kind of terrain to begin with. Now he has a head wound, blood loss, a fractured skull, and one hell of a nasty concussion. I'm amazed he's still on his feet."

"He's a brave man," Trainor says. "A lot tougher than he looks."

"I hope so." I can't hide my skepticism. "If he can make it to the bridge, we'll blow it behind us. Then we'll have a chance."

"A chance."

"If he gets over that bridge, I'll carry him to the LZ." Trainor looks back at me. "You would, wouldn't you?"

"Watch where you're going," I tell her. "Let's talk about you. How did the Mujahedeen take you?"

"I try not to think about it," Trainor says. "I was an idiot."

"Tell me."

"Why do you want to know? There isn't much to tell."

"You're *not* an idiot," I tell her. "So there *is* something to tell."

10

ROBYN'S CAPTURE

Kagur-Ghar
Tuesday, 1000

"There *is* something to tell."

We hug the lower tree line as much as possible. Trees don't flourish on large swathes of the rock slope. We cross those areas bare-ass naked. Trainor walks in front of me, trying to stay one tree inside the line. Too far inside, and your path becomes irregular as you find yourself in a maze of roots and vegetation.

"It's a great story," Trainor says. "Stumblefucks on the Arwal."

I smile to myself. "Try me."

ROBYN TRAINOR WAS RAISED on a ranch. It was a hand-to-mouth existence for her family, no matter how hard her father and brothers worked. Ranches are a lot like corner stores. They have to finance their premises, they have to

finance their inventory, and they have to sell their
inventory.

The rancher's inventory is his livestock. He breeds
them, births them, and at the end of the season, sells them.
That's the deal, it's seasonal. A grocery store buys and sells
inventory year round. Each year, a ranch succeeds or fails
on one roll of the dice.

The Trainor ranch was small. It was a family-run affair.
Robyn's father and two brothers did most of the work. Her
mother and grandmother ran the house. Her father hired
extra hands when necessary, and Robyn helped out at
branding time. Those were happy days. Branding time was
a big party, where everyone came together.

Robyn's parents pushed her to get good grades in
school. She loved to read, and she read everything she
could get her hands on. The books she loved most were the
Kipling books she borrowed from her brothers. She imagined herself a street urchin in Lahore, playing the Great
Game against the Russians. Spying for Mahbub Ali, the
Afghan horse trader who worked for British intelligence. In
more fanciful moments, she imagined herself trading her
dusty Levi's for the sensuous attire of a harem dancer.

She cursed her inability to move with the requisite
sensuality.

When she looked at herself naked in the mirror, all her
pieces seemed to be in the right place. The problem was,
she walked like a rancher. She rode, shot and roped. Sexual
bouts with cowboys resembled combative athletic events.
Harem dancing was not in her skill set.

"Robyn," her father said to her, "you are going to
college. You are going to get a degree."

"I don't need to go to college. After school, I want to
help you around here."

"You're going to school, girl. We'll pay for it. Don't much care what you study, but you are going to get yourself a degree."

"Why?"

"You know about hedging with cattle futures?"

"In case the price falls?"

"Call that degree a hedge."

Robyn had a gift for languages. In fact, the first language she learned was Farsi, spoken in Iran. While her grandmother was alive, she and her mother spoke it at home. The second language was Dari. Related to Farsi, Dari was spoken in Afghanistan. She then learned Arabic. Finally, she developed a working knowledge of Pashto.

"You have a gift for languages." I step around a pine tree. "Why not German or French?"

"Like normal people?"

"I didn't say that."

"My grandmother and mother got me started. Middle Eastern languages. My grandmother passed away, and I practiced with Mom. I read the Arabian Nights and imagined myself as Scheherazade. Studying the languages was like travelling."

"You got here."

"Not right away. One day after I graduated, my Dad called me in and told me he was selling the ranch. He was sick and my brothers couldn't manage it. I begged him not to, but he said it was time. My brothers moved to the city and got regular jobs. When Dad died, he left what little money he had to Mom, so she could live in the city near my brothers.

"Dad thought it would be easy for me to get a job with a degree, but it wasn't. I joined the army. It worked out well."

"As all can see."

Trainor laughs. "It worked out well... for a while."

"How did you get this assignment?"

"I was able to get into a program for interpreters. It wasn't specific to this region. But I also qualified infantry, and that allowed me to go on patrols. I joined a Cultural Support Team. As troop strength was reduced, so was the number of CSTs. I asked to stay, but I was the only woman working a handful of patrols."

"Didn't patrol activity decline?"

"It did. The ratio of local troops to Americans rose every month. Back in the day, there were exclusively American operations. Then it went to one-to-one. Now it's six-to-one."

"Was it six-to-one the day you were taken?"

"Worse. There were three of us, and an understrength platoon of Afghan National Army."

The ANA inspire little confidence. During the war against the Soviets, whole divisions deserted, often taking their weapons with them.

THE VISIT to Arwal village did not go well. The ANA officer and three Americans sat with the village elder in his *hujra* and spoke of the aid the government would bring. Fertilizer and improved irrigation. The elder was cold to Trainor, despite her wearing a headscarf and her introduction as Second Lieutenant Elwyn Beatty's translator.

"My forces will protect you from the Taliban," the young ANA lieutenant told the elder.

"Your presence brings us great comfort," the elder purred.

The Americans sat cross-legged, eating from plates

laden with a suspicious-looking stir-fry. It was a poor village. Their hosts were not serving their best meal, but it was rude not to partake. Trainor loaded her dish with pita bread that had the taste and consistency of rubber. She choked down a bit of goat meat.

"Tell him," Beatty said to Trainor, "we finished much work, but have had to wait for more supplies. Construction crews will return next month to complete the irrigation system."

Trainor translated the lieutenant's message into Pashto. The elder smiled and nodded. Jabbered for a full five minutes. The lieutenant gave Trainor a quizzical look.

"It's a shopping list, Sir." Trainor kept her expression neutral. "He's trying to get as much as he can from us."

"The fucker's selling our aid on the black market," First Sergeant Otis Cray grunted. "Ask him where all the young men have gone."

Trainor translated, edited out the truculence in Cray's tone.

"The young men are in the mountains, grazing the goats." The elder smiled and waved his hand in a broad arc. The sweep of his arm was meant to encompass all the slopes that glowered upon the village.

"Bullshit," Cray said. "They're bandits or militia. Tell him we have seen Taliban operating in the neighborhood. Are they Najibullah's men or Shahzad's?"

The elder jabbered, gesticulated some more. Beatty and the ANA lieutenant listened intently. Cray tried to hide his disgust.

"He says Najibullah is Mujahedeen, not Taliban. Neither have been seen for several weeks. One of Najibullah's caravans passed through more than a month ago, carrying opium. Abdul-Ali Shahzad visited several weeks ago, but did not stay."

Cray was not convinced. "Did Shahzad have strangers with him, ones who spoke Arabic?"

Trainor translated, and the elder shook his head furiously.

Another lie. Cadres of foreign fighters forged passionate young Afghans into Taliban.

"I don't think we'll get much more out of him, First Sergeant," Beatty said.

"No, Sir. I don't think we will."

"We should leave if we want to return to the base by nightfall," the ANA lieutenant said.

The group said their goodbyes. Stepped outside into the shadow of Arwal village. A colossal layer cake of houses stacked against the side of the mountain. The ANA troops, thirty men in all, formed a column and moved out. The Americans joined them, and the elder saw them off with a cheery wave.

The air was cold, but Trainor grew hot and sweaty. It was a long hike south from Arwal village. She lowered her headscarf and tied it about her throat. Walked bare-headed. The ANA platoon stretched out in a long file. The three Americans were positioned a third of the distance from the rear guard, and a third of the distance from the point. Second Lieutenant Beatty was with the forward elements of the platoon. Trainor and First Sergeant Cray trudged with the rear.

They walked past a mile of irrigated terraces. Crops of beans. From the side of the riverbank, the terraces rose like a giant staircase on the side of the mountain.

"We're not doing any good," Cray said. "That old buzzard is lying through his teeth."

"I sympathize with him." Trainor looked over her shoulder and squinted. The sun was lowering in the sky. In Kunar, the sun had to climb the mountains every morning. In the evening, it did not have far to fall before the valleys darkened. "They're caught between us and the Taliban. He knows we can't protect him, so he's nice to our face. Makes what money he can, then tries to keep the Taliban happy."

"Do you think he shares the money with his people?"

"He's not driving a Rolls-Royce, First Sergeant."

"Shahzad's in town," Cray muttered. "That means Al Qaeda."

"He said Najibullah passed through as well."

"Oh, great." Cray sneered. "A regular drug-runner. Najibullah and Shahzad. I get a little glow of joy every time those bastards rub each other's boys out."

The column had passed the terraces of Arwal village. The dirt road became little more than a trail that sloped onto a set of foothills. They were on the southern edge of the mountain. When they crested the hills, the trail disappeared entirely. The column descended toward the next valley.

"Something's not right, First Sergeant." Trainor was confused. The terrain, the angle of the sun as it sank in the west, was wrong. She couldn't put her finger on it.

From its origins in the Hindu Kush, the Arwal River flowed south through Afghanistan. There, it split into two branches on either side of Arwal-Ghar. The West Arwal continued to flow south-by-west. South of the mountain, it took a dog-leg east to meet the East Arwal. The East Arwal meandered south-by-east. It entered Pakistan before bending sharply, and crossing back into Afghanistan to rejoin its mate. The ANA forward operating base was located at the confluence of the two branches.

Cray was too old a hand to dismiss a subordinate's concerns. "What's the matter, Trainor?"

"We're heading for base, which should be due south. The sun should be setting to our west."

The first sergeant looked about himself. "We're heading for the river," he said. "You can make it out, right over there."

"Yes, but why is the sun shining over our shoulders?"

Trainor felt her stomach hollow. She drew her compass from a cargo pocket and checked their bearing. The blond hairs on her forearm were reddish-gold in the light of the setting sun. "Shit. First Sergeant, the ANA have been leading us to the East Arwal."

"What the fuck, can't they read a compass?"

"Their lieutenant's been using the river as a landmark. He forgot it *bends*."

"If he ever knew. Are we in Pakistan?"

Trainor checked her bearings. "No, First Sergeant. But —*they* are."

She pointed to the forward elements of the platoon.

Cray swore under his breath. Keyed his squad radio. "Six-Two Actual, this is Six-Two Bravo."

"Go ahead, Six-Two Bravo."

Beatty was fresh out of ROTC. He'd had one course in land nav and was following an ANA second lieutenant into another country. Nominally allies of the United States, the Pakistani army was friendly with the Taliban

"Actual, your column is in Pakistan. Stop and get them turned around. Right now."

"What do you mean, Pakistan? The river's right over there... Oh, my God."

Trainor watched the second lieutenant look to his right, then straight ahead. Saw horror on his face. He raised his right fist to signal the column to halt. The first sergeant did the same.

Gunfire rattled. AK47s blazed away. Cray went down, blood spurting from his shoulder and groin. Half a dozen ANA, including their officer, died in the same volley.

"Contact left!" Beatty raised his M4 and engaged.

The Mujahedeen had been stalking the ANA platoon. When they saw the platoon drift off course, they rushed to get ahead of their prey. The patrol had come off the mountain and were on an escarpment, sloping gently to the riverbank. There was vestigial forest to their left... the southernmost tip of Arwal-Ghar. The Mujahedeen used that forest, no more than seventy-five meters from their targets, to set the ambush.

A second group of Mujahedeen attacked the ANA column from behind. Their fire was slaughtering the rear guard. "Contact rear," Trainor yelled.

Improvised, the attack resembled a reverse-L ambush. The Mujahedeen had been presented with a gift. They took full advantage.

Mujahedeen charged the column, firing single shots and short bursts. Beatty was hit three times. His front plate stopped one round. Another drilled his shoulder. The third hit him in the throat, two inches above his chest plate. He went down, coughing blood.

Cray was in extremis. The groin wound had severed his femoral artery, and he was bleeding out. Trainor tore open a battlefield dressing and slapped it over the wound, but the blood spurted from around the edges. It was like trying to plug a garden hose with a wad of Kleenex.

The Mujahedeen ran at the column from the left and behind. Trainor watched Cray's eyes roll back in their sockets. She let go of the dressing, snatched at the rifle she had dropped on the rocks.

A Mujahedeen carrying an AK47 rushed at her and kicked her in the chest. The force of the impact knocked the breath from her body. She tumbled onto her back. The man pinned her to the ground with his foot, shoved the muzzle of the AK47 in her face.

All around her, the firing had dwindled to sporadic single shots. She realized the Mujahedeen were finishing off the survivors.

Staring down the black muzzle of a rifle, Robyn Trainor closed her eyes and prepared to die.

"HAD you never been to the village before?" I ask.

"No," Trainor replies. "Our platoons were fresh into the valley. In fact, the Arwal was considered relatively safe. The three sides… ours, Najibullah's, and Shahzad's… tended to avoid action in the valley. It was a kind of neutral zone."

"Were you the only survivor?" I ask.

"Yes," Trainor says. "I'm surprised they didn't tell you at the briefing."

I'm not. The reason I wanted her story was because Stein, General Anthony, and Koenig glossed over it. Their focus was on Colonel Grissom. To them, Sergeant Robyn Trainor is nothing more than a pawn. An excuse to conduct face-to-face negotiations over the fate of a country.

"You were lucky."

"I think so. I have a theory about that."

"I'm all ears." We arrive at a tangled obstacle of exposed roots and brush. Trainor holds onto a tree branch for support, starts to swing herself out onto the slope.

"Come right back," I warn her. "We don't know where that Taliban patrol is."

Trainor takes one step onto the bare slope, hops nimbly back inside the tree line. I give her a twenty-foot head start, then follow. A sniper surprised by her quick movement might be ready for me.

Concealed by the tree line, I breathe more easily.

"They wanted to capture an American woman," Trainor continues. "I took my headscarf off, and my hair stood out. They were careful not to shoot me."

"An American *and* a woman," I observe. "It wasn't luck."

"No," Trainor says. "It wasn't."

11

SNIPER DUEL

Kagur-Ghar
Tuesday, 1100

The trail ahead opens onto a thirty-foot stretch of mountainside. Hubble stops and raises his right fist.

I crane my neck to scope out the situation. A landslide carried away a triangular section of the slope. There are pine trees forty feet above the cleared zone. Their root systems are exposed, hanging over the edge in a dirty tangle.

"Five-Five Charlie, this is Five-Five Sierra."

"Go ahead, Sierra," Hubble says.

"What do you think?"

"The slope looks solid enough." Hubble studies the open ground with suspicion. "Suggest we cross one at a time."

Koenig's voice crackles onto the squad net. "Five-Five

Charlie, this is Five-Five Actual. Go ahead when you're ready."

Rifle slung across his chest, Hubble ventures onto the slope. Tests the mix of loose red earth and black shale. He finds a stable purchase, picks his way across. Ten feet. Twenty feet.

Hubble's body jerks, and he pitches over the side. A gunshot echoes from a great distance.

Trainor gasps.

"Fuck." Koenig drops to one knee, strains to get a better view. "Where did that come from?"

"Didn't see a flash." Takigawa presses himself against the trunk of a pine tree. Scans the dark slope of Parkat.

Takigawa didn't see the flash because he wasn't looking in the direction from which the shot was fired.

First I squeeze past Trainor, then Koenig. "Wait one," I tell him. "I need to see for myself."

I crouch next to Takigawa.

"Son of a bitch has the angle," Takigawa says.

"He's picked himself a spot."

Takigawa glances at Hubble's body, broken on the rocks below. Then he stares across the no-man's land at the safety of trees thirty feet away.

"Can you find a spot with a clear shot?" Takigawa asks.

"Depends on where he is, doesn't it."

Mentally, I transport myself halfway across the chasm. Where Hubble was standing when he was shot. I look out at the long whaleback of Parkat. Let's say the bad guy has a Dragunov, effective to eight hundred yards. The distance from where Hubble was shot to the opposite point on Parkat looks a thousand yards. With winds, cold temperatures, and barometric pressure to correct for. Trigonometrically, that implies any other position on Parkat will be outside the sniper's effective range.

"I don't care how good he is," I say. "He's pushing it."

At a thousand yards, under these conditions, hitting Hubble with one shot involved as much luck as skill.

Above us stands a wall of pines, where the landslide ripped a chunk out of the forest. "That's the best spot. Climb to those trees. Let me know when you're set. I'll draw his fire."

Takigawa chuckles. "Dude, you're the legend."

I shrug off my rucksack and plate carrier. Fish a laser rangefinder from a side pocket. With the M110 slung across my back, I plunge into the forest and climb the wooded slope.

"You know what I'm thinking?" Takigawa discards radio protocol.

"I can guess."

"Remember that sniper who got the world record for the world's longest kill?"

"What about him?" I grunt, testing each handhold and foothold. I'm twenty feet above the trail. The stand of trees over the chasm is obscured. I keep climbing.

"He took five shots to get the hit."

I laugh. "Yeah, what are you going to do at two miles. Walk the shots right into the mark."

"This isn't quite that bad," Takigawa says, "but dude, it's an ugly shot."

When I've climbed forty feet, I edge sideways.

There, I see the trees hanging over space. The soil is loose, the trees could go at any time. The trees above look sturdier, their root systems intact. Crab-like, I make my way higher and to the right.

Fifty-five feet above the trail, the going is easier. The

red soil is firm under my feet. There are spaces between the trees that give me a view of the opposite mountainside.

I shrug off my field jacket. Roll it into a ball and go prone. I open the rifle's bipod, stuff the rolled-up jacket under the toe of the rifle's stock. I aim the laser rangefinder and take a reading off a large boulder on the opposite slope. The atmospheric conditions are good, the fog has burned off. The stone is reflective, there's nothing to impede the beam.

One thousand and sixty-five yards.

Back at base, I had zeroed my rifle for four hundred yards, calculated the appropriate holdovers for different ranges. Calculated the temperature and barometric pressure adjustments at eight thousand and fifteen thousand feet. Interpolated values for intermediate altitudes.

Long-range shooters consider those variables. The ammunition and breech temperature. The Coriolis effect. It sounds cool to speak about the spin of the earth affecting your firing solution. In fact, all those factors can be accounted for in a straightforward manner. In the field, the number one reason shooters miss—is wind.

The wind is the question. It's the most difficult variable to evaluate when calculating a firing solution. It changes speed and direction randomly. It can behave differently at different distances between the shooter and the target. Of all the variables that affect a shot, the wind is the least subject to mathematical assessment. Instrumentation can help, but the most vital asset is the shooter's experience in judging the shot.

The mirage in my scope ripples from the bottom of the scope to the top. The wind is moving either toward me, or away. In this case, shooting across a valley, it could mean the wind is swelling from the base of the valley and rising toward me. It could add lift to the bullet.

This makes things easier, but not much. It means I don't have to adjust for windage, but I will have to adjust my holdover. And there is no way to know by how much. Not until I take the first shot.

This is why a semi-automatic sniper rifle is nice to have.

I flick the safety off.

"Ready," I say.

"I'm going all the way across, dude. Only doing this once."

Takigawa steps onto the bare slope like a tightrope walker. Rifle slung across his chest, left hand extended for support. He takes three quick steps. I force myself not to watch him. Both eyes open, I stare through the scope at 3.6x, intent on detecting a muzzle flash.

There. A flash. Takigawa is still moving. I twist the magnification to 10x.

When AK47 rounds go by, they *snap*.

A Dragunov round going by sounds like the *crack* of a bullwhip. A noise that says, *I'm here to fuck you up*.

Sweating, I search for the shooter. Will he displace? He's cocky. Another flash, and a spatter of rock behind Takigawa. Another whiplash. The Delta skips his way across the open space.

Crazy bastard's *dancing* on the slope.

The barrel of a Dragunov draws my eye. I follow it to the face of a Taliban marksman. I let my breath out, squeeze the trigger.

Crack.

I'd give a year's pay for a spotter. Strain to see my bullet trace—the vapor trail the round leaves in the frigid air. The semiautomatic M110 might moderate the recoil enough to make it possible. There—arcing high. A foot above my target's head, the splash of earth on the slope.

Miss.

The shooter heard my shot. He has no idea how close I came, but he's looking through his scope at me. There's another flash from the Dragunov. I hear the sniper's round drill a pine tree behind me—the whack of an axe.

Wind's rising from the valley floor in a straight line relative to my position. I adjust my holdover, fire a second time.

The shooter has his right eye to the Dragunov's scope, my bullet drills his left. His head jerks and blood sprays the foliage behind him. Another Hajji steps into view, reaches for the rifle. I fire a third time. The heavy caliber round hits him in the left side, under his arm. Blows out his heart and lungs. The second man crumples on top of the first.

Takigawa is across. Koenig crosses after him.

I sweep Parkat with my scope. Nothing. Two men down, the others determined not to present targets. I fold the bipod, shrug on my field jacket, and sling the rifle. Half jump, half slide down the mountainside. A torrent of loose shale and pebbles precedes me. I run into Lopez.

"All clear?" Lopez is tending Grissom. "I can cross with the colonel."

"Got their first string," I say. "Go for it. Hang onto each other."

Lopez and Grissom set off across no-man's land.

Trainor hands me my plate carrier.

"You'd better get across," I tell her.

Without a word, the girl follows Lopez. I watch her stop half-way and stare at Hubble's motionless form.

"Don't fucking *stop*," I yell. "Keep going."

As if to reinforce my irritation, a bullet smacks the rock wall two feet from Trainor.

I fasten my plate carrier and shoulder my ruck.

"Go ahead," Ballard says. "Looks like you got their best shooter."

"They sling enough lead, they're bound to hit something."

I turn and cross the gap.

12

REAR GUARD

Kagur-Ghar
Tuesday, 1300

Relieved, we gather on the other side of the landslide. "Let's go," Koenig says. "Trainor, stay with Breed. Grissom with Lopez. Otherwise, increase dispersion to twenty yards. Takigawa on point. I'll take slack."

I turn to Grissom. "How are you, Colonel?"

Grissom is exhausted, his eyes unfocused. "I'm fine. Let's keep moving."

Lopez's stare says it all. I might have to carry the colonel on my back

Sobered, we move out.

"You okay?" I ask Trainor.

"Do you get used to seeing people dead?"

"Depends. You'll have a lifetime to think about it," I tell her. "If we get out of this alive."

The sight of the dead heaped on a battlefield affects you forever. The sight of one man, like Hubble, crumpled in death, affects you more. That man who was once full of life now lies like a broken doll. There is something terribly human about a warrior alone in death.

"You've killed a lot of people, haven't you?"

People avoid asking me that question. Those in the business know the answer. People at home don't ask. There's an inhibition that kicks in whenever the uniform, the job, and your posting are discussed. Those people are dying to know, but they don't know *how* to ask.

Trainor does not suffer from such inhibitions.

"I've killed enemies of the United States."

Trainor digests my answer. "What's it like to kill someone?"

"You writing a book?"

"Breed, I want to know."

Trainor's sincere. I suppose a sincere question deserves a sincere answer.

"I don't think much about it. In the moment, you do what you have to do. Up close, you look at the bad guy's hands. If he's got a gun, you have a split second to decide. If he's a threat, you kill him. At a distance, you have time to think. The nature of the threat, the rules of engagement. The process is clinical."

"It's business as usual for you."

"When you're in the moment, yes. You think about it afterwards. Sometimes years later."

For a long time, Trainor walks in silence. "Why did you leave the army?"

That's striking too close to home.

"I might tell you, one day. This isn't the place."

"I don't mean to be nosy."

Trainor's like a little girl, drawn to this most savage part of the world for all the wrong reasons.

"That's alright."

I watch the lithe sway of Trainor's hips as we cover ground. The shine of her blonde ponytail. Her hair would have been cut much shorter when she was taken. I like her... that odd mix of tomboy innocence and an adventurous spirit.

She's not ready to hear what caused me to leave the army.

We hike in silence for hours. Halfway across the north col, I imagine us reaching the bridge. The Deltas are moving well, and Robyn has little trouble keeping up. She's in good physical condition, altitude-adapted, and isn't carrying sixty pounds of weapons and gear.

Grissom is the problem. He's already stumbled twice, and Lopez has had to support him over the most treacherous sections of trail.

"TAKE FIVE," Koenig says.

I join the captain, Lopez, and Grissom.

"I'm fine," the colonel insists. "A bit of rest, good as new."

"I'm not a doctor," Lopez says, "but your concussion is getting worse."

"How does a concussion get worse?" Grissom sounds skeptical.

"The brain is swelling. After an injury, it swells some, then it swells more. It has to finish swelling before it gets better." Lopez shakes his head. "Colonel, your balance is off. I'm not sure your eyes are focusing properly."

Koenig leans on his rifle. "Okay. The colonel stays next to Lopez. I mean, right be-fucking-side him."

Grissom lifts his face to Koenig. "Captain, I'm going to be fine."

"Colonel, we're going to take you home."

I'm not a doctor either, but it's obvious the colonel's getting worse. He's putting on a brave face. Thirty feet away, her back to a tree, Trainor watches us like she knows what is being said.

"Captain. Breed." Grissom's tone is commanding.

"Yes, Sir."

"Whatever happens to me... you must get Sergeant Trainor back."

"Understood, Colonel," Koenig says. "She knows the deal."

"Trainor *is* the deal."

What an odd thing to say. Has the game changed?

Koenig grits his teeth. "You'll make it, Colonel."

We turn away from Lopez and the colonel. Under my breath, I address Koenig. "He can't go on much longer. He's slowing us down, and the Talis are gaining on us. We'd better think about a stretcher."

"Can he make it to the bridge?"

"None of us can answer that."

"We play the hand we're dealt," Koenig says.

For once, I agree with him.

We set off. I look back along the trail, watching for signs of pursuit. I see nothing, but they are there. The problem is Shahzad's main body may have reinforced Taliban from the village.

"How is he?" Trainor asks.

"Grissom? His concussion is getting worse."

I take Trainor's thin shoulders in my hands to steady her. Squeeze past, and go to Koenig.

"We need intel."

"What are you talking about, Breed?"

"We need to know if Shahzad's main body has joined those Talis behind us."

"How do you propose to do that?"

"I'll hang back and scope them out. Meet you at the bridge."

"Can you make it in time?"

"I move faster alone than in column."

Koenig looks thoughtful. "Okay. But if we cross that bridge and you're late, we'll blow it without you."

"I wouldn't expect anything else."

We're traversing a forested stretch of the slope. I step off the trail and climb twenty feet, careful not to leave signs of my passage. I look back through the trees. Trainor stares at me before turning away. Lopez remains focused on the colonel. Ballard smiles and flashes me a peace sign.

The little column moves on. I lie flat, cover myself with branches and leaves. Lie still, barely breathing.

I'd kill for a ghillie suit.

A column moving in good order should have flank guards. I would set them if I had the men. The terrain isn't suitable, but that doesn't mean an effort shouldn't be made. If Shahzad has set flank guards, there's a chance they'll stumble across me. If I'm as good as I think I am, they'll pass within five feet and not notice.

Ten minutes pass, twenty. Half an hour, and I sense movement on the trail. The disturbance of loose shale.

I peer through the leaves and watch the first Taliban pass, hugging the tree line. A prudent compromise. They're not marching inside the forest because they have nothing to fear from snipers on the opposite slope. Nor are they marching in the open, because they don't want to develop bad habits.

These are tough, no-bullshit killers. AK47s at low ready, chest rigs crammed with spare mags. It looks like every fifth man is carrying an RPG slung across his back.

At least fifty men pass, with more on the way.

Shit.

Launch tubes. SAM-7 missiles, NATO codename Grail. These are the bad boys that took out the Apache. There is a risk they could reach our exfil helos from the north face of Kagur-Ghar.

More men with assault rifles. Others carrying heavy rucks full of spare ammunition. Others carrying water. This is Shahzad's main body. Troops with specialized functions. Riflemen, RPG gunners, SAM operators, a logistics train. Men who carry spare ammunition and water for the others.

At least sixty men have passed. There is no end to them.

Maybe it's time to slink away. It could take an hour for these guys to pass.

Wait. They are carrying mortar tubes. Soviet-era 82 mm mortars. Two groups of six men each. One with a mortar tube, another with a bipod, a third with the baseplate. Three men with rucksacks crammed with mortar bombs.

Our odds are dropping fast.

If I spot Shahzad, I can end this with one shot.

In my mind, I reconstruct Shahzad's photograph. Now that I know his main body is after us, I will watch for a chance.

I crawl away from my blind, inch deeper into the forest. Sixty yards from the trail, I rise to a squat and start to move. Faster now, but careful to remain silent. I'm not walking through the brush, I'm swimming through it. Cleaving through foliage so as not to leave signs of my passing. A hundred yards from the trail, I rise to my feet and begin hiking. I head north. I want to overtake the lead elements of Shahzad's force.

One man can move faster than two hundred. Ten minutes pass, and I stop to listen. Nothing. If only for a moment, I want to turn the tables on Shahzad. Our rear guard, Ballard, is half an hour ahead of me on the trail.

The gloom of the forest lightens. I see daylight through the trees. I reach the tree line, and it's exactly what I was looking for. Fifteen feet of barren rock slope, with the tree line resuming on the other side. Down-slope, a half-slice cone of rock spreads to the base of the mountain. Koenig's party would have crossed it more than half an hour ago, and Shahzad's will have to in the next few minutes.

I cross the fifteen feet to the forest on the other side. Two hundred feet below me, Shahzad's force will have to cross a *hundred* feet of slope. That's a thirty-yard kill zone. I find a thick tree trunk jammed against a large boulder. Raise my rifle, brace it in the V between the tree and the stone. I throw my shoulder against the bark, a solid stance.

Five minutes pass and a Taliban fighter steps onto the slope. Turban, AK47, chest rig. I dial the magnification on my scope back to 3.6x and lay the crosshairs on his face. The scope is zeroed at four hundred yards, and he's sixty yards away. I adjust my holdover.

I watch the man start to cross. Sweep the scope to the dark forest from which he emerged. Two more fighters there, one with a hand-held radio to his ear.

Command and control. I let my breath out and squeeze the trigger.

A supersonic crack and the man with the radio crumples. The radio drops from his hand and bounces down the slope. Without hesitation, I swing the muzzle to the man standing next to him and fire again.

Hit.

Blood sprays from the back of the man's neck and he collapses.

I switch my aim back to the man on the slope. He scrambles to reach safety on the other side and I fire. *Miss.* The bullet ricochets off a boulder down-slope.

Fire again. *Hit.* The man drops his rifle and cartwheels down the mountainside.

Shouts from the forest below. The rattle of AK47 fire. Bullets thrash the trees to my left. They're guessing where I am.

Three more men at the forest edge. Two kneeling, firing AK47s. A third scanning the tree line, looking for my muzzle flash. He's the senior of the three. I lay my crosshairs on his belly and fire. *Hit.* The bullet slams into his chest and he drops.

The men below are jabbering in Pashto.

One points at me.

Another comes from behind, an RPG over his shoulder. The men shout and wave to clear the area behind him. I take my rifle from its support and duck behind the boulder. There is a swoosh, the sound of the rocket firing. A boom, and it's like a giant has boxed my ears with cupped hands. On the other side of the boulder, an orange fireball blossoms. A wave of heat breaks against the rock and washes over me.

Lucky they hit rock. Soon enough, they'll fire at the trees, or over my head. The Talis figured out how to modify an RPG's self-destruct mechanism. To detonate the rocket at ranges inside 950 meters—fusing the weapon for airburst. I have cover against direct fire. Indirect... not so much.

I displace, move thirty feet down-slope. Find cover behind more rocks. Raise my rifle.

Fire. *Hit.*

The Taliban shift their aim, cut loose on full auto. A crew breaks out a belt-fed PKM and thrashes the trees around me. The bullets whack into tree trunks, scatter chips of bark, split thick branches, and rain splinters on my head. More shouts. Glimpses of shadows scurrying inside the tree line—ghosts climbing the slope.

I hold the high ground. They have to climb to my level or higher. Another vertical envelopment. The mountain men are masters of these tactics.

Muzzle flashes twinkle across the sloping tree line.

A popping sound. Burning bright red, a flare arcs toward me. The PKM and two dozen AK47s ranged along the tree line zero in on my position. Not rambling waves of suppressive fire. Deliberate aimed fire. The PKM gunners fire eight and ten-round bursts. The Tali infantry know what they are doing.

I hurl myself away from the edge and crawl back into the woods. There is the whoosh of an RPG and another blast, fused to explode in the trees. The forest above me shakes, tree branches splinter into matchwood. A miniature sun flares overhead—waves of heat and concussion slam me against the earth.

My shoulder burns with pain. I roll on my side. A piece of glowing-hot shrapnel has torn my uniform and embedded itself in my flesh. I press my thumb against it and flick it aside. My skin and the fabric of my uniform are smoking.

Thirty feet downhill, I turn back, raise my rifle. Taliban are struggling to cross the barren gap.

Fire. One man goes down.

Fire. *Miss.*

Fire. *Miss.* The bullet whines off rock.

Motherfucker.

I'm shooting offhand, my breathing labored. I lurch against a tree, peg the rifle to the bark.

Fire. *Hit.* The Taliban fighter slams against the rock face, tumbles. Other Taliban withdraw to the safety of the woods. More AK47 fire zeroes in on me. RPGs streak through the air, rocket motors crackling.

I turn and melt into the forest. The tree line behind me is blasted into splinters. The concussion knocks me to my knees and elbows. I stagger to my feet, run like hell.

13

THE BRIDGE TO LANAT

Kagur-Ghar
Tuesday, 1500

Every breath is agony. I key the mike on my squad radio.

"Five-Five Actual, this is Five-Five Sierra."

I'm gasping in the thin air.

"Go ahead, Sierra," Koenig says.

The team will have heard the gunfire and explosions. In these otherwise quiet mountains, there is no missing them.

"Shahzad main body twenty minutes behind you. One hundred and fifty men. AKs, PKMs, RPGs, SAMs, mortars. Repeat, SAMs and eighty-two mike-mike mortars."

"We can't move any faster."

"Get across the bridge. I'm coming fast, make sure you don't shoot me."

Shahzad knows we're making for the bridge. He knows if we get across, we'll blow it. It's a rope bridge, poorly maintained. There has been a bridge of one form or another over that ravine for hundreds of years. The warlord's logical move is to blow it before we get there.

"Five-Five Sierra, is that you?"

Ballard. Forget stealth. I'm making as much noise as I can so Ballard will hear me coming.

"Yes," I gasp. "Hold your fire."

I make my way downhill on the forested slope to the lower tree line. A shadow figure waits for me, silhouetted against the sunlit stones and lighter vegetation of the opposite slope. Ballard peers at me through his birth control glasses.

"Breed," he says.

"They're fifteen minutes behind me," I say. "Twenty, tops. We can make the bridge before they do."

Ahead of us, Lopez and Grissom are hurrying along the trail. Grissom has one hand on Lopez's right shoulder.

"I'll stay with you," I say to Ballard. "If they catch us, you and I will hold them off."

"Roger that."

EIGHT YEARS AGO, I crossed that bridge. I remember it well. Thrown across a great ravine, two hundred yards long, six hundred feet deep. A rope bridge, it hung from four great wooden pillars on either side of the gorge. Pillars forged from pine trees, topped at fifteen feet, the bark scraped clean from their trunks. The bridge was eight feet wide. The ropes that held it were as thick as my thigh.

There's a sound like a jet taking off, or a rocket being fired. An explosion ahead of us, around the curve of the mountain.

"Mortars," Ballard says.

"Five-Five Sierra, this is Five-Five Actual."

Koenig.

"Go ahead, Actual."

"We see the bridge. They're shelling us."

"Get across. Cover from the other side."

"How the hell are they directing fire?"

Shahzad's mortars are indirect-fire weapons. The gunners can't see the explosions from around the curve of the mountain. Someone has to spot the fall of their rounds and direct the mortarmen to walk their fire into the target. Right away, I know where the observers are hiding. The patrol on the opposite mountain has a clear view of the bridge.

"They're spotting from Parkat," I shout. "Get moving."

More rushing sounds. Incoming mortar fire. Shahzad figures his artillery will catch us before his men. The mortar rounds burst in sets of two, one on top of the other.

"Shahzad's trying to destroy the bridge," I tell Ballard. "Come on, we have to cross."

We round the curve of the mountain. The slope has been leveled from the tree line, and the southern approach is a flat clearing.

Our team races for the bridge. Takigawa is first across. He hurtles pell-mell over the swaying bridge, his boots clattering on the planks. A brace of explosions rock the near approach. Koenig and Trainor hurl themselves to the ground. They are showered with dirt and rock.

Koenig gets to his feet and sprints across the bridge.

Another rushing sound. A loud whoosh. Not too different from the sound of an RPG being fired, but a hundred times louder. Another explosion in front of Trainor. A geyser of earth and rock. One of the supporting pillars is hit. It cracks like a tree split by lightning.

Trainor, caught trying to rise, is blown flat by the

concussion. Debris and fragments of rock shower her prone figure.

"Fuck."

It's Lopez. He and Grissom have thrown themselves flat on the rocks.

"Breed, the bridge."

Ballard's pointing, but he doesn't have to. The ropes have been torn from the split tree trunk. The bridge hangs from two pillars on the far side, but only one on this side. The long sweep of planks tilts sharply from halfway across the gulf, to our edge of the chasm.

"Trainor, Lopez." I wave to get their attention. "Forget it. Get back here."

"We're fucked," Ballard says.

"Maybe not." I work the angles as more mortars land on the clearing. Lopez and Trainor each grab one of Grissom's arms and drag him away from the bridge.

I key my squad radio.

"Five-Five Actual, this is Five-Five Sierra."

"Go ahead, Sierra."

"The bridge is impassable. We have to make for Landing Zone Three."

"How?"

"We have to descend to the valley, cross to Lanat, and climb from there. You can either continue to LZ Two, or meet us at LZ Three."

Standard operating procedure. Before any operation requiring exfil, several options are identified and articulated. If exfil from LZ One fails, the team moves on to LZ Two, a set number of hours later. If that fails, a pre-arranged exfil from LZ Three is attempted at another fixed time. Takigawa and Koenig can either abandon us and go for LZ Two, or try to meet us at LZ Three.

"Wait one, Sierra."

More explosions. Shrapnel splinters the remaining pillar supporting our end of the bridge. Loud as gunshots, the ropes supporting the span snap. The bridge tumbles into the chasm, dangles against the north wall of the ravine. Koenig comes back on the radio. "Sierra, we will meet you at LZ Three. What are your intentions?"

"We're going to circle back across the west face of Kagur-Ghar and head down-slope. If we can't use the bridge, neither can the Talis. You can cover our withdrawal."

"Roger that, Sierra. Maintain contact. Good luck."

"Five-Five Sierra, out."

Koenig and Takigawa are our ace in the hole. Safely across the chasm, there is no way Shahzad can outflank them. The best he can do is rake them with suppressive fire and shell them with mortars. But—he only has two mortars. *One* man—Takigawa, with a sniper rifle, can pin Shahzad down. Takigawa has limitless options on Lanat to displace and cover the far side of the gorge.

So long as he has ammunition for the heavy M110.

Ten magazines and as many stripper clips.

Koenig can help. I wish we had thought to bring a light machine gun.

The mortars continue to hammer the approach to the bridge. Fountains of rock and dirt are blasted from the clearing. The first fused airbursts shower the space with shrapnel and cartwheeling tree branches thick as a man's thigh.

Trainor, Lopez and Grissom join us at the edge of the forest.

"We're going to try for LZ Three," I tell them. "We

have to get moving. Koenig and Takigawa will cover us
from Lanat."

Grissom hangs his head.

"We have no choice," I tell them. "But we have been
lucky so far. Now, we get cover from the other side of the
gorge."

"Breed... you're hurt." Trainor brushes the side of my
face. Her fingers come away slick with a pink fluid. "What
is this?"

The concern in her voice, the tenderness of her touch,
surprises me.

"I was a few feet from some RPG blasts," I tell her.
"Overpressure ruptures blood vessels in the ear. Nothing to
worry about now—we have to get out of here."

Koenig and Takigawa can buy us at least an hour. There
are two ways for Shahzad to pursue us. First, he can force
his way through the clearing at great cost. Second, he can
have men climb the steep ridge that separates the east and
west faces of Kagur-Ghar. *That* option could delay pursuit
for hours.

"Better lucky than good," Ballard says.

"Best to be both," I tell him. "I'll take point. Then
Trainor. Lopez and the colonel next. You're rear guard."

14

FLIGHT FROM THE BRIDGE

Kagur-Ghar
Tuesday, 1530

Sweat pours down my face. The fluid trickling from my ears rolls down the sides of my neck and under my collar.

I lead our small band away from the clearing and onto the west slope. We throw caution to the wind, move as quickly as we can manage on the rock face.

The view from the west slope is vastly different. The expanse of the Kagur Valley spreads at our feet. Two miles in the distance lies snow-capped Shafkat. A high tree line above which little or no vegetation grows. Forested flanks, and a jagged lower tree line where trees have difficulty growing on rock faces.

It's often easier to climb a mountain than it is to descend. In fact, when climbing, it's wise to plan for a retreat. If your way is blocked from above, and you have no retreat, you're fucked.

Years ago, I traversed the east slope of Kagur-Ghar. I
don't know the west face. Now I have to look for a trail off
the mountain. There must be a few. The bridge was built to
make it easier for travelers and goatherds to cross to Lanat
and back.

From where I stand, I can't see the whole west face.
The trail we are on continues straight south, back the way
we came. There's every chance it joins the goat trail we
used to escape from Kagur village. That's no good to us.
LZ Three is in the opposite direction.

The trail must have its own forks and switchbacks.
Paths that lead higher, to the old Soviet outpost demolished
in the eighties. Paths that lead back to the valley. Most of
these trails are no more than a foot wide.

The lower levels of the west slope are heavily forested.
Over the millennia, heavy snow melts swelled the Kagur
River and deposited sediment and fertile soil on the mountainside. Piled onto the underlying rock. At higher eleva-
tions, there's less soil, and weather conditions are harsh.
Cold air, snowfall, and high winds. There are fewer trees,
much more bare rock. Huge boulders jut from the face.
Jagged rocks of all shapes and sizes. Some are larger than
five-ton trucks.

Crack.

An M110. Takigawa engaging. The shot is followed by
an overwhelming volume of AK47 fire. The abrasive rush
of incoming mortars.

I step off the trail, follow a faint path. It's heading south
to the village. The wrong direction, but it leads off the face.
At lower levels, I'll double back.

Trainor's voice is edged with fear. "How long can
Captain Koenig hold them off?"

"As long as he and Takigawa have ammunition."

"How long will that be?"

"Depends how many men Shahzad is willing to sacrifice."

I listen for the crack of Koenig's M4. He's firing single shots. Takigawa, in particular, will be scoring one-shot kills at a range of two hundred yards. Indeed, he has enough ammunition to wipe out Shahzad's force.

"Listen." I struggle to keep my balance on loose rock.

"What do you hear?"

"Shooting."

"What don't you hear?"

Breathing heavily, Trainor says nothing. Astonishing how exhausting climbing downhill can be, how hard your muscles have to work to keep your balance. You find muscles you didn't know you had.

"Do you hear any explosions?"

"No."

"Shahzad's run out of mortar rounds," I tell her. "I'm sure he has more with his rear elements, but it will take time to bring them forward. That's good for Koenig. Good for us."

The trail disappears. Washed out by rain. Maybe it was a trail only in my imagination. I slip on loose shale, and my feet go out from under me. Next thing I know, I'm on my ass, skidding down a slope. My left arm is stretched to one side for stability, my heels scrape furrows in the shale as I try to control my fall.

A cry above me. "Shit."

Trainor must have fallen. At the base of the sharp incline is a huge boulder. I slam into it with one boot, bend my knee to take the shock.

"Look out," Trainor calls.

I look back. She's lost her balance. The reason I slid

down in a straight line was the stability provided by my left arm. I could use my arm that way because I'm wearing gloves. Otherwise, the long slide would have flayed the flesh from my hand.

Trainor has no such protection. She doesn't dare throw her hand out, and her momentum causes her to tumble. She's pitched onto her side, rolling like a barrel kicked downhill. I hear her grunting with each impact. I could move out of the way. Instead, I brace myself. She slams into me like a cannonball.

I grunt.

Trainor rolls off me. "Sorry."

"Do this too often, we'll have to get married."

The girl gives me an odd smile.

"Breed, have you ever considered…"

"What?"

"How does Shahzad know we didn't *all* make it over that bridge?"

"He doesn't know. Nor does he know we were making for LZ Two, or its exact location."

Trainor smiles with satisfaction. "We have more time."

"Maybe. Shahzad has choices to make. If he wants to get onto Lanat he only has a couple options, and one of them is to come this way."

"Hey," Lopez calls out. "You guys gonna sit there admiring yourselves or get out of the way so we can come down?"

Trainor and I scramble aside. Lopez and Grissom link arms and descend the slope on their asses, careful not to lose control. When they get to the bottom, Ballard follows. Like me, he uses one hand and arm as an outrigger.

"Let's take five," I say. "Ballard, bring the long-range radio, get me comms. Let's raise Two-One Alpha."

Two-One Alpha, General Anthony's headquarters. As Trainor has pointed out, we have a little extra time. The sound of gunfire continues to echo from the direction of the bridge. It is not lost on me that Koenig, the unit commander, no longer has the ability to contact Bagram.

I lead Ballard a short distance away from the others. He takes a knee and switches on the radio.

"Two-One Alpha, this is Five-Five."

"Go ahead, Five-Five."

I take the handset from Ballard.

"This is Five-Five Sierra. I need to speak with your actual." I glance over at the others. Fifteen feet away, Grissom is slumped against a boulder. Not resting against it. *Slumped*. He looks like he is well into his last reserves of energy. I shift my gaze toward the snows of Shafkat, blinding white in the sun.

The voice on the other end has the high, tinny quality of electronic communication. "Don't know if he's available, Sierra."

"*Make* him available. If he misses this call, he *will* be pissed."

"Wait one, Sierra."

Ballard rolls his eyes.

The voice that comes on next is terse, authoritative. There is no question it belongs to Lieutenant General William Anthony. "This is Two-One Actual."

"Sir, we have been in contact with Shahzad's main body. Estimate one hundred and fifty hostiles armed with AKs, RPGs, SAM-7s, and eighty-two mike-mike mortars. Five-Five Charlie KIA. We have been separated from our actual and Five-Five Oscar. At the bridge to Lanat. We are going to bypass LZ Two and seek RV at LZ Three."

"Say disposition Shahzad main body."

"Bridge destroyed by mortar fire. Shahzad does not know location LZ Three, but he can guess. Will follow western route to reach Lanat."

The general hesitates. "Better. LZ Two is not viable against SAMs. We cannot risk exfil by air without local air superiority."

My stomach clenches.

"Two-One Actual, we can achieve superiority with fast movers."

"Negative," the general says. "Helos would be sitting ducks."

"General, we must exfil by air. Principal One is wounded."

Again, the general hesitates.

"Sierra, you must evade enemy main body. We cannot exfil without local air superiority. Keep me informed."

"Sir, Principal One *is* the mission."

"We are well aware of that, Sierra." The general's voice could cut steel. "Proceed as instructed."

Trapped, I want to run. Instead, I say, "Roger that, Two-One Actual. Five-Five Sierra out."

I return the handset to Ballard. "Shit."

"Breed, that's impossible."

I look across the valley to gauge the distances involved. "Those SAMs lay an umbrella with a radius of two miles. If we get terrain features between us and the missile, or if weather conditions blind the sensor, it can be done."

"It's a long shot."

"We have to try," I say. "No way the colonel is making it out of here on foot."

15

DEEP RECONNAISSANCE

Kagur-Ghar
Tuesday, 1600

I form up our ragged little column. Grissom's condition worsens with every step. Koenig and Takigawa continue to buy us time, thinning Shahzad's ranks. The sound of firing from the bridge grows distant. Sporadic. Koenig and Takigawa are conserving ammunition. Shahzad must be sending a detachment down the east face to flank Koenig. A small group, meant to move fast.

"Five-Five Kilo." I speak into my squad radio. "This is Sierra."

"Go ahead, Sierra."

"Keep an eye on the ridge above us. Shahzad might send a unit over the top."

"Roger that, Sierra. If he does, I'll catch them in silhouette."

"Hold fire. You'll see them, they might not see us."

Ballard is good. He will watch our backs. I need to find a way off this damn mountain.

General Anthony's reluctance to exfil by air is understandable. Peace negotiations stand at a delicate juncture. The loss of an Apache will make the papers. I imagine the general is struggling to keep a lid on it. The loss of more American lives and air assets would be embarrassing.

Yet—the General Anthony I've known most of my working life would take the risk. Out of loyalty to his men, and to accomplish the mission. I tell myself the general did not rule out exfil by air. He told me to create a situation safe for helos to land.

That much was in character. The general found good men and gave them room to run. He always had with me.

IT WAS EIGHT YEARS AGO.

The pretty staff sergeant ushered me into Brigadier General William Anthony's office. The great man was sitting behind a polished desk. Spread upon the tabletop were the parts of several sniper rifles.

A Husqvarna 6.5 mm Mauser, an M42, and a Winchester Model 70. The Model 70 looked like a Pre-64. The general knew his rifles.

I saluted. "Chief Warrant Officer Breed reporting as ordered, Sir."

"At ease, Breed."

The general was examining the bolt assemblies of the three weapons. We shot together regularly. The M42 and Mauser were his standard weapons. The Winchester was a new acquisition. General Anthony's firearms collection was as legendary as his collection of women. A qualified sniper himself, by God he knew how to use them.

Rifles *and* women.

"The Swedes got it right, Breed. They saw the superiority of the Mauser action and refused to mess with perfection."

"Yes, Sir."

"Winchester, too. They took the best bolt action in the world and dropped it into an American platform." I knew better than to interrupt the general. "Remington wanted to *improve* things. The 700 series is a great rifle, but flawed."

"I think they've ironed out the bugs, Sir."

"Have they?" The general held the M42 bolt to the light, inspected its lugs. "I suppose they have. But the difficulties were unnecessary."

The general sighed and put the bolt down. Stood, and rose to his full six feet, two inches. Lean and hard. He regularly joined operators on forced marches and combative drills. The old man held his own against sergeants half his age.

"I need you for a mission." General Anthony strode across his office to a giant wall map of the region. Waved me over. The map covered Afghanistan, Pakistan, western China, and Tajikistan.

I joined the general and waited for him to continue.

"We all know about poppies," the general said. "Afghanistan's economy runs on poppies. No other crop has the economics. The margins on wheat and beans aren't enough to support the farmers. Every square mile of arable land is devoted to poppies. Opium production, Breed, is Afghanistan's number one industry. Sixty billion dollars a year."

Of course, we all knew about poppies. Poppy fields grew within spitting distance of our airfields and operating bases. The dollar value of the crop shocked me. Anthony registered the surprise on my face. Smiled.

"Sixty billion a year, Breed. Opium finances the Afghan economy. It finances the government, it finances the Taliban. These people are not peasants. They run a sophisticated international business. *Most* drugs entering the United States enter through Mexico. *Most* drugs entering Europe and Russia come from Afghanistan."

"Sir, I've always wondered…"

"Don't be shy, Breed."

"There are poppy fields right outside the wire. Why don't we raze them?"

"Afghan drugs don't enter the United States, so the US government doesn't give a rat's ass. We, the military, have focused on kinetic aspects of the campaign. Left the war on drugs to the ANA. We give them money, they do the razing. The ANA, of course, are corrupt and ineffective. I reckon it's time we shook the box."

Nowadays, you'd expect a PowerPoint presentation. General Anthony was old school. He gestured toward an acetate overlay. Arrows were drawn in blue felt-tip marker from Helmand province, extending west into Iran. Red arrows from the south flowed north of Kabul, into the harsh mountain passes of Kunar and Nuristan. Reached through Badakhshan into Tajikistan and Pakistan. One long arrow stretched through the finger of the Wakhan Corridor, all the way to China.

"Drug smuggling," General Anthony said, "is all about routes. Highways over which caravans can pass. All the routes into Iran are over open ground, much of it desert. Look at Tajikistan. What do you see?"

"A third of the frontier is a no-brainer," I replied. "Flat ground, a nonexistent border. You can cross in a pickup truck. But—you stand out like a sore thumb. You *could* lose six out of every ten loads. That's not viable. The eastern two-thirds is mountainous. Melts into the Hindu Kush. There are no effective borders."

The general gestured at the map. "That's right. The western border is much easier to interdict than the eastern. In fact, the western border remains invested with units that had been the Northern Alliance. Enemies of the Taliban."

"The borders are nothing more than lines on a map," I said. "The tribes don't recognize them. They cross freely. In the winter, ninety percent of those mountains are impassable. We don't go there."

The general looked troubled. "Breed, I won't admit this in front of the men, but we are losing."

"Sir?"

"The outposts we maintain in those high mountain valleys are subject to terrible attrition. Morale among our regular troops is plunging. Rules of engagement designed by civilian authorities limit their scope for action. We don't have enough men to ensure victory, yet the men we have in those outposts make great targets."

"Is there no solution?"

Anthony pointed to the red arrows on the map. "I asked for more men. Until my requests are granted, I have to strike at the Talis any way I know how. These are the opium smuggling routes into Russia. Through the high mountain valleys, into Pakistan, China, and Tajikistan. Similar routes carry arms and explosives back."

"What about money, Sir?"

"The proceeds of the trade are laundered through offshore banks and held in Pakistan. The Talis are not peasants. Their technology is sophisticated. They receive assistance from Al Qaeda."

The general was setting the stage. He was about to come to the mission. I remained silent, gave him time.

"I intend to interdict their opium caravans," he said. "To do that, I need to know their business as well as they do. I need the intel only deep penetration reconnaissance can provide.

"Breed, your mission is to lead a team north from the Arwal valley. Through the northern passes into Tajikistan. You will plan for three months on the trail. You will follow the caravans wherever they lead. You will map the caravan routes, plot the enemy's bases. Locations of drug supply, processing and distribution. Arms trading. Training of enemy personnel. I want you to write the book. Make me an expert on the trade."

My heart pounded at the thought of three months in the mountains. Avoid contact at all costs. Spend a hundred percent of the time spying. It was a brilliant mission.

"I'm keen to get started, Sir. I assume you will allow me to do the detailed planning."

"Of course. Take any three men you choose."

"Keller, Lenson, and Hancock."

The general smiled. "I expected no less."

"They are the best."

I took my team down-range. We hiked through the Arwal, the Kagur, all the river valleys. We moved like ghosts in the mountains. Followed the Taliban. For three months, we lived off pre-positioned caches of supplies. Water, food, ammunition, fresh clothing. Hiking in the Hindu Kush inflicts wear and tear on the most durable uniforms. Regular tumbles on rocky slopes can leave you half-naked until you reach the next resupply cache.

More than once, Taliban found our trail and we had to shake them. I don't think they cottoned onto what we were doing. They were not onto us long enough to see the larger canvas of the mission.

On one occasion, we ran head-on into a Taliban patrol. There was no warning, we collided. I passed both their point man and their slack before any of us realized what had happened. I shot their number three man, and Keller shot both their number one and number two. In the fight that followed, we killed eight Taliban without suffering injury ourselves.

When the GPS told me we'd reached Tajikistan, I took a deep breath and stepped over the line. The air smelled no different. The earth and rock were no different. We pushed deeper.

Photographs, notes, annotated maps. I wrote the book General Anthony wanted. All the way from Kunar to Tajikistan and back.

When we returned to Bagram, General Anthony spent a month debriefing us. The debriefs were the strangest I'd ever experienced. We turned over all our material to the general. All the originals, no copies. Then he sat with us individually and as a group to review the after-action reports.

No one from the general's staff was present. No adjutant, no G-2, no one. We conducted private, top-secret briefings for the general. Tutorials on the drug and weapons trade in Afghanistan.

When we finished, the general took away all the material and sent us out again.

"This time," the general said, "you are going to China."

"The Wakhjir Pass."

"A low-intensity drug smuggling route." The general planted his hands on his hips. "An artery conducting opium from Afghanistan to western China. The mission is not limited to the pass. You are to identify all the routes in use. Take as much time as you need."

The general drew an X on the border between Afghanistan and Pakistan. "This will be your last pre-positioned supply point. We cannot send air resources into China. If you get caught there, you are on your own. No dog tags, no identifying unit patches or badges of rank. Nothing."

"Roger that, Sir."

"Breed, this is top secret. Your mission is to make me an expert on the drug traffic between Afghanistan and China."

That mission almost killed me. The Chinese caught wind of us and maneuvered to seal the border. We fought two engagements. Escaped through Pakistan-controlled Kashmir. There must have been collaboration between the Chinese, Pakistanis, and the Taliban. For the better part of a week, we dodged hunter-killer units in the mountains.

Did they know we were American? They must have. We were the only ones with the interest and the balls to be there. Our first mission into Tajikistan drew no attention. The mission into China rang some bells.

I wrote the book.

Personally briefed the general.

We never spoke of the missions again.

Now, eight years later, I pick my way over the rocks. Trampled stones form a narrow trail—barely suitable for mules and goats. On either side of the track, a carpet of pointed rocks and treacherous scree. I consider rigging a safety line, dismiss the idea. Taliban regularly cover this ground unassisted.

The disturbing conversation with General Anthony takes me back to those long patrols.

I watched to see what developed from the missions. You never forget a pair of journeys that occupied eight months of your life. Six months on the trail and two months of rigorous debriefs for the general's eyes and ears only.

US forces conducted more drug interdiction missions. Ambushes and air strikes on caravans. The attacks never made a dent in the opium traffic. A full-blooded effort could have stopped four out of ten loads coming through the Hindu Kush. I doubt we stopped two out of ten.

I had other missions on my mind. My team conducted nightly direct action raids on high value targets. I attributed our lackadaisical performance against the drug trade to a bureaucratic failure in the big green machine.

Why am I thinking about them now? Certainly my experience conducting those operations is the reason the general sought me out.

I can't escape the feeling that a circle is being squared.

16

THE CARAVAN

**Kagur-Ghar
Tuesday, 1600**

T he sound of gunfire no longer echoes from the bridge. We need to follow the trail lower, and find an off-ramp that takes us north. All I see below are craggy outcrops of stone, boulders as big as Humvees, and dense pine forest. Flowing mercury, the river snakes through the valley.

The trail we're on is narrow, at the edge of a rocky face. It plunges precipitously to trees at the base of a deep ravine. I lead our group in a loose file. Trainor follows close behind. Lopez and Grissom trail us by sixty feet. Ballard brings up the rear sixty feet behind them.

My attention is focused on the trail. The terrain is treacherous, one careless moment can be your last. Every few hundred yards, I raise my eyes and sweep the valley. I scan the brooding face of Shafkat and traverse north. Clench my teeth.

There, in the distance, a column of horsemen is making its way south. At least forty riders, in a file that stretches along the bank of the river. There are as many pack mules as horses in the caravan. Sure-footed animals burdened with cargo.

Shahzad's Taliban, or Najibullah's Mujahedeen. Impossible to tell.

I key my mike. "Five-Five Kilo, this is Sierra."

Ballard's voice crackles. "Go ahead, Sierra."

"Interrogative. Do you see a caravan, your five?"

"Affirmative, Sierra. Doubt they've seen *us*."

"They are between us and Parkat. This could get sticky."

"Your call, Sierra."

"Keep an eye on them, let's play it by ear. Sierra out."

Trainor is staring at the caravan with sharp eyes.

"Najibullah's or Shahzad's?" I ask.

Trainor shakes her head. I turn away and continue on the trail.

"Colonel!"

At Lopez's shout, I jerk my head.

Grissom has left the trail and is crawling out onto a huge outcrop, a promontory of black stone. From where we stand, the stone table onto which the colonel has crawled looks straight down four hundred feet onto the tops of pine trees, themselves a hundred feet tall.

What the fuck is the colonel doing?

Lopez follows the colonel onto the promontory, careful to pick his way among the rocks. One mistake will plunge either man five hundred feet down the west face.

At the edge of the promontory, Grissom stands, stares at the caravan.

Lopez reaches the colonel and grabs him by the

shoulder straps of his plate carrier. Grissom turns, tries to push the sergeant away.

The two men struggle. Trainor steps off the trail to follow the two men onto the outcrop. I scramble along the track, step in front of her. Hands on her shoulders, I hold her back. Feel my boots slipping on loose shale.

Trainor stares over my shoulder, struggles. "Breed, let me go."

I clutch the girl tight. "No, you'll make things worse."

Can't see what's happening. If I lose my balance, Trainor and I could both fall.

A man screams—Trainor cries out. "No!"

I look over my shoulder in time to see Grissom disappear over the edge.

Lopez stares after the colonel. He takes a breath, turns, and picks his way back to the trail. Together, he and Ballard join me and Trainor.

"The colonel's dead," Lopez says.

Trainor breaks free of my grip, launches herself at the medic. "You son of a bitch."

I grab the girl, struggle to restrain her. Viewed from the narrow trail, the five-hundred-foot drop is dizzying.

"He fell," Lopez says. "He crawled out over those rocks when he saw the caravan."

"Bullshit," Trainor snaps. "You could have held him."

"He lost his head." Defensive, Lopez steps back. "He jerked away from me, then he was gone. I saw him hit a tree, fall further."

At the image, Trainor cringes.

I turn to Ballard. The comms man was sixty feet behind Lopez and Grissom.

"It happened fast, Breed. That is how it looked."

Trainor's fuming. She turns on Ballard. "Are you blind?"

Ballard looks stunned.

Lopez throws up his hands. "Fuck you, Trainor."

"Cease fire, all of you." I'm watching the team fall apart. "Trainor, it was an accident. Now, we need to know. Are those Najibullah's men, or Shahzad's?"

The girl looks around our little group. Glares at Lopez. "I can't tell from this distance," she says.

"They can cut off our move to Lanat," I tell her. "We have to know."

Trainor jerks away from me. "I can't help you."

Fuck. I need this girl to be a soldier, not a petulant child.

I fish the Leitz binoculars from a pouch on my plate carrier. Squint at the sky. The sun is well past its peak and shining on our slope. To keep reflections from giving our position away, I snap honeycomb shades onto the lenses. Scan the column.

The usual Taliban and Mujahedeen garb. Turbans, waistcoats, chest-rigs, and high boots. They ride tall in the saddle, assault rifles slung over their shoulders. The pack mules must be carrying weapons and explosives. Further along the riverbank, a long column of infantry follows the caravan. No indication they've seen us.

I hand the binoculars to Trainor. "Try. Who are they?"

Trainor raises the glasses to her eyes and scans the caravan. Hands them back to me. "I can't say."

She barely looked. I can't tell if she's hiding something, or plain pissed. I want to shake some sense into her.

We have Shahzad behind us, and a mounted force in the valley. If the caravan belongs to Shahzad, our route to

Lanat has been closed. We can try to slip through, but it will be risky.

What if the caravan belongs to Najibullah. I'm not sure he'll be any better than Shahzad. Sure, he's negotiated a peace deal. The envoy he negotiated with took a five-hundred-foot dive onto the rocks. How will he react to that. He might decide to take us *all* captive. He might kill us, keep the girl, and start over.

What did Grissom say.

If anything happens to me, Trainor is the deal.

I turn on the girl. "Grissom knew he was in a bad way. He said if anything happened to him, you were the deal. What did he mean?"

Trainor looks miserable. Shrugs. "I know all the details."

"Were you present at the negotiations?"

"Not all of them. Grissom told me after."

"You know the details, but not the nuance. It'll be difficult for a new negotiator to step in. *Trust* is crucial. Najibullah won't be familiar with someone new."

"That's *right*." Trainor bares her teeth. Her voice is a snarl. "Trust *is* crucial. No, Najibullah *won't* trust a new guy."

"Cough it up, Trainor. What did Grissom mean when he said you were the deal?"

"Fuck off, Breed."

"We have a right to know."

Trainor's hostility dissolves. She looks pensive. "I have the details. And releasing me is *part* of the deal."

"Trainor." Ballard's voice is gentle. "If you know something, tell us. We could all die out here."

"There's nothing more to tell."

Not good enough. Trainor is holding back, but I can't figure her out.

I'm tired of running, and I need a place to think.

Someplace we can reach before dark. A defensible strong point.

I know just the place.

17

SOVIET OUTPOST

Kagur-Ghar
Tuesday, 1700

The Soviets knew enough to seize the high ground. Back in the eighties, they flew a company of crack paratroopers onto the north peak of Kagur-Ghar. Built an outpost. The Taliban heard the helos fly in one morning, and the fortress was there by nightfall.

The south summit was higher, but snow-capped year round. The north peak afforded the paratroopers a commanding view of the entire Kagur River valley. It was above the tree line, occupied a position that gave defenders a 360-degree killing zone.

I intend to occupy that strong point.

We can't go back because of Shahzad's main body. We can't make for Lanat because of the caravan and mounted Mujahedeen.

I step off the trail and start climbing. Full of confidence, energy surges through my limbs. The photograph of Kagur-

Ghar is fresh in my mind. In half an hour, we can reach the tree line. From there, it will be easy to make our way to the peak.

The pace I set is fast enough to exhaust the fittest trooper. I'm still shaking from the confrontation at the promontory. Trainor all but accused Lopez of murder. Neither Ballard nor I saw what she thinks she saw. I can't blame Lopez for being pissed.

Trainor is sucking wind behind me. No casual chit-chat now. Either she's still upset by Grissom's death, or she's being beaten to death by the altitude and physical exertion. I will give her this much—she is holding her own. Higher and higher we climb. Without Grissom holding us back, we cover ground at a faster pace. Above the tree line, I find a trail that leads to the summit. Not directly, because such a route would be too steep. Rather, it snakes across the face at acute angles. A series of dizzy switchbacks. First south, then north, then south again—always higher.

I pick my way over rocks and boulders. Now, incongruously, over a huge log. A felled tree trunk. I sit on it, raise one leg, and rest it on the log. Prop the butt of the M110 against my thigh, lean my forehead against the barrel. Watch sweat drip from the tip of my nose. Gasping, Trainor joins me.

"How did this get here?" Trainor asks.

No question… she regrets her outburst. She's offering a peace pipe.

"Soviets." I lift my face to Trainor, hold the rifle barrel with both hands. "They hauled logs from the tree line by helicopter. Used them to build the fort."

Trainor rests her hands on her knees and bends over. "Why, Breed. Why bring us here?"

"This elevated position dominates the valley. It's a

defensible strong point. From here, we can hold off two hundred Talis."

I lower my leg to the other side of the log and roll over the obstacle in one smooth motion. Climb higher.

"*Fuck.*" Behind me, Trainor levers herself over the log. I'm pretty sure she's not swearing at me.

More logs are scattered over the mountainside. Many are splintered. When the Soviets abandoned the fort, they set off explosive charges, scattered debris everywhere.

I reach the top as the sun crowns the summit of Shafkat. We're ten thousand feet above sea level and the air is cold. The setting sun bathes the mountain in blood-orange light.

Take out my binoculars, sweep the valley. Looks like the caravan will make camp for the night. The Mujahedeen are setting a lager on the embankment of the Kagur. Watering the horses. They must be Shahzad's men... they are making no effort at concealment.

Sweep right. Nothing from the direction of the bridge. An illusion. Koenig and Takigawa have disengaged. Shahzad will have split his force. A small unit descending the east face to flank Koenig. The main force following the contour of the mountain to the west. Will they see signs of our passage?

Exhausted, Trainor collapses next to me. "What do you think?"

"I think everybody is going to ground for the night."

Lopez is the next to reach the peak. He casts his eyes around. "Be it ever so humble."

The Soviet outpost isn't much to look at. Never was. Two bunkers, a cookhouse, a magazine, and slanted chutes blasted in the rock—to wash toilet waste downhill. The smaller of the bunkers was for officers, the other for the enlisted. The sleeping quarters doubled as storage space for supplies. RPGs and ammunition for mortars was stored in the magazine bunker in case the Mujahedeen got lucky with a mortar round.

When the Soviets blew everything up, they did a pretty good job. The quarters are little more than a pair of dugouts sunk five feet into shallow depressions in the rock. The log and stone walls are still there. They rise three feet above the depressions.

Each roof had once been constructed of logs laid across the walls. Each log was lifted by helicopter from the tree line. In some cases, the Soviets used a double layer, to provide extra protection from mortar attack. The magazine had a concrete roof with rebar, and logs on top. Pitch was slapped between the logs for insulation. The whole affair was covered with canvas tarp to provide a measure of waterproofing. When the Soviets' charges went off, the rock reinforced the walls, and directed the blast effect skyward. A good eighty percent of the roofs are gone, scattered over the mountainside. A few of the logs fell back into the living spaces.

I key my squad radio. "Five-Five Actual, this is Five-Five Sierra."

No response.

Ballard trudges the last few steps to the mountaintop.

"Five-Five Actual, this is Five-Five Sierra."

"They're out of range," Ballard says. "I can get them on the high frequency set."

"Let's do that."

Ballard shrugs off the ManPack, deploys its five-foot whip, and establishes comms. I turn to Lopez and Trainor. "We can hold off a company from here if we have to," I say. "Keep a lookout. Lopez on the west face, Trainor on the east. Watch each other's back."

Lopez and Trainor glare at each other. Sullen, they walk to their positions.

"Five-Five Actual, this is Five-Five Kilo," Ballard says.

Nothing.

"You got the right frequency?"

"Yes." Ballard twists a dial on the set. "We can reach them, but they can't reach us. Their squad radios aren't powerful enough."

"Let me get this straight," I say. "They can hear us, but we can't hear them. If I speak into that handset, there's a good chance Koenig will hear, though he can't respond."

"Exactly. Incoming bursts on the squad frequency will trip their receivers. He'll try to respond, but it'll take him a minute to realize you can't hear him."

I motion for the handset and Ballard hands it over. "Five-Five Actual, this is Five-Five Sierra. Listen close. You can hear me, but I cannot hear you. Have spotted Mujahedeen caravan in valley between us and Lanat. LZ Three is no-go, we cannot RV. Am sheltering for the night, will advise intentions in the morning. Repeat. Will advise intentions in the morning."

"Fair enough," Ballard says.

"Best we can do," I tell him. "Let's raise the general."

Ballard has no trouble reaching the general. The 25-Watt HF ManPack bounces waves off the ionosphere, straight onto Bagram. I provide a terse update of our situation. No embellishment is required—it's a clusterfuck.

"Bring Principal Two home." If General Anthony is tearing his hair out, his voice gives no indication. "Use your discretion. Improvise."

"Yes, Sir. What about Five-Five Actual?"

"If they are at LZ Three on schedule, we will exfil, subject to local air superiority."

"Yes, Sir."

"Keep me posted. Two-One Actual out."

Ballard switches off the radio. We exchange glances. Trainor and Lopez are keeping watch on the slopes. It is my first chance to be alone with Ballard since Grissom's fall. "What happened out there?" I ask. "You had the clearest view."

"I don't know, Breed." Ballard looks uncertain. "The colonel was getting worse. Unsteady on his feet. Half the time, he used Lopez for support. Then he saw that caravan, broke loose, and stepped onto the outcrop. Lopez went after him, tried to pull him back. The colonel kind of... flailed. They struggled for a second. The colonel fell."

"Did you see the way Trainor looked at Lopez?"

"Trainor thinks Lopez killed the colonel." Ballard grimaces. "Dude, her reaction was fucking bizarre."

"She's calmed down," I tell him.

"Trainor freaked out once." Ballard shakes his head. "That's once too many."

18

ZAREK'S BASE CAMP

Kagur-Ghar
Tuesday, 2000

The wind howls on the mountaintop. Ballard stands at the wall of the enlisted quarters and covers the west approach. Lopez covers the south. All around us, the rocky slope drops off in a symmetric cone. Both men are wearing their helmets and NODs. The Taliban cannot approach undetected.

"Four hours," I say. "Trainor and I will spell you at midnight."

I descend the steps of the officers' dugout and find Trainor leaning back against one of the walls. She's sitting on the floor, arms folded across her chest, trying to stay warm. The dugout provides protection from the wind.

She's staring at the sky.

Resentment and anger have bled from her features, leaving grief. She has been crying. In the moonlight, the tracks of tears shine on her dusty cheeks.

Nights are dark in the Hindu Kush. Villages are lit by lanterns. Precious fuel is conserved. In the mountains, the faintest glow can give away your position. Something as simple as lighting a digital watch can get you killed. A cigarette is a magnet for snipers. In the valley, the caravan has lit cooking fires. Cocky bastards.

Without light pollution, a clear night is beautiful. The sky is an ocean of stars. "Do you see the Big Dipper?" I ask.

"Yes." Trainor points. "Right there. If you follow it, you get—the North Star."

One of the logs that formed the ceiling has fallen back into the space. I sit on the floor across from her and lean against it.

Exhaustion is stamped on the girl's features. Her blond hair has been drawn back in a careless ponytail. A tangle of loose strands hangs to her shoulders, gets in her eyes.

"You were right," I tell her.

"About what?"

"I do love it here."

"You got a first name, Breed?"

"Yes."

Trainor stares at me. At last she chuckles. "You can call me Robyn."

"I'm not sure that would be appropriate."

"Why? You're not a serving officer. You're a *consultant*."

She's playing with me, and I don't mind.

"Robyn," I say, "you're a tough girl."

"Not five minutes ago."

"How well did you know Grissom?"

"How long have you known these men?"

"Are we trading now? Two days."

"You were brought in from outside. Why would they do that?"

"I know the land. Now—how well did you know Grissom?"

Robyn zips her field jacket to her chin and tries to duck into it like a turtle. "Reasonably well, over the last six months. He was a good man. I liked him."

"Eighteen months, Zarek held you. Did you ever try to escape?"

Darkness. I study Robyn's expression by the light of the moon and stars. She exhales, and her breath fogs instantly.

"I knew you'd ask me that."

I shrug. "You'll have to answer at your debrief."

Robyn chews her lip. "Alright," she says. "I tried to escape—once."

"Tell me."

She does.

THE MUJAHEDEEN who captured Robyn hooded her, and marched for three days along the banks of the Arwal. When helicopters passed overhead, her captors rushed her to the cover of the tree line.

Robyn was exhausted. On the fourth day, the Muja-hedeen mounted horses and put her on a pack mule. The trail sloped upward. Her captors took her ever higher into the mountains. Deeper into the Hindu Kush.

When they stopped, the Mujahedeen jerked the hood from her head and pushed her off the donkey. Hands bound behind her back, she fell to the ground with a thud. The men around her laughed.

The shock of the impact rattled her bones. Robyn felt like she had been beaten.

They had arrived at another village. High in the mountains, surrounded by snow-capped peaks. The village, of rock and logs, rose majestically from the river valley. It was bigger than other villages they had passed. There were stables for horses, barns to store feed. Caravans ran as long as grain could be stored in the north... When the grain was gone, the last caravan left. The animals wintered in the south.

The Mujahedeen moved aside deferentially as a rider approached. Staring at Robyn, he dismounted and handed the reins to one of his men.

The man scrutinized Robyn.

Robyn squinted at him.

The man was six feet tall, with a pointy beard, handlebar mustache, and sharp features. There was a bit of gray in his beard, he must have been in his mid-fifties. He wore a traditional tribal turban... black, with dark red trim. His trousers were tucked into high leather boots. His dress consisted of a black *perahan tunban* in the northern style, over which he wore a crimson leather waistcoat.

Over his shoulder was slung a Dragunov, a Russian sniper rifle with a polished wooden stock. A heavy weapon, but he was a big man. The rifle's sling was decorated with red, black and white beads. His chest rig was of the Chinese Type 56 pattern. Pouches for three magazines in front, smaller pouches at the sides. The Chinese rig was canvas, this one was hand-stitched leather.

"What is your name?" the man in black demanded.

Robyn was shocked he spoke English.

The Mujahedeen didn't seem to know she could speak Pashto. Robyn decided it might be wise to conceal the skill. She would listen and learn all she could.

"Robyn Trainor. Sergeant, United States Army."

"Sergeant Trainor." The man enunciated each syllable. "I am Zarek Najibullah. These are my men, and you are my guest."

Insurgent, drug trafficker, warlord.

Najibullah conveyed an aura of majesty.

Two of the Mujahedeen helped Robyn to her feet and cut the cords that bound her hands. They stood aside, and she stared. Refused to dust herself off.

An old man, with a white beard shaped like a shovel, pushed his way through the crowd. He stepped close to Robyn and slapped the side of her head. She raised her hands to protect herself. The man jabbered in Pashto and made to strike her a second time. He was screaming at her to cover herself. Robyn pretended not to understand.

Najibullah waved him off with a sharp command. More Pashto, and one of the men produced a length of white cloth. He draped it over Robyn's head.

"The village imam." Najibullah's tone was apologetic. "You must keep your hair covered."

Robyn adjusted the cloth protectively. "Let me go. The US military will find us, and you will regret the day you took me."

Najibullah laughed. "They have been searching for a week, Sergeant Trainor. A hundred miles south."

"How long are you going to keep me here?"

Najibullah smiled. "Today you must wash yourself and rest. This afternoon we will speak. Tonight we shall dine."

Robyn fumed.

"Ghazan," Najibullah commanded in Pashto. "Take her to Wajia."

. . .

"THAT VILLAGE MUST HAVE BEEN a base camp," I say. "Far north in Badakhshan, close to Tajikistan."

"Yes," Robyn agrees. "Three days' hike and seven days' ride north of Arwal."

"American units don't go there. The Soviets never built outposts further north than this one."

"Why not?"

"Look at it. Impossible to resupply, except by air. Patrols have to traverse rough mountain country. Our fittest troops aren't cut out for this. The Soviets learned, abandoned it. We learned the same, *much* further south. In Kunar."

"People live there," Robyn muses. "They're happy. They know nothing else."

"I doubt life there has changed much in two thousand years."

"Zarek and his lieutenants felt secure enough to bring their families there."

"Yes," I say. "It sounds like he was confident enough to turn you over to his women. Tell me about Wajia."

"Wajia was lovely. In many ways, she was everything I wanted to be."

I'm sure Robyn is smiling in the dark. A sad, wistful smile.

19

ROBYN AT BASE CAMP

Kagur-Ghar
Tuesday,1800

G hazan was a big man of fifty, with a bushy black beard, and granite features. He wore a white turban, dark blue waistcoat, and a canvas chest rig. Each pouch was big enough to pack two magazines, which meant he had six thirty-round banana mags strapped to his chest. The side pockets were crammed with F1 *limonka* hand grenades.

He led Robyn to a big house at the foot of the mountain. Standard construction for the region. Walls of flat stones, piled high in columns. Windows and doorways buttressed with logs and planks. A metal stovepipe chimney stuck out of the roof. It would be sealed with pitch. The front door was intricately carved, but without a lock. This house was big, like a duplex, with two front doors. Robyn wondered if two families lived there.

A curtain was drawn from one of the windows, and a

pair of striking blue eyes peeped out. Slender brown fingers let the curtain fall back into place. Blue eyes were sometimes found among Afghans. It was a striking genetic trait.

Ghazan slung his AK47 over one shoulder. His worn brown boots crunched on the stone approach to the house. Robyn looked back. Najibullah and the men were unburdening the mules and stabling the horses. The imam was glaring at her.

A woman in a black *burqa*, with gold trim about the headpiece, appeared at the front door. Her eyes shone with the light of youth. There was no question she was the one who had peered from behind the curtain.

"You have a guest," Ghazan said in Pashto.

"The lord told me to expect her," the woman replied. Her voice was soft and melodious.

Robyn's ears burned. Her abduction *had* been planned. Zarek had made arrangements for a woman captive.

The woman ushered Robyn into the house.

Daylight shone through large windows into the main room. There were shelves, a fireplace, mats and cushions. Compared to other houses Robyn had visited, this dwelling was well-appointed. It belonged to a man of status.

The layout was traditional. There was an open staircase that led to a basement. There were three doorways, one to the left of the front door, and two on either side of the back wall. All were covered with screens made of cloth, or beaded curtains.

"I am Wajia," the woman said, hand on her chest. She spoke Pashto, but the gesture made her meaning clear.

"Wajia." Robyn responded in English. "I am Robyn."

"Good." The woman gestured to one of the doorways at the back of the room. "Come with me."

Wajia pushed through a curtain and led Robyn to

another room, half as large as the living room in front. This was a woman's room, with sleeping mats and wooden chests against the walls. Robyn was surprised to see a back door in one corner. The mountainside was *not* the back wall of the house, as Robyn had first suspected. Rather, the house had a proper back wall, constructed of logs and stone. There must have been an alley behind the house, leading to communal toilet facilities.

Robyn turned in a slow circle, to take in the room. The woman took off the *burqa* and laid it on top of one of the chests.

The Pashtun woman turned a knob on a gas lantern. The light pushed the shadows back into the corners. Robyn sucked a breath.

Wajia was thirty, five years older than Robyn. Her hair was long and brown, her eyes a supernatural blue. Freckles dusted her cheeks, a complexion the color of milk chocolate. She had high cheekbones and a wide mouth.

Her dress was overwhelming in its femininity. She wore a *firaq*, a kind of blouse, with orange and yellow vertical stripes. It was tucked into an orange *shalwar*... baggy, gathered at her waist and ankles. Her shoes were flat and sensible, with thick rope soles to cope with rocky terrain.

"You're beautiful," Robyn said, in English.

Wajia looked puzzled.

Robyn smiled. The smile conveyed what she wanted Wajia to know.

Wajia smiled. She gestured toward clothing stacked on another chest. It had been prepared for Robyn's arrival. In a corner, on the stone floor, was a basin of water and towels.

"Clean yourself," Wajia said. She did not expect her Pashto to be understood, but she made motions with the towels and water. "Dress."

Robyn could smell the stink of her camouflage uniform, dusty and stiff with dried sweat. She felt like she had been shredded by days on the trail.

"Thank you," she said, in English. She nodded her head, smiled her appreciation.

Wajia returned Robyn's smile. Pushed through the curtain and left Robyn alone.

The back door beckoned.

It was too soon to attempt an escape. Robyn took off her plate carrier, wondered why Najibullah had allowed her to keep it. He must have wanted to afford her a measure of protection in the event of a firefight. Of course. He had abducted her for a reason.

Robyn stripped and bathed. Washed and dressed herself in Pashtun clothing. A white *firaq*, with baggy sleeves, tight cuffs, and a high collar. A turquoise *shalwar*. A dark blue *chador* or head scarf. She was also given a veil that she would wear in the presence of men other than Najibullah.

Wajia showed her into the main room, where they sat on mats and drank tea.

Najibullah joined them.

"We shall speak English," Najibullah told her. "Wajia does not speak English, but she knows what I am about to tell you. Afterwards we shall go to my *hujra* and meet my lieutenants."

"Alright," Robyn said.

"You will share quarters with Wajia," Najibullah said, "You will be part of my household."

Robyn's stomach clenched. She knew things about fundamentalist Islamic culture. The thought of becoming a harem slave was a childhood fantasy, but the prospect of experiencing the reality was terrifying. "How long will you keep me?"

Najibullah ignored her. "I have negotiated your status with the village imam. In this home, and in this village. Wajia is my wife. You are a captive of my right hand. And a guest. There are rules."

"A captive of your right hand."

"You were taken in battle, therefore you are a slave." Najibullah spoke as though her status was obvious.

"If you touch me," Robyn said, "you had better not sleep. I *will* kill you."

"I am allowed four wives," Najibullah continued, unimpressed, "and as many captives of the right hand as my finances permit. That is a substantial number, I assure you."

Dear God, Robyn thought, *he is going to rape me.*

"You are also a guest." The warlord spread his arms expansively. "I intend to hold you for ransom, and it behooves me to support your value. I shall do that by maintaining you in the condition in which you were found."

"Can I be a slave *and* a guest?" Robyn asked.

"Within this house, you may go about with your hair uncovered. You may go about in traditional clothing. Outside the house, you will keep your hair and face covered at all times. Is that understood?"

"Yes."

"I will have the head of any man who dares to gaze upon your naked face. Put on your *chador* and come with me."

Wajia helped Robyn don her *chador*, and fastened her veil.

Najibullah led her through the front door into the sunlight. They walked forty feet to the other door she had noticed earlier. Inside was another sitting room. Rectangular, twenty by thirty feet. Two doorways in the back wall, widely spaced. Unlike those in the living room next door, these were solid wood. Two cold fireplaces, one at each end. Thick mats were arranged around the walls. Fifteen men sat, eight on one side of the room, seven on the other. Najibullah and Robyn sat cross-legged in the middle of the row of seven.

This was a Pashtun *hujra*. Robyn knew what they were, but this was the largest she had seen. It was a tribute to Najibullah's affluence and prestige. The outer walls were of stone, at least a foot thick. The interior walls were paneled with wood, and carved. The windows had clear glass, and curtains that were drawn to let daylight into the room.

"Men are not permitted in one's house," Najibullah said. "This is my *hujra*, a place where I receive guests. Where we can be served by women, and allowed our time. You are here as an exception."

"Why?"

"Because *you* are the order of business."

Three women in *burqas* entered and served tea. When everyone had a cup before them, the women left pots of tea on a low table and withdrew from the room.

Robyn looked around the room. Ghazan was there, seated across from Najibullah. The other men ranged from thirty to fifty in age. All were bearded and dressed in Pashtun clothing. They laid their chest rigs on the floor next to them, and rested their AK47s against the walls.

"The first phase of the operation is complete." Najibullah addressed the room in Pashto. "Adim Fazili, speak of Shahzad's movements."

A young man in his early thirties straightened. "He knows we have the girl. As you are aware, he shadowed you through the attack on the American patrol. A small band of his men followed as you travelled north."

"And now?"

"They have sent three men back to report your movements."

"Well done, Adim." Najibullah continued, "What of his main force?"

A third man, with salt in his beard, waved his arm. "They remain in the tribal lands. Al Qaeda is paying him well to protect their training camps. Every day they grow stronger."

"Does he spare no forces to protect his caravans?"

"No more than usual," the gray-bearded man said. "The drugs move north, the explosives move south. Unimpeded."

Najibullah looked displeased. "What of ours, Baryal?"

"American helicopters attacked Dagar's caravan yesterday. He was forced to scatter. Small groups will make their way south independently."

"Losses?"

"A quarter. It could have been worse. Dagar did well, lord."

Najibullah stroked his beard. "Very well, we shall progress to Phase Two. This is Sergeant Trainor. We are going to ransom her. Where are the nearest Americans?"

"There are Americans at Nangalam," Adim Fazili said. "They are at the Afghan National Army post."

Nangalam, in Kunar, is a village on the bank of the Pech. It is the southern terminus of the Kagur and Arwal river complex that extends all the way to Badakhshan. The US Army had tried to turn it over to the ANA, but the Afghans couldn't hold it. A year later, the Americans returned to occupy the base.

"One of you shall make an overture," Najibullah announced. "Right now, they do not know whether the woman is alive or dead. They need to be advised she is alive. We have her, and will return her for compensation. Who will go?"

"I will go," Adim Fazili announced.

"No, I!" roared Ghazan.

"I will go," Baryal shouted.

Najibullah laughed. He turned to Robyn and switched to English. "Each one of these men," he told her, "wants to take news of your capture to the Americans at Nangalam. It is a dangerous journey. They may be attacked by Shahzad's Taliban, by Americans, or by the Afghan National Army."

"Why would Taliban attack Taliban?"

Najibullah laughed. Turned to the room and spread his arms. "She calls us Taliban."

The room broke out in laughter and hoots of derision.

"I don't understand," Robyn said.

"We are not Taliban," Najibullah told her proudly. "We are Mujahedeen. Shahzad is Taliban. Schooled in the Wahabi madras of Lahore. You Americans must learn the difference."

He was right, Robyn thought. All Taliban were Mujahedeen, but not all Mujahedeen were Taliban.

Najibullah turned back to his officers. "How shall we prove to the Americans that we have this woman?"

"Cut off a finger and send it to them," Baryal called out. The group roared. Robyn flinched.

"We shall cut something off," Najibullah muttered. He clapped his hands.

Robyn fought down the bile that rose in her stomach. She was going to fight. By God, she was not going to let these savages cut pieces off her.

A woman in a *burqa* entered. With deference, she approached.

Robyn shrank back. "Don't you dare."

"Cut her fingernails," Najibullah snapped.

The woman produced a small ceramic bowl and plastic bag from the folds of her *burqa*. Knelt on the floor in front of Robyn.

"Give her your hands," Najibullah commanded.

Heart pounding, Robyn held her right hand out. The woman produced a large nail clipper and trimmed Robyn's fingernails. When she had done both hands, she shuffled the clippings from the bowl into the plastic bag and sealed it.

Najibullah took the bag from the woman and dismissed her with a wave of his hand.

"Your DNA is in the US Army registry, is it not?"

Robyn was impressed by Najibullah's sophistication. Had the idea come from a Westerner, she would not have remarked it. Coming from this savage, the idea of providing DNA evidence of her captivity seemed worthy of awe.

"This—" Najibullah shook the bag "—will prove we have the woman. The Americans' science will tell them it belongs to her."

"They will not know she is alive," Ghazan objected.

"Let them wonder," Najibullah laughed. "Not knowing will make the Americans twice as desperate to find out."

Robyn knew it was true. The army would recover the bodies, find hers missing. The media would be full of the news. An American woman missing in action. Heaven and earth would be moved to find her.

"Adim." Najibullah held out the plastic bag. "Take twelve men and bring this to the Americans at Nangalam."

The young man got to his feet and took the nail clippings from Najibullah. "What compensation should we ask, lord?"

Najibullah laughed. He turned to Robyn. "What will

America pay to get you back? A million dollars? An independent Nuristan? Perhaps the President's head on a golden plate."

"Nothing." Robyn's voice was firm.

"Nothing." Najibullah squinted at her. "Do they value your life so little?"

"We do not bargain with bandits. The United States will *take* me back."

"We shall see." Najibullah turned back to Adim Fazili. "Ask nothing," he snapped in Pashto. "Let the Americans tell us what *they* think she is worth."

"YOU COULDN'T HIDE your knowledge of Pashto forever," I say.

"No, but Zarek was proud of his English." Robyn's expression softens with the memory. "He learned it at the French *lycée* in Kabul when he was a boy. He speaks seven languages."

"Seven."

"Yes. Pashto, Dari, Farsi, Arabic, English, French and Russian."

I struggle to make out Robyn's expression in the dark. "Dari?"

"Yes, it's a dialect of Farsi. Eighty percent of Afghans speak Dari or Pashto. We practiced together."

How cozy.

"How did they find out you speak Pashto?" I ask.

"By accident."

20

ROBYN'S PLAN

Kagur-Ghar
Tuesday, 2000

The wind howls outside the ruins. It must be terrible for Lopez and Ballard. We should be trying to sleep, but I cannot tear myself away from Robyn's story. Something was never right about this mission, but I can't put my finger on it. The secret may be in this girl's story. The secret may save our lives.

"The Mujahedeen were using you to barter," I tell Robyn. "That made escape more important."

"Zarek had something special in mind. I had to try."

There is no mistaking the determination in Robyn's tone. She continues her story.

ADIM FAZILI WENT to select his patrol, and prepare for the trip to Nangalam. Najibullah took Robyn back to the living space. As they left the *hujra*, Robyn smelled the aroma of chicken cooking on a grill. Wajia and two other women were preparing a meal outside the front door.

"Ghazan is my right hand," Najibullah said. "Baryal is my left. Their houses are on either side of mine, and those are their wives. They are preparing supper for all of us. We dine in an hour."

Robyn felt a sudden urge to join the women. "Let me help them."

Najibullah laughed. "There will be ample time for that. You will help Wajia with her work and much more. Now, let us take this opportunity to speak."

He led her into the living room. The shadow of the mountain was creeping across the house. Najibullah lit a pair of lanterns and set them on tables, one at either end of the room. He reclined on cushions by the wall.

"Take off your *chador*," he instructed Robyn. "Let me see you."

Robyn took off the *chador*, folded it, and set it on a table. She turned to Najibullah, found herself shy. She shook her hair out and presented herself to the warlord. She knew her hair would shine golden in the light of the lanterns. She was not a beautiful girl, but she knew she was pretty enough, in a tomboyish way. The *firaq* and *shalwar* were too feminine for her. She did not know how to stand to show herself to advantage.

"Sit," Najibullah said. "There are things of which we must speak."

He reached over and grabbed a cushion from the floor. Tossed it to her, motioned to a spot in front of him. Obediently, she set the cushion on the floor and sat cross-legged, facing her captor.

"We are Mujahedeen," Najibullah said. His manner was pedantic. "We are engaged in a great jihad. Russians,

Americans, all unbelievers must depart our land. We are good Muslims, but we do not subscribe to the strict rules of the Wahabi. Do you know what the word 'Taliban' means?"

Robyn knew, but shook her head.

"It means 'student.' The leaders of the Taliban were trained in madras in Pakistan. They seek to impose the strictest form of Islam on our country. If you walked outside like that, with your hair unbound, the Taliban would have you flogged to death."

"I've seen too much of that," Robyn said.

"Not by my men. We know that for Afghanistan to prosper, we must move beyond these strict laws. We will not forsake the teachings of the prophet. But the Quran can be interpreted in a number of ways, as can your Holy Bible."

"Women are stoned to death."

"And men beheaded. When the punishment fits the crime. This country is going through a terrible internal conflict. America has blundered into it, as foreigners always do. This village has been one of my operating bases for the last three years. It was Shahzad's before that. How do you think the village imam survives?"

"He's caught between you, isn't he?"

"Of course. These villagers have not survived three thousand years of war without becoming masters of deceit. All must accommodate the ways of soldiers who pass."

Robyn shook her head. "You make it sound like you have all the answers."

"No, Sergeant Trainor. I do *not*. But at least I understand the questions."

"What is the question?"

"Afghanistan is in a theocratic civil war."

Robyn stared, and Najibullah laughed. "You see? You

have never heard the matter described in such terms. It is true. We are in a civil war between Wahabism and a more enlightened Islam. Only one side can win."

"Your side."

"I do not intend to lose." Najibullah straightened. "Now. Go help Wajia. I will retreat to my room for afternoon prayer."

SUPPER WAS A COZY AFFAIR. Wajia brought in Najibullah's share of the meal. Ghazan's and Baryal's wives each took their husbands' food to their houses. Bowls of vegetables, rice, and cubes of grilled chicken were set on the floor. The meal was far more palatable than the stir-fry of goat and vegetables served at Arwal.

"Why did she join the army?" Wajia asked Najibullah.

Najibullah translated the question for Robyn.

"I couldn't find a job," Robyn answered. "I figured the army would teach me things."

"Your army allows women to serve with soldiers."

Robyn shrugged. "We know villagers in Afghanistan are sensitive about men questioning women in their homes. Women soldiers like myself are brought along to make things easier."

"I know of this," Najibullah said.

"Not many of us remain."

"Yet you continued to serve in such a capacity."

Najibullah stroked his beard.

"Yes."

"Why?"

"I do not wish to return home."

Najibullah clucked. "Home is all any of us has. Without family and tradition, we are nothing."

Robyn swallowed. "Where else can I be of use?"

After the meal, Robyn and Wajia took the dishes and cooking pots to the river to wash. They carried buckets of fresh water back to the house for drinking and cleaning. She began to appreciate why the most senior men and village elders occupied homes at the base of the mountain. Gravity. One didn't need to climb the steep flights of steps.

Najibullah slept in one of the back rooms. Wajia and Robyn shared the other.

That first night, Robyn began planning her escape.

Wajia had shown her how the back door opened to an alley between the mountain and the back wall of the house. Robyn stepped outside, closed the door behind her, and surveyed the passage. The houses above were supported by rock, and stilts that extended to the levels below. One had to squeeze between the stilts, these great wooden columns, and the face of the mountainside. Go far enough in one direction, and one came to Ghazan's house. Travel in the opposite direction, one would pass the back of Baryal's. Beyond lay the communal toilets.

There were narrow spaces between the houses. Robyn crept to the front, where she had a clear view.

The escarpment stretched twenty yards from the village to the fast-running river. On the ground level were a number of large houses. There were stables and a corral. She looked right and left. There, on either side, were steps that led to the higher terraces.

Every village had sentries. This village had at least two. One at either end, close to the river. From there, they could watch the big wooden bridge that provided access to the far bank. They covered both banks, the steps, and the upper terraces.

From her place of concealment, Robyn could not tell if there were more sentries posted on the higher levels.

She crept back to her room, careful not to disturb Wajia.

ROBYN BEGAN to leave the house every night. She studied the sentries' behavior. She saw they could not focus on both the riverbanks and the village at the same time. In the mountain blackness, on a moonless night, it would be easy to climb the steps when they were not looking.

She would have to escape onto the mountainside. Cover as much ground as possible during the day, and make her way to the river by night to drink. She began to hide food inside her boots. She would make her escape in her camouflage uniform. Draw a dark *chador* over her head to hide her light-colored hair.

There had to be sentries on the upper terraces. Robyn dared not venture onto the escarpment at night to see where they might be posted. Rather, every time she went with Wajia to the river, she swept the village with her eyes, trying to spot armed men on watch.

Always, she saw one or two. Never in the same place. She had to assume they would also be posted at night.

The distance from the terrace to the tree line was no more than fifteen yards.

It was a chance she had to take.

21

ROBYN'S ESCAPE

Kagur-Ghar
Tuesday, 2000

"I had to wait for the new moon," Robyn says. "I used the time to plan, and hide food."

People who live in cities are used to streetlamps. They are often surprised by how bright moonlight can be when cast across an open space. Soldiers standing exposed on a riverbank or mountain slope make easy targets.

"Were you able to identify the positions of sentries on the terraces?"

"No." Robyn shakes her head. "I had to assume they were roving. But I knew they were there."

THE NEW MOON CAME. Robyn waited till the early hours of the morning. She dressed in her camouflage uniform, drew a dark brown *chador* over her straw-colored hair.

Robyn stepped to the back door. Glanced over her

shoulder at Wajia's sleeping form. She felt a pang in her heart. Wajia had tried to befriend her. She hoped Wajia would not get into trouble.

It was a soldier's duty to escape. Robyn crept out of the house and along the alley.

The distance from Najibullah's house to the steps was a hundred yards. Robyn located the two sentries by the river-bank. Slowly, she lowered herself to the ground and began to crawl. She moved deliberately, with her chest and belly close to the ground. Within twenty yards, her knees and elbows felt raw.

When she reached the foot of the steps, she knew the easy part was over. She waited for the sentries to look toward the riverbank, then sprinted uphill for ten seconds before throwing herself flat against the stone. She held her breath, rolled on her back, swept her eyes over the terrace. There... on the third level, a sentry leaned against the side of a house.

Three points of reference now. She waited till all three men were looking away, then sprinted for ten seconds. She reached the top, flattened herself on the first terrace. The sentries by the river were no longer the greatest threat. She had to watch the sentry on the third level. Find other sentries she assumed were high on the terraces.

Robyn lay flat, watched, and listened.

There. A man stood on the edge of the second terrace, looking out toward the river. He stared at the glistening black ribbon for a long time, then looked to the sentry by the house and waved. She rolled on her side and hid her face.

Fifteen yards.

Robyn fought the temptation to get to her feet and run.

Instead, she rolled onto her belly and crawled. Six inches at a time.

Twenty feet and she looked back. The man on the second level was looking toward the river.

The man on the third level was staring at her.

Robyn's heart stopped. She turned her head to the side and hid her face. Held her breath and waited. Counted three hundred seconds.

The night was silent. when Robyn looked back, the man was looking toward the river again. She shut her eyes briefly, kept on crawling.

When she reached the tree line, she wanted to run. Forced herself to crawl further, past the first trees. The village was quiet. She had no compass, but on a clear night, she knew how to use the stars.

Ten minutes later, she got to her feet and began to hike. She moved slowly, watching her step. The forest floor was treacherous. Gnarled roots snaked in all directions, fighting for purchase in the rocky soil. It was rough going, but she found herself reassured by the familiar smell of pine needles. She pressed her hands flat against the trunks of trees for support. Felt bark under her fingers. Every fifteen minutes, she stopped to listen for the rush of water from the river.

First light, Robyn moved faster. The Mujahedeen were born to track in these mountains. She looked over her shoulder, moved so as not to disturb the foliage.

She pressed on, trying to cover as much ground as possible before sundown. Her legs burned and grew heavy from the difficulty of balancing on the undulating forest floor.

Robyn decided to do the unexpected. She turned west, deeper into the forest. Harder going, uphill. She was careful not to break any branches. After half an hour, she stopped and laid herself on the ground next to a fallen log. The sun was setting, and the forest was cloaked in shadow.

She sensed a disturbance in the forest. The soft brush of sleeves against bushes, the click of a sling's swivel against metal. The sounds of a small group of men pacing themselves.

The men passed her. Now she had a problem. They were not going to return to the village that night. They would camp out for another day at least. Until they decided they had lost her, or until she blundered into them.

Blundering into them was a real possibility. They would surmise she would stay close to the river, and now they were between her and freedom. If she kept going south, they would cut her off. If she headed further west, she would get lost.

Robyn went to ground.

IT WAS close to dawn when Robyn woke, shivering with cold. Though she had food in her cargo pockets, she could not satisfy her gnawing hunger. She was thirsty. Her mouth and throat were dry, and she could only swallow her saliva with difficulty.

Robyn struggled to her feet and made her way to the river. Fifty feet below, black waters coursed over rocks in the riverbed.

The mountainside was an obstacle course of boulders. Huge rocks with grotesque shapes jutted in all directions. Some were half-buried in the mountainside. Others were piled together like mounds of rubble, ready to slide into the river with the removal of a single stone from their base.

Descending in the dark was suicidal. Desperate from

thirst, Robyn groped her way around the largest boulders. Extended her legs and tested each foothold.

Halfway down, she slipped and skidded fifteen feet on her ass. Slammed into a boulder, lost her balance, pitched sideways. Hit a pile of loose shale and rolled. The roll saved her. Had she fallen down a vertical face studded with rocky outcrops, she would not have escaped injury.

She stared at the stars. Strained her ears to detect any sign of pursuit.

Silence.

Robyn stood and tested her arms and legs. She was scraped and bruised, but otherwise unharmed. She staggered across the escarpment to the riverbank, threw her legs over the edge, and lowered herself till her boots found purchase. The waters were high enough to fill three-quarters of the riverbed. The water's edge was ten feet from the bank. The rocks were slippery, but she knelt on all fours, and ventured out. Took off her *chador* and plunged her face into the rushing water.

Ice cold, like a hose directed at the side of her head.

She threw her head back and shook water from her hair. Then she cupped her hands and drank. She found a large rock, worn smooth by the waters. Sat and closed her eyes.

The sky over the western mountains was the color of salmon. Fog flowed over the waters and filled the riverbed. Robyn got to her feet. Her hair and the fabric of her uniform crackled with frost. Like a kerchief, she bound the *chador* loosely about her neck.

She took chicken and rice from her cargo pockets and ate. Crawled into the fog bank, found the running water, and drank some more.

The sun cast its golden rays over the mountainside she had descended. She had been so preoccupied with her hunger and thirst she forgot she would have to climb back. She would be exposed on that slope. Safety lay in the forest, beyond the tree line.

Robyn climbed out of the riverbed, slipping on wet stone. Once on the bank, she stood and brushed herself off. She sucked breath, froze. Four Afghans with horses stood on the escarpment, staring at her. How could she have missed them? The fog, and early morning frost. The sound of rushing water must have muffled their approach.

How could one tell a Mujahedeen from a Taliban? Were they Najibullah's men, sent to find her, or Abdul-Ali Shahzad's? Perhaps they were bandits. Perhaps they were villagers. There was no way to tell. They were dressed alike, with white turbans, waistcoats, and chest rigs. Dismounted, they carried AK47s.

Two of the men strode toward her.

Robyn ran. It was useless to run on the riverbank. They would catch her with the horses. She sprinted for the mountainside, twenty yards away. Reached it before they did, started to climb.

They caught her before she got ten feet up the slope. She felt a hand grab the back of her belt and yank her off-balance. Cried out and fell backwards against a man who turned, deflected her weight, and left her to crash on her side. Another man kicked her in the belly and she doubled over into a fetal position. In seconds, one man had pinned her arms from behind. The other was tearing at her belt.

Robyn kicked at the man. He threw his weight on her, balled his fist, and struck her face. Robyn spat blood.

Overcome with panic, she screamed in Pashto. "No! No! Stop!"

The belt came undone and the man struggled to jerk off her pants. Robyn thrashed, but he pinned her down and continued to struggle with her clothing. "Stop it," she shrieked. "Help me!"

Thwack.

The man holding her arms let go. Something wet and fleshy spattered her face. She heard the bullwhip crack of a high-powered rifle echo from the mountain walls.

Robyn realized the man holding her arms had been shot. She had heard the sound of the impact before the sonic boom of the bullet.

The man struggling with her pants straightened. Robyn turned.

On the riverbank, a quarter of a mile away, a lone figure sat on a horse. A rifle was raised to his shoulder. Off-hand, he fired again.

Another *thwack.* The head of the man at her feet exploded.

A third man raised his AK47 and cut loose. Robyn recognized the distinctive heavy drumbeat of an AK on full auto. Effective at maybe a hundred yards. The fourth man swung onto his horse, unlimbered his rifle, and charged.

The lone figure fired again at the galloping bandit. Missed.

The man on foot dropped his mag and pulled another from his chest rig.

Thwack.

The round hit the man center-mass before he could reload. He dropped like a sack of grain.

The rider with the AK47 was charging at full tilt. The only way to close the distance and get inside the AK's effective range.

The lone figure spurred his horse, fired again. Another gunshot, and the bullet knocked the attacker right off his mount. The horse, without its rider, bolted.

From start to finish, the engagement had lasted less than a minute and a half.

Robyn struggled to one elbow. Humiliated, she tried to cover herself. The lone mounted figure cantered toward her. She recognized the black turban with red trim, and the red waistcoat. Zarek Najibullah carried his Dragunov with one hand on the pistol grip, muzzle pointed skyward.

That was damn good shooting. Mounted, off-hand, at four hundred yards. Five shots, four hits, one from a gallop at a moving target.

Robyn squinted at Najibullah. Brushed dust from her face. Her hand came away wet with blood. From the man who had pinned her arms.

"Sergeant Trainor," Najibullah said. "You are full of surprises."

Robyn blinked. "What?"

Najibullah smiled. "You speak Pashto."

Robyn was shaking. Her pants and underwear were down around her knees. She struggled to pull them up. All she wanted was to cover herself.

The warlord sat on his horse and circled her. Watched her struggle to fasten her belt with quivering fingers.

"Shall I have you flogged, Sergeant Trainor?" he asked.

"You'll do what you want."

"Give me your word you will not run away again."

Close to tears, Robyn stared at him.

"I've seen women flogged in the villages." Robyn shudders. "I agreed."

"You didn't have a choice," I tell her. "You had to go back."

"He gave me one of the horses from the men he had

killed. Watched me mount it, liked that I knew how to ride. He made me wear the *chador*, escorted me back to the village. The imam tried to make trouble, but Zarek ignored him.

"Wajia said I'd been foolish, that there was nowhere to go. Zarek and the men thought my escape was entertaining. They expected me to run."

"Entertaining."

"These are hard men, they lead hard lives. They find sport in things modern Americans don't understand. Hunting, racing horses cross-country, telling stories. Most Afghans are illiterate, but they respect a man who can deliver a good story."

"Did you keep your word?" I asked.

"Yes. Everyone knew bandits tried to rape me. The men accepted Zarek's decision not to have me beaten. I kept my word, and the village welcomed me. Of course, I was a woman, and had to respect their restrictions. Zarek gave me a lot of room. While we waited for Adim Fazili to return, Zarek took me riding, hiking. He wanted to learn all he could about our culture."

Trainor's narrative disturbs me. There are ways to obtain information. Trainor's relationship with Najibullah sounds way too cozy. The fact that he'd rescued her from being raped mattered a lot to her. Everything he did was tailor-made to gain her trust.

"I know what you're thinking," Trainor says. "He should have beat the shit out of me and locked me in a box. You think he wanted information. I'm telling you he didn't care. He had his own agenda."

"Alright," I say. "I believe you."

But I don't.

22

EXFIL AND AMBUSH

Kagur-Ghar
Wednesday, 0400

I call a council of war.

The four of us take a knee in the center of the enlisted bunker. Robyn and I are short on sleep after our long talk.

"What's the plan, chief?" Ballard sounds alert and rested.

"I want to try something the Talis won't expect."

"I like it already," Lopez says.

"Okay. We're going to violate the most basic rule of infil-exfil. We are going to leave the way we came."

A special forces team does not leave an area of operations by the same route it entered. The simple fact is, should the enemy become aware of the infil, he will deploy forces to guard it.

"Do you think they know you came by way of Shafkat?" Ballard looks skeptical.

"I'm not sure," I admit. "But any forces around the village and Shafkat are likely to be weak. We'll use the smaller bridge. Cross the river a mile to the north, avoid the village entirely."

"What about Shahzad's main body?" Lopez asks.

"We'll stay a step ahead of them. I'm willing to bet they humped all night to close on Koenig and LZ Three."

"Will the general try to exfil LZ Three?"

"Only if the helos don't run into SAMs. It's also possible Shahzad doesn't have SAMs deployed on Shafkat. Better for us."

"What's our Plan B?" Ballard asks.

"We're on Plan E now," I say. "There is always something else to try. If helo exfil fails, we'll melt into the forest below the tree line. Walk out."

"Alright," Ballard says. "I'm in."

Lopez gets to his feet. Snorts, rolls his shoulders like a boxer stepping into the ring. "Why not hike out right now?"

"This mission is time-sensitive." I glance at Robyn. "Exfil by helo is the preferred option."

Ballard raises Bagram on the high frequency radio. General Anthony comes on the air almost immediately. I doubt he has slept.

"If we start now," I tell him, "we can reach our insertion point on Shafkat an hour after daybreak. It's on the west face. If Shahzad has SAMs in the village, the peak will shield us."

"It's worth a shot," the general agrees. "I'll arrange the extraction team."

"Five-Five Sierra out."

Next, Ballard switches to the squad frequency. Koenig cannot respond, but he might be able to receive. Twice, I transmit my intentions. Sign off, get to my feet.

"Let's roll."

I CHANGE our order of march. Lopez, armed with his HK416, takes point. I follow in the slack position with my M110. Unarmed, Robyn follows me, while Ballard acts as rear guard.

We set off down the trail. Except for Robyn, who stays close to me, we space ourselves ten yards apart. We wear our NODs, and there's still enough moon in the sky to help light the way. We move at a fast pace. I want to reach the village before first light.

I force myself to relax, settle into an economical gait. Shahzad came after us with his main body. That means he left a token force at the village. With luck, crossing further north, we'll bypass them completely.

Lopez stops and raises his right fist. Beckons me to join him.

"Check me," Lopez says. "Is this the right waypoint?"

I double-check his coordinates. Compass and GPS.

"Yes, we need to divert here."

Lopez departs the trail. Slows as he picks his way across the slope. I follow him by three or four yards. To steady herself, Robyn occasionally grabs my shoulder. Each of us tries to follow in the other's steps.

We reach the riverbank. Our land nav was not shabby. We stand fifteen feet from the bridge.

It's smaller than the one at the village. Sturdy, built from thick wooden planks.

I wait for Lopez to cross before I follow him. We make our way over the bridge one at a time and gather at the tree line.

The moon is bright enough to illuminate the riverbank.

I cringe at the thought of standing there, like a duck in a
shooting gallery.

Lopez moves out, heading for the trail we used the
previous night. He moves slower than before. A British
slow march, weapon at high port. All his senses are primed.
This is the kind of pace one uses on a jungle trail, alert for
ambush and booby traps.

The village rises from the opposite bank on our left. It's
dark, not a flicker of light. The riverbanks are moonlit, but
we are walking close to the tree line. We should be invisible from the village.

Lopez throws himself to the ground. I hear a snap and
see a muzzle flash from the direction of the trail. Throw
myself down. More muzzle flashes, the drumbeat of AK47
fire. We're thirty yards from the trail. There must be two
dozen Talis ranged between us and the mountainside.

We're on the X.

Lopez returns fire, single shots. I hear the sharp crack of
an HK416 behind me. Ballard has joined the fight.

We have to get off the X. Two choices. Either assault
the ambush and throw the enemy on his back foot, or seek a
strong point and call for help.

The enemy outnumbers us eight to one, and we are on
open ground.

"Ballard," I yell. "Make for the village. Strong point.
Trainor next. Lopez, cover our withdrawal."

Ballard sprints for the bridge. His form is silhouetted
against the glittering water. In the light of the setting moon,
he casts a long shadow on the riverbank. His boots clatter
on the bridge—he's across. Robyn runs after him. Stumbles, falls, struggles to her feet, and keeps running.

My stomach hollows. Was she hit?

Robyn's across. I race after her. Bullets snap around

me, ricochet from rocks on the bank. Behind me, Lopez switches his rifle to full auto and hurls a blistering volley of automatic fire at the ambush.

On the other side of the bridge, Ballard drops to a kneeling position and starts shipping rounds. I sprint across. Lopez displaces, the last to withdraw.

Weapon raised, I race over the escarpment toward the village. Half expect to be shot from one of the houses.

Nothing.

The Talis arranged the ambush on the west bank. They didn't leave any of their men in the village. Too much risk they might be hit by the shooters across the river. A conscious decision was made to guard the trail and let the village go.

I reach the house where Robyn and Grissom had been held captive. Short-stock my M110 and push the door open. Enter, covering the left cut. Clear. Blood-soaked mats. A wide, amoebic stain on the floor—from the man I shot yesterday. I pivot, covering the right cut. Clear.

There is no time to properly clear the house. Kagur is an enemy-controlled village, and the villagers are armed. I toss a grenade into the side room. Another into the basement.

Explosions from the side room and cellar. The curtain billows into the living room.

I turn, raise my rifle, and fire at the muzzle flashes across the river.

Breathless, Robyn hurtles through the door.

Lopez dashes across the escarpment. Enters the room, smashes one of the windows with the butt of his rifle. He switches back to semi-auto. Together, we cover Ballard's withdrawal from the bridge.

Ballard tumbles into the house.

"Get comms," I tell him. "Right fucking now."

Robyn takes Ballard's M416, goes to a window, breaks the glass.

I grab her by the back of her collar, drag her down. "What the fuck do you think you're doing."

"I can fight."

"Like hell. You are the mission. Get on the floor and stay there."

"Two-One Alpha," Ballard calls into his handset. "This is Five-Five Kilo."

"Go ahead, Five-Five Kilo."

"Troops in contact, Kagur village. Grid reference, Yankee Romeo 803 675. We have two-five hostiles. Require immediate air support and evac."

"Copy, Five-Five Kilo. TIC, two-five hostiles. QRF good to go. Be advised—final approval my actual."

I grab the handset. "Two-One Alpha, tell your actual, if we don't get support A-S-A-fucking-P, there is no mission. Out."

Ballard and Lopez fire from the windows. I fire from the door.

We have one thing going for us. Two dozen Talis are going to have a hard time charging across that bridge. They maintain a sustained volume of fire from the opposite bank. Like rain, bullets spatter the stone walls of the house.

"We need a way out." Ballard drops a mag, reloads, thumbs his bolt release.

"That house on the left," I say.

"What about it?"

"Right next to the steps. From that house, we can get onto the slope."

"Where are the villagers?"

"Taking cover. Be careful, around here every civilian has a gun."

Lopez grunts. "Dawn's breaking. We can hold them off until help arrives."

He's right. The sky is lightening. The air is cold, and tendrils of fog creep along the surface of the river. The stones on the riverbanks glisten.

The radio crackles. "Five-Five Kilo, this is Two-One Alpha."

Ballard snatches the handset from its cradle. "Go ahead, Two-One Alpha."

"We have UAV eyes on your poz."

Of course, General Anthony would have tasked a drone to loiter over Kagur. From the moment the exfil from LZ One went bad.

"Give us the news," Ballard snaps.

"Estimate one hundred Taliban infantry approaching from the north, larger caravan one mile behind."

"Damn." I grab the handset. "What about air support?"

The general's voice comes on the air. "This is Two-One Actual," he says. "Those Talis have SAMs. We cannot risk exfil by air."

"Two-One Actual, request immediate gunship support."

"Negative, Five-Five Sierra." The general's voice assumes a tone of finality. "You are on your own."

I toss Ballard the handset. Robyn stares at me, open-mouthed.

Back to the doorway. Bullets spray from the right and splinter the frame. I duck back inside. With cries of *Allahu Akbar*, Taliban rush across the bridge. Other Taliban, the vanguard of Shahzad's main body, are firing from our side of the riverbank.

"Fuck." Ballard drops the handset and turns back to the

window. Rains fire on the Talis crossing the bridge. One man falls, then another. The Talis on the other bank provide a base of fire. The ones coming on our side are free to maneuver against us.

"Not going to wait for another hundred and fifty Talis to get here," I say. "Ballard, Trainor, run for that house. I'll follow. Lopez, you're rear guard."

Ballard needs no urging. Shouldering the radio, he squeezes past me. He's through the door and running like hell. Robyn starts to go, but I hold her back. "Wait till he gets there, he'll give us cover."

More Talis rush the bridge. Emboldened by covering fire from their comrades on our side of the river. I raise the M110 and fire. Another two crumple onto the bridge's planks.

Gunfire spits from the house under the steps. Ballard has reached the strong point and cleared it. I grab Robyn by her plate carrier and push her out the door. "Go," I tell her.

Sprinting without the burden of a heavy ruck, Robyn covers ground quickly. One hand on the door frame, I step into the open and run after her.

AK47s fire from both sides of the river. Once again, it's like we are on the X, sitting in an L ambush. Ballard and Lopez fire their HK416s in response. Accurate, aimed fire.

I'm gasping, running with the weight of a sixty-pound ruck on my back.

Robyn cries out, pitches face-down.

I drop to her side. Grab her shoulder, roll her over.

"I'm hit," Robyn says. Her eyes are glassy.

"Can you stand?"

Bullets snap around us. I put my arm around the girl, help her to her feet. She's walking like a zombie.

Fuck it. I let my rifle hang from its sling, sweep Robyn

over my shoulders in a fireman's carry, and lurch the remaining fifteen feet to the door. The muzzle flash of Ballard's weapon is blinding. Inside, I drop Robyn on the floor.

"Where are you hit?" I ask.

"In the back."

I roll her over, examine her plate carrier. There is a hole in the canvas, a dent in her back polyethylene plate. I can stick my thumb in the damn thing.

But—the bullet did not penetrate.

"You're okay," I tell her. "Plate stopped the round. You got blunt force trauma."

It was a hell of a shot in the dawn light. Center mass, between her shoulder blades, a bit to the right of her spine. There is a chance her right scapula's cracked, but I doubt it. Whatever injury she has, it isn't as bad as having her heart and lungs shot out with a high-powered rifle.

A hell of a shot—or dumb luck.

Lopez charges through the door. "Damn," he gasps. "They are right on my ass."

"This is not looking good, chief." Ballard continues to fire single shots. He is picking off Talis crossing the bridge, but he cannot stop them all. Through the door, I can see a large force approaching from the riverbank. They are fanning out, investing the village.

We've been lucky. AK47s on full auto are inaccurate. Muzzle climb makes the weapon all but uncontrollable. The shot that nailed Robyn was the lucky shot to end all lucky shots.

"Do we run for the hills, chief?" Ballard drops another mag. Reloads, thumbs his bolt release, fires. A man fully integrated with his weapon.

I take a breath. Raise my rifle, dial the scope to 3.6x, scan the Taliban massing in the village.

Shahzad. If I can find him, I can end this with one shot.

"Either of you guys make Shahzad?"

"Negative," Ballard says.

Lopez scans the village with his optical sight.

"Negative."

Ten minutes ago, I was thinking of running for the hills. Now all I want to do is kill the Taliban leader.

There he is.

The man in the photograph. Al Qaeda's ally in Afghanistan, Abdul-Ali Shahzad looks more like a priest than a warlord. Long gray beard, *karakul* cap. Sharp, black eyes. Eyes that look like they are staring right into me every time he glances in my direction. He's standing in the doorway of a house, a hundred yards away. Waving, barking orders.

I lay the crosshairs on his head, adjust my holdover.

Shahzad gestures. I swing my rifle to see what is occupying his attention.

My blood runs cold.

It's a Tali, AK47 slung across his chest. Over his shoulder, he carries an RPG. The rocket is pointing right at me. Its warhead can crack the stone wall of this house. Not sure it will penetrate, but I can't take the chance.

I squeeze off the round. There is a puff, a bright pink mint. The man with the RPG drops.

Swing my rifle back to cover Shahzad.

The warlord is gone.

23

ZAREK'S ENTRANCE

Kagur Village
Wednesday, 0630

I can't find Shahzad.
Taliban are gathering behind houses at the top of the escarpment. Others are crossing the bridge from the far side, taking kneeling positions on the riverbank. It's like every fourth or fifth man carries an RPG on his back. A long firing tube, and a pointed warhead. Other men carry spare rockets.

"We should run for it," Ballard says.

I shake my head. "It's light enough to see. They'll blow us off the mountain before we get halfway up those steps."

"I ain't surrendering, chief." Lopez draws his Mark 23, stuffs the pistol in his waistband. "It's like that dude Kipling said. Save the last round for yourself."

I look through my scope, searching for the Taliban warlord.

No sign of Shahzad. There are other men who look like

squad leaders. They are getting ready to rush us. An RPG barrage first. No idea how many RPGs this stone wall can survive. They'll follow with an infantry charge.

"Ballard."

"Yes, chief."

"Can we call a Broken Arrow... Napalm the whole village?"

"Negative. There's ROE. Civilians hiding in these houses."

I draw my Mark 23, hand it to Robyn. "You're living Kipling now, Sergeant."

The girl's eyes meet mine. Wide, blue, all pupil. "I wouldn't trade it for anything."

I brace myself against the door frame. Raise my rifle. Decide which leaders to kill first. Robyn has not seen enough killing. When you have killed enough, the act loses any special quality. It's a job. You are left with nothing but the husks of men from whom life has been taken.

Shouts from the Taliban.

An RPG sizzles toward us.

I squeeze the trigger. One of the leaders falls.

Ballard ducks as the rocket's warhead explodes against the outer wall. Orange flames flare against the windows, and a wave of heat breaks over our heads. The house shakes, and clouds of dust burst into the air from cracks between the stones. I fire again. Another leader jerks, blood spurting from his neck.

Another RPG explodes. The concussion rocks me back as I am about to fire. I struggle for balance, raise my rifle. Can't reacquire my intended target. Shoot an RPG gunner instead.

More shouting, a different timbre. The Taliban are turning this way and that, shouting to each other. There is a

sound like thunder. The rattle of automatic fire. Many of the
Taliban are turning away from us, pointing their weapons in
the opposite direction. Some run for the steps leading to
higher terraces, others run for the bridge.

"What's going on?" Lopez continues to fire, picking off
fleeing Taliban.

I ignore him, swipe my scope back and forth, looking
for Shahzad. The big kahuna, the apex of command and
control.

"They're running," Ballard breathes. "My God, they're
running."

They are. A hundred or more Taliban, fleeing across the
bridge, swarming up the steps. Fighting each other to reach
the tree lines on either side.

Ballard shoots a man running across the bridge. The
Talib jerks, pitches over the side. Lopez fires on the men
running up the steps. I have never seen men climb stairs so
fast. Already, two dozen have reached the first terrace.
They are either running to the tree line, or disappearing
behind houses for cover. Looking for stairs and other ways
to get onto the mountain.

The village and riverbanks go quiet. Cordite smoke
drifts in the breeze. Three dozen Afghans on horseback
approach. More men on foot follow behind them.

One man at the head of the cavalry stands out. Dressed
in black, with a crimson waistcoat. A brown leather chest
rig. Muzzle pointed skyward, he carries a Dragunov in his
right hand.

Zarek Najibullah.

Robyn steps close, lays her hand on my shoulder.
Squeezes.

"He's here."

· · ·

ROBYN UNDOES her headscarf from about her throat, covers her hair. Steps around me and through the door. "Let me," she says.

Arms spread wide, Robyn approaches the mounted men. Addresses Najibullah in Pashto.

The warlord's men remain mounted, rifles ready. Wary, they cover the opposite bank and mountainside for snipers. Najibullah exchanges words with Robyn. Turns to his men and issues commands. Mujahedeen swarm the steps and begin the process of clearing the village.

Najibullah addresses Robyn.

Robyn turns to me. "Zarek wants you to come out," she says. "No harm will come to you."

"We can't trust this guy," Lopez says.

I carry the M110 low ready. Step through the doorway. "I don't think we have a choice."

Ballard and Lopez follow me outside.

"Tell him we thank him for his help," I say. "He has our gratitude."

Najibullah responds in English. "You have rescued Sergeant Trainor from Abdul-Ali, and kept her safe. That is thanks enough."

"We have to bring her to Bagram."

"Colonel Grissom is not among you."

"We lost him yesterday."

Najibullah sighs. "That is terrible news. It is now more urgent that Sergeant Trainor complete her journey. You understand?"

"Yes. Our people cannot bring helicopters to this valley as long as Shahzad has SAMs in the hills."

Najibullah laughs. "I have them, too. In fact, I need them more than Shahzad."

What's that supposed to mean?

"We have to walk out," I tell him.

"You shall ride out. I came to free Sergeant Trainor, you have rescued her for me. Therefore, you shall ride to Nangalam under my personal protection. Make no mistake, Shahzad will shadow us the entire journey."

Najibullah dismounts. A practiced, graceful motion. He slings his rifle and goes to Robyn.

"We shall dally here an hour or two. My men are clearing the village, and we must finish any Taliban who are wounded. Make yourselves easy, enjoy a meal. I must speak with Sergeant Trainor alone."

That's a slap in my face. What the heck is this Afghan warlord doing, speaking with an American sergeant without leave? I start to object, but Robyn silences me with a sharp glance.

Fuming, I watch Najibullah take Robyn by the arm and escort her to the house where she had been kept prisoner two days ago. Now, Mujahedeen guards flank the door, AK47s locked and loaded. The warlord ushers her into the structure, closes the door behind them.

"Son of a bitch," Lopez snarls.

"Take it easy," I tell him.

One of the riders, a big man with a bushy black beard, laughs. "Do not worry, American. My lord and Sergeant Trainor know each other well."

"FIVE-FIVE KILO, this is Two-One Alpha, over."

The high frequency radio crackles from where Ballard left it on the floor of the house. We drag ourselves inside, and Ballard grabs the handset.

"Leave it," I tell him.

"They want to know our status," Ballard says. "Fifteen minutes ago, we were about to be overrun."

I don't know how I feel about General Anthony. The man I knew would have sent air support. Risked the loss of an aircraft. Today, he left us hanging out to dry. I haven't had time to process the events of the morning. Until I do, the general is on his own.

"The general can wait."

First the general pisses me off, then Najibullah and Robyn. Goddamn, the army has had its share of deserters go over to the Talis. One guy travelled all the way from California to get religion. Another guy walked off post one night and joined the enemy. Thousands of civilians from western Europe travelled to Syria and Iraq to join IS.

Robyn Trainor is acting too much like one of those fruitcakes.

And yet—she *is* the mission.

24

THE SWIM & THE HUNT

Kagur Village
Wednesday, 0730

I order Ballard and Lopez to check their weapons. Together, we take empty magazines and reload them from stripper clips in our packs. Ensure our chest rigs are loaded out. We've been good with ammunition. Only Ballard and Lopez spent time on full auto, and then for brief periods.

When we have finished packing our gear, we break out cold MREs and wolf down what passes for breakfast. Twice more, Two-One Alpha comes on the air. Twice more, I shrug him off.

"Breed." It's Robyn, standing at the door.

"Is Zarek finished with you?" I hate the petulance in my tone.

"Yes, he is," Robyn says. "Come for a walk?"

She's holding out a peace offering, but she's controlling the situation. I don't like it.

I get to my feet, sling my rifle across my chest. "Why not."

Robyn steps outside. I turn to Ballard. "No contact until tonight," I tell him. "If anything urgent develops, hit me on the squad radio."

We walk out of the house. "Where's Zarek?" I ask.

"In the house," Robyn replies. "He has his men pray in rotation."

"How devout."

"He is, actually." Robyn exchanges words in Pashto with the big, black-bearded Mooj. "That's Ghazan. He's a good guy. I told him we were walking to the riverbank."

"A good guy?"

"Yes. He was one of Zarek's first followers, when he was but a child. They fought the Soviets together."

Together, we walk to the bridge. The Mujahedeen look at me with as much suspicion as I regard them.

I stop at the bridge and stare at the girl. "Robyn, you look way too comfortable with this bunch."

"What do you expect, Breed. I lived with them for a year and a half."

"That's the point. You were a hostage, a POW. You guys treat each other with familiarity. There's such a thing as consorting with the enemy."

Robyn leans against the railing of the bridge. "They aren't the enemy, Breed. The United States is going to do a peace deal with Zarek Najibullah. Abdul-Ali Shahzad wanted the deal. When his negotiations collapsed, he sought to screw Zarek by kidnapping me and Grissom."

"How did he find out? The back-door negotiations were secret. Grissom was supposed to be negotiating your release, not peace in Afghanistan."

"I don't know. Shahzad could have killed me and Grissom. That would have ended the peace deal. But he wanted Zarek. They've hated each other for thirty years. Instead of killing us, Shahzad took us prisoner and used us as bait. Stuck us in that house over there, took his main body a mile north, and set an ambush."

"No coincidences, then. Grissom saw Najibullah's caravan yesterday. Crawled out onto the promontory to signal him. That's when he fell."

"Grissom must have suspected it was Zarek, but I doubt he was sure. The caravan was a long way off. I couldn't tell, looking through your glasses."

Robyn's lying again.

"In any case," she says, "everything has worked out well for Zarek and the United States. He'll escort us to Nangalam and be on his way."

I shake my head. "There is no peace deal, Robyn. Until everything is agreed, Zarek remains the enemy."

"You can look at him that way, Breed. But—I promise you, he is on our side. He wants this deal as much as we do."

"What is the deal?"

Robyn looks at the Mujahedeen watering their horses. "I suppose it won't hurt to tell you the broad strokes. The United States leaves Afghanistan. The Afghan National Government leaves Zarek's Mujahedeen to keep peace in the provinces. Together, they push Shahzad out of the country. Keep Al Qaeda from using Afghanistan as a staging area."

"What else is in it for Zarek?"

"The Afghan government is weak. The ANA won't fight for the leadership."

"Zarek thinks they'll fight for him?"

"He knows they will. Zarek will run the country—and the opium trade."

An audacious proposition. In Afghanistan, opium is a sixty-billion-dollar-a-year industry. A peace deal with America will be followed by a civil war to bring it under the control of one man.

"Of course," I say. "The opium trade."

"Yes. You can trust Zarek as far as Nangalam, Breed."

"Don't you have a problem trading drugs for peace?"

Robyn shrugs. "Grissom did the trade, with the authority of the United States government. Grissom and I are messengers. No, I don't have a problem with it. Opium's been traded out of Afghanistan for thirty-five-hundred years. They smoked it in the *Arabian Nights*."

I suppose I don't have much of a problem with it either. The United States has spent too much blood and treasure on this war. Afghan opium supplies junkies in Russia and Europe. Let *them* sort it out.

"How did you and Zarek get to be so close?"

"Zarek proved escape was hopeless. I made the best of the situation, lived with him and Wajia. Zarek took me hiking and hunting while we waited for the back-channel to develop. It took a long time before Grissom became involved."

"Hiking and hunting?"

"Yes. Zarek and his people are more progressive than the Taliban. So long as I kept myself covered and demonstrated submissive behavior, no one objected. Zarek took me on long walks and rides in the mountains. Wajia didn't want to go. Well… the imam objected, but not too loud."

I can't believe my ears. "Zarek Najibullah took you hunting."

Robyn smiles. "Have you ever hunted Himalayan ibex, Breed?"

THE APRIL after she was taken, Baryal came to Zarek's house. The two men spoke for a while, then Baryal left. Zarek came inside, rubbing his hands together. "My scouts have spotted ibex on the high slopes. I am going to bring one back."

Wajia and Robyn stared at him. The warlord's eyes twinkled. "Do you want to come, Sergeant Trainor?"

Robyn had hunted with her brothers. Harvested deer with a Winchester '94. She wanted to go with him.

They left early the next morning. Zarek took his favorite mount, and Ghazan loaned Robyn a mare. A sturdy pack mule carried their water and camping gear. They dressed for cold weather, for winter had not yet released the high slopes from its grip.

"We shall find them well above eight thousand feet," Zarek told her. "Possibly as high as ten. There will be snow on the ground."

"I have never seen an ibex," Robyn said.

"It is the Himalayan ibex," Zarek told her. "They are found where the Himalayas meet the Karakoram and the Hindu Kush. The juncture of three countries. Here, we find our share."

For most of the journey, they stuck to the river valley After a day's ride, Zarek found a campsite. They built a fire, ate their rations, and drank tea. They went to bed, and rose early the next morning.

It was time to go to work. They fed and watered their mounts, then tethered them out of sight, in a copse of trees. Zarek slung his Dragunov and led her up the mountain.

They hiked at a steady, ground-eating pace. Zarek did not consult a map. The area was well known to his scouts, and Baryal must have given him a good description of where to find their quarry. It did not take them long to climb above the tree line. They found themselves on a rocky slope, barren but for clumps of dry brush. They pressed on, often knee-deep in snow.

"The ibex's ears are sensitive," Zarek warned her. "From now on, we must not speak. They will be around the curve of this slope."

Zarek and Robyn crept around the mountain. There wasn't a tree in sight. Zarek put his hand on her shoulder and pointed.

There, separated from them by a shallow draw, were a dozen Himalayan ibex. Barely visible against the dark brown moonscape of the mountainside. They were heavy animals, with thick slabs of muscle. Their coats were dark, their horns light brown. Scimitar-shaped, with lateral ridges that marked their age. The males had great, long horns. The females had smaller, thinner horns.

Beautiful animals. Powerful and graceful. They climbed effortlessly, sprang from rock to rock. Stopped to forage.

Two hundred and fifty yards separated Zarek and Robyn from their prey. Zarek lay prone, rested the barrel of his Dragunov on his pack for support. Robyn lay next to him. He handed her a pair of old Soviet binoculars.

Robyn had done enough hunting to know the range was not a problem. At two hundred and fifty yards, the ibex were well within the Dragunov's performance envelope. No, the problem was the wind. It whaled off the Hindu Kush, blowing snow into a fine mist. It gusted left-to-right, then reversed, in a devilish game of cat and mouse.

Zarek took his time, judging the shot. He could estimate, from the blowing snow, the wind's speed and direction. He waited patiently and assessed its reversals.

Crack.

The crash of the gunshot echoed across the mountains. One of the animals, a large billy, jerked and slid back on its hind legs. The other animals bolted, ran in all directions. Some disappeared over the crest. Others stopped, searching for the source of the disturbance.

Zarek kept the animal he had shot in his sights, ready to deliver another blow. The animal flopped onto its side and lay still.

"You got it," Robyn breathed.

Zarek turned his face to her and grinned.

"Come, Sergeant Trainor." Zarek got to his feet without touching her. His voice was warm. "Let us look at the animal we climbed all this way to kill."

It took them hours to butcher the billy. Hard, sweaty work. They gutted and skinned the animal. Zarek was pleased with Robyn's facility with a blade. The skill with which she kept the animal's fur from tainting the meat. They sliced the choicest cuts from the animal and packed them carefully. Stained with blood, covered with the animal's stink, they carried the prize on their backs.

Three thousand feet lower on the mountain, the air grew warmer. Drenched in blood and sweat, they came to a waterfall. Blue-and-white water poured from the peaks. Snow melt cascaded into a pool carved into the rock by centuries of erosion.

Zarek leaned his rifle against a boulder and undressed in front of her. Mouth dry, legs trembling, she watched. Naked, he stood before her and laughed. His body was a scar-scape of wounds. It looked like it had been blasted and torn, bare-handed, from the stone that surrounded them. He straightened and dove into the pool.

When Zarek surfaced for air, he shook out his long hair like a wet dog. Treaded water and stared at her. Said nothing.

The Dragunov was within Robyn's reach.

Zarek dared her with his eyes.

Robyn struggled. Came to a decision. She was fascinated by Zarek's body. Wanted to run her hands over the scars. Told herself she should know better. But—she took off her headscarf, then her boots. When she was naked, she stood on a smooth stone at the edge of the pool. Her body was white against the rock. She raised her arms over her head and dove in.

The shock of the ice water was like a thousand silver needles lancing Robyn's body. The pain was delicious. Every inch of her skin was jolted awake. She surfaced with a scream.

Robyn treaded water and laughed.

Zarek stared at her and broke into a grin.

For fifteen minutes, they swam. Blue with cold, they crawled out and dried themselves. Robyn was especially discolored because of her fair skin. They put their clothes back on.

Robyn wanted Zarek, but he didn't touch her.

He was entitled. She was a captive of his right hand.

That night, Robyn collapsed from exhaustion. Before sleep overcame her, the last thought to cross her mind was that she felt happy.

EMBARRASSED, I ask, "Why are you telling me this?"

Robyn's eyes search mine. "You're worried something

I've done will compromise the mission, or the safety of the team. Understand—this is why Grissom and Zarek trusted me."

My squad radio crackles. "Five-Five Sierra, this is Five-Five Kilo."

Ballard. *Shit.* "Go ahead, Five-Five Kilo."

"Our actual is here. He got chased off LZ Three, just arrived at the village."

"Where are you, Kilo?"

"Outside the house. Actual is on the horn to Two-One Alpha right now."

Damn. Koenig's back, and he's on the radio to General Anthony.

"I told him we were occupied with the Mooj," Ballard continues. "We haven't had time to report."

"Thanks, Kilo. We'll be back soon."

"No sweat. Five-Five Kilo out."

25

ZAREK'S TALES

Kagur Valley
Wednesday, 2200

The Mujahedeen camp is surreal. Zarek posted sentries along the riverbank, in the forest, and on the mountainsides. Then he had cooking fires lit. A flagrant invitation to Shahzad to launch an attack.

Rifles slung across our chests, Takigawa and I walk among Zarek's men. Koenig posted Lopez and Ballard for security. One by the river, the other on the bank.

We walk through Zarek's Casualty Collection Point. It is a makeshift aid station where medics tend wounded fighters. Men injured during the fighting at the village. We are surprised the senior medic is a trauma surgeon trained in Islamabad.

There are not many wounded. Shahzad ordered his men to break contact as soon as Zarek's cavalry made an appearance. I doubt we've seen the last of the Taliban and their embedded Al Qaeda advisors.

"Look at this." Takigawa stoops to pick up a discarded glass ampoule. Hands it to me. Black Chinese characters have been stenciled across its side.

I hand the vial back to the sniper. "Pakistan-trained doctors, Chinese morphine and antibiotics. Everything short of a field hospital. This is a professional outfit."

Takigawa plows calloused fingers through his long hair. Adjusts his baseball cap. His helmet hangs from the back of his ruck. "You have to respect the enemy," he says. "They have the training, the supplies, the commitment. We can't kill our way to victory."

"Depends what you mean by victory," I tell him. "I don't think we can ever conquer these people. But we can keep Al Qaeda from using this place to attack America."

"You think this peace deal buys that for us?"

"I think it's a chance to declare victory."

"By shaking hands with Najibullah."

"Dude, that decision has been made way above our pay grade."

Zarek sits at one of the fires, surrounded by his lieutenants. Robyn and Koenig sit in the circle.

I like the sound of crackling flames, and the smell of sharp wood smoke in the cold mountain air. I can't help but worry about our exposure. Zarek knows lighting fires is like waving a red cape in front of a bull. "How many mortar rounds did Shahzad lay on you?" I ask Takigawa.

"A lot, brother. He plastered us for half an hour."

The thought of Shahzad shelling Zarek's beach party makes me cringe. "Let's hope he's run out."

"He couldn't have carried that many rounds without

pack animals," Takigawa says. "I think he only had what his infantry could carry."

Zarek sees us approaching, raises his hand in greeting. "Breed," he calls. "Takigawa. Join us."

I address the warlord. "You know Shahzad has eighty-two-millimeter mortars?"

"Of course." Zarek spreads his arms magnanimously. "So have I."

"Isn't this beach party a little risky?"

"Yesterday, we heard your battle from the valley," Zarek laughs. "Abdul-Ali spent more mortar ammunition than he had men to carry them. Did he use mortars at the village? No. *Inshallah*, none remain. Now sit with us. Rest."

I don't care that Najibullah and his men saved our hash this morning. Nine hours ago, these Mujahedeen were the enemy. The distinctions between Mooj and Tali do not move me. They all hate us. With Grissom gone, the deal is at risk. As far as I'm concerned, these people could turn and cut our throats.

We join the group gathered around the warlord. The circle is three deep, and Zarek orders his men to make way. I'm impressed he remembers our names. I'm sure he did not hear Takigawa's more than once. He is one switched-on leader.

Zarek is telling a story. He speaks in English, for the benefit of the Americans. I know what he's doing. He's charming us. A good leader is always on the job.

Takigawa and I sit cross-legged, clutching our rifles like lovers. It's not unusual. Zarek's men have their AK47s close to hand. Najibullah has set his Dragunov on the ground beside him.

Koenig looks out of his element.

Robyn is the only comfortable person in our party. She leans forward, gazing with rapt attention, hanging on Najibullah's every word. She murmurs in Pashto, translating the warlord's story. Her voice is barely above a whisper, and the Mujahedeen strain to listen.

"These stones have been washed in blood for three thousand years," Zarek says. "Foreigners have always wanted this land. At times they managed to capture it, never have they managed to hold it. We have been put on Earth by Allah to defend this place. The prophet has shown the way to jihad, and I have been chosen to lead the faithful."

Zarek doesn't say who chose him. The implication is that Allah himself laid his hand on Najibullah's shoulder.

"A man's wisdom grows with his years," Zarek says. "When I was but a boy, I fought the Soviets. With a rifle in one hand and a rocket on my back. One day Soviet gun-birds chased me and my comrades, into a draw. There was no escape.

"I stood alone on the rock. Pulled cloth over my nose and mouth, for the dust was choking me. I raised the rocket to my shoulder and faced the gun-bird. As close as I am to you. I fired, and the rocket pierced its head like a lance. Exploded within its skull. The gun-bird shuddered, but did not fall from the sky. Smoke poured from the beast as it turned and fled."

Zarek has a way with words. Enthralled, Robyn continues her translation.

"The other gun-bird breathed fire. The rocks around me splintered, and my comrades were cut to pieces. I was the only one of our little band on his feet, yet I survived. I fell, unconscious. The Soviet soldiers took me to their jail in Asadabad. For months, they did many things to humiliate me, and cause me pain. Who can humiliate one who knows that one day, he will stand naked before Allah?"

Koenig looks bored. Takigawa, a pure warrior, sits captivated. Robyn's eyes glisten, wet with tears.

"They broke me in body, but not in spirit." Zarek is careful to meet the eyes of each person in his audience. "Not *once* did Allah leave my side. For public execution, they had me transported to Kabul. My brothers awaited their chance, and fell upon the Soviet caravan. *Mashallah.* The earth was watered with the blood of the infidels."

"You were meant to escape," Robyn says.

"It was the work of Allah," Najibullah pronounces. "I have always been, and remain, naught but a servant of his will."

THE HOURS TICK BY. We eat and drink. Ghazan and Baryal take turns telling stories. Ghazan of the days when he and Zarek fought the Soviets in the high mountain passes. Among soldiers, the talk comes to Soviet tactics. Their use of motorized units to drive Mujahedeen into traps laid by paratroopers.

"They were always late," Ghazan says. "I became convinced Soviets could not make good timepieces, because they could never synchronize their attacks."

Zarek laughs. "The paratroopers were good fighters. They were tough. They did not know the land well, but they could climb. Once, a company of Soviets climbed a mountain and attacked us from the rear. We never expected them to climb the mountain. We waited for helicopters that never came. When the paratroopers attacked, we were taken by surprise."

"The helicopters were devils," Ghazan says. "The gun-birds would hunt and kill us. They often used two or three gun-birds to kill a single man."

"Until our American friends brought us the missiles," Zarek smiles.

"Stingers," Koenig says.

"Yes," Zarek nods. "Stingers. You gave us many of these missiles, and we lanced the gun-birds. The missiles were more effective than the rocket I used, the day the gun-bird cornered me in the draw. The Stingers won the war for us."

"Then the Americans tried to buy them back," Baryal sneers.

"Oh, yes." Zarek warms to the topic. "America is so rich it gave us many missiles. Then, after the war, they feared we would use missiles against commercial aircraft. So they bought them back."

"The threat was genuine," I tell him.

Zarek shakes his head. "No. There were crazy Muja-hedeen. Among us, there were fanatics, trained by the Wahabis—Saudis—in the madras. They would use the missiles. *They* did not sell their missiles back. They have caused much trouble for you *and* for our country."

The warlord's tone grows pedantic. "Understand," he says to Koenig, "my people were pleased the war ended. There were no Americans on our land. No Soviets. There was no need for jihad. The Saudi Mujahedeen began a civil war. They found reasons for the jihad to continue."

"You let them stay," Koenig says.

"Taliban let them stay," Zarek corrects him. "America continues to interfere in matters it does not understand. Look at the opium. America concerns itself little with opium. Why is that? Poppies are grown in vast fields outside American air bases, yet you do nothing. You bomb my caravans three times more frequently than Shahzad's. Yet—it is Shahzad's opium that finances the war against you."

Zarek stares at Koenig. "Why do you bomb me more than Shahzad?"

"I don't know that we do."

"I run a business. I count the loads." Zarek takes a bite of mutton, chews carefully. "Counting is not difficult."

"If that is true," Koenig says, "and I am not certain it is, you and Shahzad are doing something differently."

A crafty gleam in his eye, Zarek says, "*Someone* is doing something different."

I think back to my missions into Tajikistan and China. I studied the routes, the players. I studied Najibullah and Shahzad, wrote the book for General Anthony. I saw no difference in their operations.

"To America," Koenig shrugs, "one load of opium is like any other. You all make war on us."

"Methinks not for much longer." Zarek smiles. "There will be peace. America will take its guns, its money, and its young men. It will leave this land, and jihad will be no more. Many problems will be solved when you leave. The rest we will solve ourselves."

"What about the opium?" Koenig sneers.

"What of it?" Zarek spreads his arms and opens his hands. "Afghan opium is not found on the streets of New York. What do you care? Let the English, French and Germans take an interest. They do not want to spend the money. Perhaps they do not have the money to spend. Americans love to spend money to fight other people's wars. They think it makes them loved. No. It makes them fools."

Zarek laughs. Brings his hands together and makes a

washing motion. "No, my friends, your country has no interest in Afghan opium. Are you on a crusade? The only people who have an interest in Afghan opium are those who seek profit. Then—all that matters is where the profits are used."

Robyn told me the same thing. Zarek has a point.

"We pay the ANA to raze the poppies," I offer. "It is their responsibility."

Zarek laughs. A full-bellied laugh echoed by Ghazan, Baryal, and the other men around the campfire. "You pay the ANA to raze the poppies. *We* pay them not to."

Robyn meets my eyes across the fire. Rosy from the warmth, her cheeks glow.

I told you so.

THE FIRE BURNS LOW. One by one, men drift away to sleep. Either on their sleeping mats, or in houses where they have found lodging with civilians. Koenig and I walk back to our house. We leave Robyn and Takigawa sitting with Zarek, who never runs out of tales. Stories of the high mountains and battles with the Soviets.

"Are we bombing Najibullah more than Shahzad?" I ask Koenig.

"I told him," Koenig says. "I don't know."

"Now tell *me*."

"What the fuck, Breed." Koenig stops, stares at me with his hands on his hips. "You calling me a liar?"

"One caravan looks like another from five hundred feet."

"If there's any difference, it's random. Dumb luck."

I shake my head. "Dumb luck averages out over the

years. Dumb luck averages out one-to-one, not three-to-one."

"Aren't you the egghead."

"Zarek's right," I tell him. "Counting is not so difficult."

"You'll take the word of a Hajji who has every reason to lie."

"We're on the same side, Koenig." The captain looks ready to punch me. "I don't want to be the one guy who didn't get the memo."

Koenig wrestles with his anger. "Look, Breed. I don't know, okay? If I knew, I would tell you."

It's time to mollify the captain. "Fair enough," I say.

"The Mooj said it." Koenig snorts. "Why should *we* give a rat's ass about opium?"

26

THE TRAIL TO ARWAL

North Arwal Valley
Thursday, 0800

Zarek had five of his youngest Mujahedeen lend us their mounts.

We ride in column, Zarek's cavalry first, followed by the mules and donkeys of the caravan. Mujahedeen without mounts walk beside the mules, or follow behind. Today, we enter the northern reaches of the Arwal valley. That puts us within shouting distance of ANA troops and American advisers.

The pack animals are burdened with leather harnesses that support canvas rolls of weapons and explosives. There are twenty pack animals in the train. A lot of weapons, enough to spark a major conflagration. If Zarek makes peace with the United States, who are those weapons going to be used against?

Zarek reads my mind, rides next to me.

"When we make peace with the United States," he says, "Afghanistan will explode into civil war."

"Where are these weapons going?"

"My allies in the south." Zarek waves his arm over the long train of mules. "America arms the ANA. The Taliban in Helmand are armed from Pakistan. I must arm my friends. They are well organized in Kandahar. With these weapons, they will drive the Taliban back into Pakistan, and we shall enforce the border."

"That's the ANA's job."

Zarek laughs. "Will you trust your life to the ANA?"

I say nothing.

"I thought not." Zarek chuckles. "Rest today, Breed. There will be a battle this afternoon."

"How do you know?"

"Shahzad orchestrated this to destroy peace and bring me to battle. Here I am."

"Is that why you light cooking fires at night? He will ambush you."

"Of course. But—an ambush is not an ambush when it is anticipated in all respects. Therefore, we shall do battle."

"Where?"

"You are a soldier, Breed. Where do you think?"

We're traversing a river valley. A kill zone two or three hundred yards wide in most places. With steep slopes on either bank, an X-ambush is practical. Shooters high on the cliffs will fire downslope without risk of hitting each other. But—a mounted column can ride off the X.

The ideal ambush is a box, arranged at a bend in the river. High ground on either side. The ambush force will then occupy elevated positions in the shape of a U. There will be no easy ride off the X.

"A bend in the river," I say. "Steep slopes all around."

"Very good." Zarek's expression is grave. "There was such a place a mile north of Kagur village."

"Shahzad's main body, two days ago."

"Of course. He held Colonel Grissom and Sergeant Trainor at Kagur, knowing I would come for them. Then he set the ambush."

"We spoiled his game."

"Yes. You took his captives, and he abandoned the ambush to chase you."

"But they had served their purpose. He brought you to battle."

"Ah, but with the colonel alive, a peace would be negotiated. Shahzad had to get them back."

"He didn't attack yesterday."

"We all know this river. The next best place for an ambush is a day's ride from here. The Kagur becomes the Arwal and bends to the east. Not perfect, because the valley is rather wide at that point. About a quarter of a mile. The west bank is exposed."

"An L-ambush."

"As you call it, yes."

"You're going to ride straight into it."

"My men know what must be done," Zarek says. "Now *you* must understand your role."

"Tell me."

"When the battle begins, Allah will not leave my side. *You* must not leave Robyn's. See that she rides out of the ambush."

Zarek kicks his horse and rides ahead without answering. Joins Robyn. She smiles at him, and they settle into a relaxed conversation. They look and act like old friends.

I'm uneasy, riding in the open. My eyes sweep the

slopes on either side. The tree lines. Zarek is confident the
ambush will come at the riverbend. Why would Shahzad
allow himself to be so predictable?

I want the son of a bitch in my sights… I want to see
his bright pink mist.

The Americans are riding in file. Takigawa first,
followed by Lopez, then Koenig. Robyn, speaking with
Zarek, is fourth in line. I ride behind, and Ballard covers
the rear.

"Five-Five Sierra," Ballard calls over the radio, "this is
Five-Five Kilo."

"Go ahead, Kilo."

"You sure the Mooj know what they're doing? Feeling
bare-ass naked out here."

"Mooj survived here thirty-five years," I say. "Whatever happens, if we come under fire, ride. Don't worry
about the Mooj. Get off the X."

"Understood, Sierra. Five-Five Kilo out."

I've executed ambushes more often than I've experienced them. Zarek is right. The essence of an ambush is
psychological. It's surprise. When caught in an ambush,
you feel powerless. With agency stripped from you, you
either flee or freeze.

We're taught to take agency back. As soon as the
ambush hits, you stop and evaluate the situation. You do
that in a second, then you act. You take back your power,
and that is psychological. If appropriate, you attack into the
ambush. Otherwise, you move. You get off the X. If you
stay where the bullets are landing, you die. It is that simple.

Robyn laughs gaily at something Zarek has said.

The warlord smiles at her. With a tilt of his chin, he
rides ahead to speak with Koenig. Robyn looks around,
catches my eye. Waits for me to join her.

"Zarek's men are all good riders," Robyn says.

"Polo was invented in Afghanistan, wasn't it?"

"Yes." Robyn laughs. "With the heads of slain enemies for balls."

"That's a pretty heavy ball," I tell her. "A human head can weigh eight or ten pounds."

"Strengthens a man's sword arm."

I'm struck by the girl's dissociation from the horror of war. She is moved by loss on a personal basis. Her emotions swung from anger to grief at the loss of Grissom. Her tears at the Soviet outpost were real. On the other hand, battlefield deaths and executions affect her not at all.

Robyn's enjoying this too much.

"Did Zarek tell you we're going into battle this afternoon?"

"Yes. He warned me to ride to safety and let it play out."

"That's good advice."

Robyn stares into the distance. A tomboyish girl, with unruly hair. The strands struggle to break free of her headscarf. She's pretty. It would be easy for someone like Zarek, from a culture that keeps women in cloisters, to become enchanted with her. A girl next door from Colorado became something exotic in the wilds of Badakhshan.

"I'm to stay close to you," she says.

"He tell you that too?"

"Yes." Robyn smiles. "Good leaders are extraordinary judges of character. He figured toot sweet you're the American in charge."

The transparent effort at flattery annoys me. "You're pissing me off, Robyn."

"I'm not trying to." Robyn reaches out and touches my

shoulder. "You kept us alive yesterday. I respect that. So does Zarek."

"You and Zarek." I shake my head. "And this damn peace deal."

"We're the good guys, Breed. Not everybody wants peace."

27

THE BATTLE

North Arwal Valley
Thursday, 1600

The riverbend is half a mile away. I can see why this is only the second-best ambush location on the river. The valley is wide and stretches six hundred yards. The slopes on either side are gradual, heavily forested. They rise to the low northern ridges of Arwal-Ghar.

With my Leitz binoculars, I glass the valley.

I know where Shahzad will position his fighters. Fifty on the slope overlooking the bend, a hundred on the approach. Zarek has stretched out our caravan. With twenty yards between animals, the mule and donkey train is over a quarter mile long. The mounted Mujahedeen are similarly dispersed. Looking back the length of the caravan, I can't see Zarek's infantry.

The effect is to stretch Shahzad's forces thin. With one hundred and fifty men, Shahzad can cover four hundred and fifty yards of front. Zarek's stretched column is at least twice that. If Shahzad goes after the mule train, he has to let Zarek's cavalry through. If he attacks the cavalry, he will miss the long line of mules, donkeys and infantry.

The problem with the dispersal is obvious. With his men strung out over a half mile of valley floor, Zarek can't mount a concentrated attack.

Von Clausewitz called it the *Schwerpunkt*. Every maneuvering plan should have a center of gravity. Its main thrust against the enemy. As far as I can tell, Zarek's force doesn't have one.

Zarek's right about one thing. Five Americans won't swing this battle. Our best bet is to ride around the bend as quickly as possible. Get out of the effective range of Shahzad's AK47s and RPGs.

"Five-Five Sierra, this is Five-Five Oscar."

Takigawa.

"Go ahead, Oscar."

"Are you feeling like a duck in a shooting gallery?"

"Yes. Everybody stay close to the river. We'll be well out of effective AK47 range."

"Just what I was thinking," Takigawa says.

"You know what I'm thinking, Oscar?"

"Where would you be if you were Shahzad."

I smile to myself. Takigawa and I are snipers. Trained to decide a battle with a single bullet. Neutralize the enemy's leadership.

"I'd be where I can see both the approach and the bend. That leaves out the long bar of the L. He'll be on the foot, not the toe."

"Yeah," Takigawa agrees. "I don't see how we can get a good angle on him."

"The best angle is right in the shooting gallery," I tell him. "Out of AK47 range, well within M110 range."

"You got full metal jacket balls, my friend."

"This is Five-Five Actual," Koenig breaks into the conversation. "Let's not clutter the radio net."

I go silent without acknowledgment. Look at Robyn riding twenty yards ahead of me. Delivering Robyn unharmed is my first priority, not hunting Abdul-Ali Shahzad. But—maybe I can do both.

Ghazan is riding twenty yards ahead of Robyn. The black-bearded Mooj raises a small walkie-talkie, the equivalent of our squad radios, to his ear. Low-power FM sets, line-of-sight comms good over three-quarters of a mile. The Taliban and Mooj make extensive use of these.

Zarek's small-unit leaders have been using their walkie-talkies as we approach the riverbend. They expect to be hit at any moment.

"Oscar, this is Sierra."

"Go ahead, Sierra."

"Any time now."

Battles rarely develop like you expect. Some begin with a clamor that shocks and fills you with terror. Others, like this one, develop slowly. The fighting seems to be happening a mile away until it spreads and washes over you.

Zarek's point cavalry elements are well around the bend when the first drumming of automatic fire echoes across the valley. I see other cavalry dismount, force their horses to lie down, and dive for cover. Takigawa, Lopez, and Koenig gallop to the riverbed.

The mule and donkey train stops cold.

I spur my mount forward and join Robyn.

"Come on," I say. "Let's get to the river."

The valley's six hundred yards wide, and the river's fifty yards across. From the water's edge, the range to the slope is three hundred fifty yards. A shooter with an AK has to go to semi-automatic aimed fire to be effective at that range. Shahzad's men are firing on full auto.

The riverbed is rocky. The water is not at full swell, so we tether the horses, and roll into the riverbed. Rocks and mud. The rocky ground between the flat bank and the sloping riverbed forms a low parapet. I unsling my M110 and sweep the valley with my scope.

"Are we safe here?" Robyn asks.

We'd be safer had we run past Koenig. I'm not built that way. A sniper can win a battle with one shot. I can protect Robyn *and* kill Shahzad.

"No place is safe," I tell her. "But we are better off here than the elbow of the L."

"Who are you looking for?" Robyn asks.

"Shahzad."

I have a lousy oblique angle into the elbow. I scan the tree line. Muzzle flashes twinkle like fireflies across a quarter mile of forest.

Zarek's men return fire, but refuse to charge the ambush. Two dozen Mujahedeen have allowed themselves to be pinned down.

There's a whoosh, followed by a shattering explosion on the riverbank. A spout of dirt and rock. One of Zarek's men cries out. A horse shrieks and bolts. Shahzad's men are loosing RPGs. Their rifles aren't accurate enough, so they are using rockets. Extravagant, but effective.

I lay my sight on an RPG gunner and pull the trigger. The man drops.

More swooshes. Shahzad's men are launching RPGs in salvos. White vapor trails mark the passage of rockets blasting the men on the bank. Geysers of rock and soil mark their impact. Zarek's men fire their own RPGs into the tree line. The firefight becomes a rocket duel as Zarek's RPGs explode in the trees, and wood splinters spray Shahzad's ambush party. Zarek's men have fused their rockets for airburst. The explosions shatter the pines and scatter branches in all directions.

I prioritize my targets. If I can't find Shahzad, I'll take out RPG gunners. I kill one man, who drops his weapon. Another man shoulders the tube, and I kill him too. I'll kill any man who carries a rocket. That's sending a message.

The whistling roar of incoming assaults my ears. Larger explosions shred the tree line. Red blooms and black smoke obscure the woods. The earth shakes, and the concussion pounds my ears. These are not RPGs. Zarek has laid his own 82 mm mortars further back on the riverbank. Shahzad spent his mortar ammunition on the bridge to Lanat. Zarek is deploying his to devastating effect.

I lay my scope on an RPG gunner. A mortar round explodes inches from him. Head, arms and legs fly off. The torso is launched into the air like a popping champagne cork. I lose track of the man's pieces in the whirling blender of splintered wood and flying guts.

The volume of gunfire coming from the west bank doubles. There is a high-pitched keening in the air. An amorphous sound rises from the woods. Shouting. Cursing. The woods themselves ripple. Like ants scattering from a hill, the Taliban move. The men in my sights turn their weapons on the woods behind them.

Zarek's men on the riverbank rise and charge the tree line.

Taliban break and flee in our direction.

Shit.

Takigawa sees the same movement. "Five-Five Sierra, this is Oscar. Interrogative. Why are the Talis breaking?"

"Zarek's infantry flanked the ambush from the slopes," I say. "He must have sent them around hours ago. He's got Shahzad's nuts in a vise."

"They're coming our way."

"Only place they have to run. Watch yourselves. Watch for Shahzad."

Shahad's forces are retreating along the bend in the river. Straight toward us. I hear the crack of Takigawa's rifle as he picks off Talis.

Bullets spray the rocks in front of us.

Robyn peeps over the edge of the riverbank. I drag her back and shove her onto her stomach. Sit on her.

"Damn," she shouts. "Breed, get *off* me."

"Stay there," I tell her. Taliban are running in our direction, seeking cover in the riverbed. They're more terrified of Zarek's men than they are of us.

I shoot one man in the chest, and he goes down. Two more rush us. I shoot the next in the face. The third fires, close enough for his muzzle flash to singe my face. I use my M110 as a metal bar and deflect the muzzle of his AK47. He crashes into me.

We tumble into the riverbed, and I lose my grip on the M110. His hand claws at my face. I wrestle my attacker onto his back and grab a rock the size of a bowling ball. Raise it in both hands and bring it down with all my strength. His arm deflects my first blow, so I raise the rock over my head and smash him again. With a crunch, the bones of his face give way. Another blow and his head comes apart.

The hammering of AK47 fire. A cry from behind me. I drop the rock, turn.

A Talib jumped into the riverbed. Robyn grabbed the rifle of the man I bludgeoned, shot the attacker. He drops to his knees, pitches face down.

I lurch back to the parapet. Robyn is huddled against the rocks, clutching the AK47. I grab my rifle, rejoin the fight. More Taliban run past. Takigawa fires methodically, covering us. Fleeing Taliban know where we are by now. They see the riverbed is well defended, and they withdraw to the tree line.

One of the Taliban looses an RPG. I duck under the parapet, cover Robyn with my body. A shattering explosion pelts us with rock chips and mud. My ears ring with the concussion.

Rifle over the parapet, I continue firing.

As quickly as the battle engulfed us, it sweeps on. Zarek's men are running past, chasing the Taliban. I cease fire, hoping to God they don't shoot.

"Five-Five Oscar," I yell into my radio. "Hold your fire. Friendlies."

"It's cool." Takigawa's voice is calm. "I got 'em."

Baryal runs past. He glances at me and Robyn, keeps going.

A number of Zarek's men have mounted their horses. Some of the animals have been wounded, others have bolted. The men chase the runaways.

Ghazan sits on his horse, rifle in one hand, walkie-talkie in the other.

Zarek rides past, evaluates our condition. He sees Robyn is alright. To me, he nods approval. "Once more, I am in your debt."

I watch Zarek ride off. When he has gone, I turn to Robyn.

"What did he mean by that?" I ask.

Robyn stands in the riverbed, carrying the AK47 in one hand. The wind blows her headscarf. Like a veil, it flutters across her nose and mouth. Her blue eyes stare at me.

"Haven't you figured it out by now?" she says. "After everything I've told you?"

"No more games, Robyn."

"Nothing more to tell, Breed. I'm Zarek's wife."

28

THE WARRANTY

North Arwal Valley
Thursday, 2230

Zarek made camp two hundred yards from the spot where Robyn and I had sheltered. Shahzad's force was decimated. The Mujahedeen spent the entire afternoon bayoneting the survivors and setting a security perimeter.

Every dead Talib was examined. Shahzad could not be found.

It took me hours to recover from the shock of Robyn's revelation. When the fighting ceased, we climbed out of the riverbed. The air reeked of the metallic smell of blood, the sharp scent of cordite. Zarek rallied his troops and issued instructions.

The hour grows late. Zarek and his men regale each other and Koenig with tales of the day's battle. I meet Robyn's eyes across the campfire. Jerk my head toward the river.

We rise and walk to the edge of the riverbank. Stare at the fast-moving water, flowing silver in the light of the moon. I sling my rifle, thrust my hands into my pockets for warmth.

I don't have to say a word. Without prompting or preamble, Robyn launches into her story.

DESPITE THEIR MUSLIM BELIEFS, the Pashtun are inherently monogamous. A man takes a second wife only in cases where there are deep issues with his first marriage. If a second marriage is ill-conceived, it can lead to lasting enmity between families. Blood vendettas.

Zarek and Wajia loved each other. During their twelve years of marriage, Wajia had not been able to conceive a child. She encouraged him to take a second wife to bear him children. The warlord refused. Preoccupied with other matters, he pushed off the decision.

When Zarek kidnapped Robyn, his sole intention was to use her to draw the United States into negotiations. He was playing the old game of bait-and-switch. He would open negotiations for a hostage, then segue into negotiations for peace.

Wajia found she liked Robyn. The American girl's tomboyish nature, her clumsy, self-conscious femininity appealed to the Pashtun woman. More importantly, she saw a girl who could never hope to usurp her position as Zarek's first wife. Let Zarek take the American hiking and shooting. What interest did Wajia have in such things?

The situation was perfect. Wajia studied Robyn carefully. Concluded that Zarek and Robyn would produce attractive, healthy offspring. Nor was there a question of the girl's sexual appetite, or Zarek's sexual interest.

A year after Robyn's kidnapping, Wajia broached the subject to Zarek. Indeed, she suspected Zarek and Robyn had already engaged in sexual relations. By Sharia law, he had the right to take Robyn without marriage. The issue was irrelevant.

The issue that mattered most to Zarek was political. Would marriage to an American hostage, a soldier, affect negotiations? Of course they would. The bait-and-switch had better work. Otherwise, Zarek would have to walk away, keep Robyn, and incur the wrath of America. What of it? It would not be the first time Zarek Najibullah had angered great powers. In these mountains, Zarek was lord and master, leader of the faithful.

Zarek made his decision.

One beautiful autumn day, he took Robyn riding to a secluded spot on the river. There, they picked their way onto the riverbed and sat by the flowing water.

"Come, Sergeant Trainor," he said. "Face me."

There was nothing unusual in the formality of Zarek's speech. It reflected the English he had learned as a small boy at school in Kabul. What surprised Robyn was the gravity in his eyes.

Robyn and Zarek sat facing each other, knees touching.

"Pay attention, Sergeant Trainor. I will only say this once."

"Of course, Zarek." Robyn was flustered. "What is it?"

"Very well." Zarek took a deep breath. "I am a simple man. Allah has chosen me to lead the faithful. It is my responsibility to save this land from foreigners. Westerners, and foreigners from other Muslim countries who would use this land for their purposes. More than the lines on paper Westerners call Afghanistan. All the historic lands of our peoples."

"I understand that," Robyn said.

"You have become special to me," Zarek said. "Wajia and I do not want you to leave. I want you to bear my children."

Robyn had no words. She reached for his hands and took them in hers.

"You accepted, of course." I kick at pebbles. Some loose shale on the riverbed.

"I'm happy here," Robyn says. "I love Zarek. His dreams and ambitions inspire me. Wajia is a wonderful woman."

"Did you discuss how your marriage would complicate negotiations?"

"Of course. I told Zarek there was no way I would go back. If negotiations broke down and America wanted me, they would have to come and take me. Zarek drove off the Soviets. He would drive off the Americans as well."

"How did you manage Grissom?"

"*That*," Robyn says, "became a delicate matter. In the end, we managed it very well."

Zarek and Robyn were married in the Pashtun tradition. They consummated their union, but agreed not to have children until the negotiations were complete. Grissom was to be brought to the camp in secret. Hooded so he could not locate it. Robyn's marriage to Zarek would be concealed to facilitate the bait-and-switch. There was never an intention to send her back.

Negotiations between the United States and Abdul-Ali Shahzad were difficult. America courted Shahzad because

he dominated the Afghanistan-Pakistan border and hosted
Al Qaeda. If he could be turned, it would be a major coup.

Everything went according to plan. Grissom began by
negotiating for Robyn's release. Zarek turned her release
into a rider appended to a broader peace deal. Grissom,
well aware of the difficulties that bedeviled the Shahzad
deal, was eager to learn what Zarek had to offer.

Grissom was a colonel in the United States Army.
However, it became clear that for the purposes of the negotiation, he had been seconded to the State Department and
was taking direction from State and the CIA.

GRISSOM'S CHAIN of command is crucial. "He told you
that?"

"Yes," Robyn says. "Well, he told Zarek. The Army
was aware of the negotiations, but they were only given
broad strokes. They were not involved in the details."

That was why General Anthony's briefing had been
light on details of the peace deal. All he knew was that the
US was agreeing to withdraw its remaining forces from the
country. Nor did Stein tell me everything during our breakfast at Clark.

Anthony knew little, Stein knew everything. The question now, is how much did Stein keep from me?

I turn to Robyn. "But—Grissom had to find out at some
point."

"Yes." Robyn smiles. "That was when our secret
became useful."

THE QUESTION WAS one of trust. It always would be.
Assurances would be given, documents signed. History had

proven documents were not worth the paper they were printed on unless the hearts of the men giving the assurances were true.

How could the Americans trust the word of Zarek, and how could Zarek trust the word of the Americans?

Zarek and Robyn conferred.

Robyn went to Grissom and told him she did not want to return to America. The colonel was shocked. He wanted to know why. She told him she was Zarek's wife. That she wanted to remain in Afghanistan and raise a family with him.

The colonel was beside himself. Robyn was still a serving non-commissioned officer in the United States Army. Her marriage to an enemy combatant was illegal. She would be court-martialed upon her return. At best, she would be dishonorably discharged. At worst she would spend time in Leavenworth prison.

He wished she hadn't told him. He had a duty to reflect the situation to his masters at State and the CIA.

STEIN'S A CRAFTY WITCH. All this time, she knew Zarek and Robyn were married. Now, the sixty-four-thousand-dollar question. "Did he tell the army?"

"No," Robyn says. "Grissom's background was intelligence. He was used to working with State and the CIA. That's why he was selected. I also think he was a good man. He saw me as misguided, wanted to help."

"Naturally, you and Zarek gave him an opportunity to do that."

"Yes. The conversations became fascinating. Zarek and Grissom negotiated in English. I was present to translate difficult concepts that neither man could express in the other's language. I was present as an interpreter, but also a stakeholder with a personal interest."

"I can guess how you resolved it." I shake my head. "I want to hear it from you."

"The issue was always one of trust. In other words, a warranty." Robyn stoops and gathers a handful of stones. Pitches them one by one into the river.

"Trust."

"Yes. I became the warranty." Robyn looks back at the campfires to make sure no one has approached behind us. "The deal was a risk for both Zarek and the United States. Zarek would permit me to return with Grissom. To convey the proposal to the highest authority. In return, the United States would sign the deal, and discharge me honorably from the army. If I was not so honorably discharged, the deal would be dead and the US would be left with damaged goods. The army would be forced to court-martial me. The result would be a terrible scandal. Zarek would lose his second wife, and the United States would have its machinations blow up in its face."

"Therefore, it was in everyone's interest to discharge you honorably and send you back."

"Exactly. Zarek would sign the deal and we would all live happily ever after."

"Zarek was willing to risk you."

Robyn shakes her head. "No, it was my idea."

Of course it was.

A story worthy of Kipling.

29

THE SECRET

North Arwal Valley
Thursday, 2350

R obyn and I are silent for a long time.
I work hard to process her story. Tug at the
various strands. Test them.

"On the mountain," I say, "Grissom knew the caravan
in the valley was Zarek's."

"Yes, he must have. Zarek cuts a distinctive figure when
he rides. Dressed in black, with the crimson waistcoat. I
saw him, without the help of your binoculars."

"Why did you lie to me?"

Robyn squirms. "It looked like…"

"Like what?"

"Like Lopez pushed Grissom."

"At the time, it was clear that was what you thought.
Ballard saw the whole thing, and he didn't think so."

"Look, Breed." Robyn stiffens. "Grissom told me and
Zarek there were people in the administration and else-

where that did not want to see a peace deal. Not with Shahzad, not with Zarek. No deal, period. There are people who want us to commit more forces to Afghanistan."

"That's a given," I tell her. "But—it's not worth killing for."

"I can't perform that calculation. All I know is… it looked like Lopez pushed Colonel Grissom. That meant Ballard, Takigawa and Koenig could be in on it, too."

"Didn't you suspect me?"

"I did, for a while. But it's clear you and Captain Koenig don't get along. When I learned you were brought in at the last minute, I felt a lot better about you."

"Thanks," I say. "That's not a great vote of confidence."

Robyn looks miserable. "I believe in you, Breed. One hundred percent, and so does Zarek. You have to understand. Colonel Grissom and I grew close in the short time we knew each other. This deal—Zarek, Grissom and I put it together. After Grissom died, I felt lost and alone. I could push the fear and loneliness away while we were climbing to that old fort. Made brave faces and smart-assed my way through things. The minute I sat alone in that old bunker, I fell apart. I couldn't hold it together."

I remember walking in on her that night. She'd been sobbing.

"Shahzad's force has been crushed," I tell her. " Tomorrow morning, we'll call for exfil. They will extract us by air."

"Promise me," Robyn says, "you won't tell anyone Zarek and I are married. The people who know, in State and the CIA, will reach out. Let them come to us."

"We're going to be debriefed."

"Of course. I'm not asking you to lie. I'm asking you not to tell everything. Without Colonel Grissom, I have to

wait for friends to come to me. They will, as soon as they
learn the colonel was killed."

I hesitate. But—Robyn's suspicions mirror mine. And
my suspicions mirror Stein's. I believe interests in neoconservative circles want the war to continue. I'll go so far as
to say the military-industrial lobby wants the war to
continue. But Afghanistan is a sideshow compared to Syria,
Iran and Ukraine. I'm not prepared to believe it's worth
murdering an Army colonel over.

"Okay," I tell her. "I'll play along. For a while."

"Thanks, Breed. That's all I ask."

30

DEBRIEF

North Arwal Valley
Friday, 0800

The Apaches hover over the riverbed, their chin guns levelled at Zarek's troops. The warlord signals two of his men. The Mujahedeen step forward from the tree line, long olive drab tubes on their shoulders. *Stingers.* Zarek snaps a command, and the shooters lock onto the Apaches.

Koenig stands there doing nothing.

"Ballard," I snap. "What's their call sign?"

"Black Hawk is Hawk One. Apaches are Hawk Two and Three."

I take the handset from Ballard. "Hawk Two, this is Five-Five Sierra."

"Go ahead, Five-Five Sierra."

"Safe your weapons and back off. These are friendlies."

"Five-Five Sierra, they have missile lock on us."

"You have guns on them. For the record, it's my call. Back off two miles."

"Hawk Two, copy. Your call. Backing off two miles."

The first Apache peels away. The second hesitates, then follows.

I meet Zarek's steely gaze. He nods, waves his men off. The shooters raise their missile tubes and withdraw to the tree line.

"Hawk One, this is Five-Five Sierra."

"Go ahead, Five-Five Sierra."

"LZ is clear. These are friendlies. We are ready to exfil."

"Copy, Sierra. Stand back, we're coming down."

The Black Hawk swoops down, flares for landing. The door gunners are primed for action.

"Hawk One, keep your gunners off their triggers."

"Hawk One, copy."

"Let's go." Koenig ducks his head against the rotor wash and runs to the helo. Takigawa follows, then Lopez and Ballard.

I take Robyn by the arm. Together, we run to the waiting Black Hawk and pile in. She sits on the floor, her back to the copilot. I squeeze in next to her, brace one booted foot against the minigun mount.

Koenig takes the handset from Ballard. "Let's get out of here," he tells the pilot.

The Black Hawk pilot lifts from the LZ. His rotor wash drives the Mujahedeen back. All but Zarek, who stands in the open, staring at the helicopter as it pulls away. Robyn puts one hand on my shoulder, the other on my chest rig. Leans around me.

She's not waving goodbye, but I know Robyn's eyes are drinking Zarek in. Impressing his image upon her memory.

Standing in the rotor wash, Dragunov slung over his shoulder, watching her go.

The future of a country rides on this girl's shoulders.

THE THREE HELICOPTERS fly south-by-west in a Vic formation. Our Black Hawk leads, flanked behind and on either side by the two Apaches. We race across the mountains, skirting the tall peaks of the Hindu Kush. Soon, we are hurtling over foothills. To our right rises the forbidding shark's-tooth silhouette of the Koh-i-Baba range.

My ears are stuffed by the pressure differential as the Black Hawk descends toward Bagram. I swallow hard to clear the inner chambers. Soon, I am gulping air as fast as I can, trying to equalize the pressure within and without my skull.

Robyn twists, craning her neck to look through the pilots' windscreen. I turn and register what she sees. The vast complex of Bagram Air Field. The long runway, the endless rows of parked aircraft. Everything from whale-like C-5 Galaxies to tiny F-16s. Row upon row of administrative buildings, barracks and armories.

The Black Hawk lands at the rotary wing terminal, and the pilots shut down the engines. The Apaches make for the gunship field. I look out the door. Next to the landing pad, a Special Forces sergeant stands waiting by a Humvee.

I step off the Black Hawk and help Robyn down. As soon as Koenig joins us on the tarmac, I say, "What the hell was that, Captain?"

"What are you talking about, Breed?"

"Were you going to stand there and let Zarek's men and the Apaches shoot each other?"

Koenig turns on me. "Listen, Breed. Let me remind you

those Mooj are still the enemy. As and when we get a peace deal in our hot little hands, we will cease fire. Until then, I don't trust anybody."

"You came pretty goddamn close to a firefight right there."

The sergeant approaches us, salutes Koenig. "Captain Koenig, your team is to report to General Anthony."

"Very well, Sergeant. Let's go."

Blood pounds in my temples. I want to haul off and deck Koenig. Am I being paranoid? Oversensitive because of my conversations with Stein and Robyn?

No. We have reason to be hypersensitized to danger. Robyn looks at me anxiously. The young girl who orchestrated this complicated negotiation is in the thick of it. She is struggling to process situations her experience has not prepared her to handle.

I take Robyn by the arm and help her into the Humvee. She sits between me and Takigawa. Koenig, Lopez and Ballard sit across from us in back. Koenig stares at me, fuming. Was his dereliction malicious, or an example of his lackadaisical approach to command? I am seeing threats everywhere.

Lopez stares straight ahead, unconcerned. Ballard looks troubled. He knows how close we came to exchanging fire with Zarek's Mujahedeen. He knows the escalation was unnecessary. A call to the helicopters before they approached was all that was required to control the situation.

The sergeant drives us to General Anthony's HQ. The VIP gate is guarded by two stony-faced MPs with Berettas in open holsters and M4 carbines. The sergeant at the wheel exchanges words with one of the MPs. I catch the word "pre-cleared." The MPs swing the gate open and the sergeant parks the vehicle.

"This way, Sir."

We are ushered into the ground floor of the modern annex. The corridors are clean. A stark contrast to our uniforms, filthy from three days in the mountains. We are shown the same conference room we occupied the day of our briefing. The sergeant leaves us alone with the hum of air conditioning.

Robyn looks bewildered. I sit next to her, take a load off.

The other men relax. For them, the hard part is over. This is the usual debrief, the traditional after-action Q&A. They are looking forward to a shower, hot food, and a decent crib.

General Anthony enters, a staff captain in tow. The captain opens a laptop computer, sets a digital recorder on the desk. Reads the date, location, and a list of those present into the record.

"Welcome back, gentlemen." The general's tone is curt, no-nonsense. "Sergeant Trainor, it is gratifying to have you returned to us after such a long spell in captivity.

"This will be an informal session. A more detailed debrief will follow with each of you. We are under pressure at the moment, and I need to know what happened. I understand the team was separated at the bridge to Lanat. I want Captain Koenig to relate the after-action report to the time the group was separated. Breed, you tell the story from there. Understood?"

Koenig and I respond together. "Yes, Sir."

"Very well. Captain Koenig, the floor is yours."

Koenig relates the story from the moment of our infil on Shafkat. When he reaches the point at which Takigawa and

I entered the house to free the prisoners, the general interrupts him.

"You say at this point you engaged sentries on the upper terraces of the village. How did that occur?"

"Not much to tell, Sir. Breed and Takigawa were in the dwelling. A sentry stepped from around a house on the third terrace and spotted myself and Sergeant Lopez. He raised his rifle and pointed it at us. Sergeant Lopez engaged."

"That correct, Sergeant?"

"Yes, Sir." Lopez stares at the general. "At first, I froze. Hoped he hadn't seen us in the dark. When he raised his rifle, I shot him."

"How many rounds did you fire?"

"Two or three. Short and sweet, aimed fire. I hit him, but as he went down, he fired his AK47. The sound of shooting caused another sentry on the third level to engage. After that, more Talis emerged on every level."

Lopez's story matches my own recollection. I was angry with Koenig for not doing a better job of concealing himself and Lopez. They might have waited at the approach to the bridge, rather than venturing onto the escarpment. At the bridge, the structure would have broken up their outlines, made them more difficult to spot.

"Carry on," Anthony growls.

Koenig relates how he and Lopez leapfrogged each other over the steps. How they provided cover for us from the second terrace. When he comes to the shooting of Grissom, the general stops him a second time.

"Where did the shot come from?" the general asks. "The one that hit Colonel Grissom."

"Impossible to say, Sir." Koenig straightens in his chair. "It was a lucky shot, for both the Tali who fired it, and the colonel. The Talis were firing on full auto. Connecting with the colonel was pure fluke."

Lopez pipes in. "Another inch and the shot would have blown the colonel's brains all over those steps."

Koenig continues. He relates our surprise to find Shahzad's men had SAMs. He thinks they are SAM-7 Grails. Invites me to describe how Hubble was killed, and my rear-guard action as a sniper element.

"It was bad luck your team was separated at the bridge," the general tells Koenig.

"Yes, Sir."

"Only a fool dismisses luck," General Anthony says, "but you had more than your share working against you that day."

"It also worked for us, General." I tilt my head toward Robyn. "Sergeant Trainor and the rest of us wouldn't be here today had the captain and Takigawa not been able to cover our withdrawal. They delayed Shahzad's force for more than an hour."

The general grunts. "Alright, Breed. What happened on the west face?"

I continue the story, careful to relate Grissom's death in a manner that leaves out Robyn's behavior. Her suspicion of Lopez. I wait for the others to provide further color, but they remain silent. I cannot fault them. Impressions of other individuals and their behavior are subjective. These can be articulated in one-on-one debriefs.

After our trek to the Soviet fort, the story becomes more straightforward. We were in radio communication with the general before the ambush at the village. Lopez tells of how he handled the point position.

"I was wary of an ambush," Lopez says. "That village gave me the creeps. I went past it like I was walking on eggs. I saw a shadow move in the tree line and hit the deck. Next thing I knew, they lit us up."

I continue the story, leaving out my resentment at the general's refusal to provide the least air cover. I tell of how Zarek's vanguard relieved us from the siege.

Koenig says, "After the battle at the bridge, a detachment of Shahzad's force followed us onto Lanat. It looked like they might have SAMs, so exfil by LZ Three was out. We knew from Breed's transmissions that he was trying to exfil from Shafkat, so we tried to catch him. It was then we saw that Shahzad's main body, a hundred and fifty men, was heading in the same direction."

"Carry on."

"Not much more to tell, Sir. We reached Kagur village too late to participate in the action. Najibullah's force had already beaten off Shahzad's attack. That's when Sergeant Takigawa and I rejoined the team. From then on, we enjoyed Najibullah's escort to the Arwal."

The general should have spotted a glaring incongruity.

"Shahzad's main body was in position to cut off Koenig and Takigawa on the west slope of Lanat," I tell them. "At the time, he could not have known our team had split up. Why did Shahzad turn his main body around and head for the village?"

"He was covering all his bases," Koenig says. "All morning, Takigawa and I dodged a platoon-strength detachment."

"Shahzad knew Zarek's caravan was on its way to the village. Zarek's mounted fighters were covering ground at the pace of the Mujahedeen infantry. Even so, Shahzad had to turn around and drive his own foot soldiers hard. His objective was to get to the village first. Kill us and capture

Robyn before Zarek could intervene. We held him off long enough for the cavalry to arrive."

I pause for effect. "How did Shahzad know to move his infantry so quickly?"

"We may never know the answer to that, Breed," General Anthony says. "Shahzad split his force and moved quickly. Captain Koenig's theory is as good as any."

Koenig tells of our two days on the trail with Zarek's caravan, the ambush at the riverbend, and the battle that conclusively defeated Shahzad's main body. The captain ends with our extraction earlier this morning.

Before the general can speak, I interject. "Sir, Najibullah said something I thought rather odd."

"What was that, Breed?"

"He claimed we attacked his caravans three times more often than we attacked Shahzad's."

"That's news to me, Breed." General Anthony clasps his hands behind his back and steps to the front of the room. "Have you seen any such stats, Larsen?"

"No, Sir." The captain lifts his eyes from the screen of his laptop. "I don't think we break them out that way."

"It isn't the kind of self-serving statement Najibullah would make," I offer. "He said it was not too difficult to count. Good businessmen count."

The general smiles. "Well, I reckon we bomb them where we find them, Breed."

"Yes, Sir."

The general dismisses me, addresses Koenig. "Thanks for the picture, Captain."

"If you have any other questions, Sir."

"Not at the moment." Anthony turns to Robyn. "Sergeant Trainor, it is unfortunate that Colonel Grissom did not survive to see you freed from your ordeal. I am given to understand that you are familiar with the details of the deal he negotiated with Najibullah. These men are all cleared top secret. Please share with the team."

"There is considerable detail, General." Robyn straightens in her chair. "In broad terms, the United States agrees to withdraw all its forces from Afghanistan. The Afghan National Government and Zarek Najibullah will make peace, and guarantee the Taliban and Al Qaeda will not be allowed to operate inside the Afghan-Pakistan border. It's that simple."

"And the details?

"I am to convey the details to the highest authority in DC, Sir. They will be documented in an agreement Zarek Najibullah is prepared to sign."

"The deal can't be that simple."

"It's not. There are spheres of influence, phases of implementation. Colonel Grissom was very specific. I was to convey the details to State and the highest authority in DC."

What balls. Robyn is giving General Anthony the equivalent of her name, rank and serial number.

The general wrestles with his frustration. "Very well," he says. "I am scheduled to engage in a call with State an hour from now. Captain Larsen will arrange appropriate quarters. Grab a shower, some hot chow. We'll reconvene when I have something to tell you."

The general leaves the conference room. We are left staring at each other in silence.

"Gentlemen." Captain Larsen slaps his laptop shut and pockets his digital recorder. "If you'll follow me."

31

THE BONUS

Bagram
Friday, 1300

Captain Larsen takes us back to the Humvee. The sergeant who escorted us from the helo has gone. We pile into the vehicle, and Larsen gets behind the wheel. In minutes, he is racing toward the barracks area.

"You'll occupy the same barracks you've occupied all week," he tells Koenig. I assume his statement includes me, since I was billeted with the team. "The women's quarters are across the street. With force reductions, there is plenty of room. Sergeant Trainor will have a room to herself. She'll share quarters with three other ladies, two nurses from the base hospital, and one from intel."

The Humvee lurches to a stop in front of the same drab, prefabricated huts I saw when I arrived on Monday. The street the captain referred to is a single lane, twenty feet wide.

"Sergeant Trainor's in the hut opposite yours," he says. "Sergeant, please follow me. The rest of you wait here."

Robyn piles out of the Humvee and follows Larsen to the first hut on the women's side of the street.

The captain pounds on the door, throws it open. "Man on the floor!"

He disappears inside, with Robyn in tow. Emerges five minutes later.

"Gentlemen," Larsen says, "I believe you are familiar with your quarters. You have until sixteen hundred free. Do whatever you like. I will be in touch with Captain Koenig to let you know the score."

We pile out of the Humvee, shoulder our weapons and our rucks. I'm too exhausted to move. Follow the others into the hut, go to my room, and drop my gear on the floor. Strip naked, walk bare-assed to the communal shower, and let the spray blast four days of mountain dirt and sweat off my body. I'm not alone. Koenig, Lopez and Ballard straggle in. Dressed in full combat gear, Takigawa has passed out on his bed.

I go to the sink and shave. Back in my room, I close the door, put on the civilian clothes and desert boots I'd worn from Clark. I hang up my stinking camouflage uniform. Set the M110 and plate carrier at the very back of the closet.

The Mark 23, I take from its holster. Drop its magazine, rack the slide, and perform a three-point check. There were two spare magazines in my plate carrier. I grunt, fish them out, and slap a fresh mag in the butt. Let the slide go, lock and load. I place the spare mags in the pocket of my field jacket. Squeeze the pistol into my waistband, appendix carry. It's a big gun, but my clothes are loose enough to conceal it.

Finally, I tug open my duffel and rummage around until

I find my cellphone at the bottom. Tap my passcode, check the battery. Slip it into my pocket with the mags and go outside.

The street is empty. Wonder if any of the other huts are occupied. I walk the length of the barracks compound without encountering a soul. I wonder how Robyn is making out in her new quarters. How a Western bed feels, after sleeping eighteen months on Afghan mats. Or a shower with hot running water.

Maybe that doesn't beat skinny-dipping with Allah's chosen leader of the faithful.

The last hut in the row has a great view of the airstrip. I sit with my back to its outer wall. Watch a pair of F-15 Strike Eagles thunder down the runway and lift into the sky.

I unlock my phone, tap Stein's speed-dial, and let it ring.

It is 0430, Eastern Standard Time.

The voice that answers is alert, all business. As I knew it would be, despite the early hour. "Stein."

"It's Breed. We brought Trainor back. Grissom took a high dive off a five-hundred-foot cliff. The girl thinks one of the men on the team helped him, I can't be sure. Zarek's bitching we hit his caravans three times more often than Shahzad's. The general says he doesn't keep those stats."

"Do you believe him?"

"Hard to say. He's always been a detail-oriented guy. But—he may be disinterested in that level of granularity. To use his words, we bomb them where we find them."

"What about the deal?"

"You've been naughty, Stein. You didn't tell me everything."

"I thought you would find it more entertaining to figure it out yourself."

"How thoughtful. Yes, Robyn Trainor is an entertaining piece of work. The deal is rattling around with all those happy thoughts she keeps in her skull. Reserved for Grissom's masters at State and the CIA. Know who *those* might be?"

Stein refuses to rise to the bait.

"I'm on a conference call with General Anthony in an hour," she says. "You will all be returning to DC on a flight out of Bagram tomorrow morning. Sergeant Trainor is to be debriefed by the highest authority."

Warm fluid oozes out of my right ear. A viscous drop begins to form at the corner of my jaw. I swipe at it with the heel of my hand before it soils my shirt. The phone and my hand grow slippery.

"Oh. Little Robyn's playing in the big leagues, is she?"

"We are approaching the endgame. General Anthony indicates Shahzad is prepared to make concessions to restart talks."

"We kicked his ass all over the Arwal. He's suffered fifty or sixty KIA in the last forty-eight hours."

"He and the Taliban have hundreds, thousands more in the Tribal Lands."

"Zarek has the same in the north, and he's arming a coalition in the south. Once the US pulls out, Zarek will go to war against the Taliban right across the country."

"Get Robyn Trainor to DC, and we'll close the deal with Zarek. The administration is fed up with Shahzad's bullshit."

I can't believe it. Anya Stein is staking everything on a romantic kid.

Who's the romantic? I remember how Robyn touched

my face, her fingers wet with my blood. The concern in her eyes. The girl has gotten under my skin. But she is not for me.

"Stein, this girl thinks she is living a fairy tale. The army won't let her get away with marrying a Mujahedeen warlord. They'll court-martial her ass, lock her in Leaven-worth, and throw away the key."

"The army will do whatever the fuck the administration tells it to do. The administration will do what I tell them to do. *If* you get her back alive."

Stein is on a power trip, and I need to put some emotional distance between myself and Robyn.

"My job was to get her out of Badakhshan," I say. "Nobody said anything about babysitting the kid all the way to DC."

I can read about Robyn in the newspapers... from the veranda of a plantation house in the Philippines.

"A romantic child has her uses," Stein says.

"Where does the CIA find you people?"

Stein ignores the dig. "However—it does exceed the parameters of our agreement."

"*Our* agreement? The general thinks I work for him."

"Great. He won't have a problem with you coming to DC. You and I can add a side-letter right now. A fifty percent bonus on delivery—*to the highest authority*."

One hundred and fifty thousand bucks for a week's work. *And* they buy out my last contract. It's a good excuse to hang around Robyn a little longer.

"I suppose I *could* babysit a few more hours."

32

THE ASSASSIN

Bagram
Friday, 2300

Airplanes and helicopters take off and land at Bagram 24/7. You want to sleep, you get used to it.

I lie fully clothed in bed. Our Globemaster leaves Bagram at 0400 for the fifteen-hour flight to Joint Base Andrews. The Mark 23 rests by my right hand. Old habits die hard.

There are *some* habits we'd like to erase.

In combat, we played the Adderall Olympics. There were two lemon drop bowls on the table in the mess. One filled with Adderall, the other with Ambien. We ran the vampire cycle. Got out of bed at 1600 hours, worked out, had breakfast, and absorbed the briefing for the night's operations. Popped a couple Adderall. By 0300, we were wired to the eyeballs. Hyper-alert, ready to go out and kill the bad guys in their beds.

We ruled the night. When we got back to base after sunup, we were still high. We sat around and popped Ambien to bring us back down. Loser was the guy who had to take the most to get to sleep. If you were lucky, you lost consciousness by 0800 so you could roll out at 1600 and do it all again.

That's how the elite operate. Stroll by the barracks at noon, you'll find Delta Force passed out in their racks, or face down in the dirt, halfway to the communal outhouse. Do that for a full deployment, no one can live around you when you get home.

Ask me why I love living on a plantation in the Philippines. Sipping pineapple juice.

Now I lie in bed, staring at the ceiling, listening to the cargo planes take off and land. The interceptors are all-weather, but apart from scheduled combat air patrols, there are few strike missions this late at night.

The hut is quiet. The street outside is quiet.

That is a C-5.

That is a C-17.

That is a Huey. The distinctive thud of the ancient helo's two-bladed rotor. It's been out of service for years. Wonder who the hell is operating one out here.

That is a woman screaming.

I roll out of bed, stuff the Mark 23 in my waistband. Jerk open my bedroom door, bang through the front. There, across the street, lights are going on in the women's quarters. Another scream. Throaty—a mature woman. Not a girl, not Robyn.

A man dressed in dark clothing, wearing a balaclava, strides from the rear of the women's hut. Must have left by the back door. He looks left and right, then back. I break into a run. He draws a pistol from his jacket and fires.

There is the rapid-fire popping of a small-caliber pistol. A nine-millimeter.

I throw myself onto the pavement. Skin my knees and elbows. The muzzle flashes fade. The man runs for the long road that borders the runway.

A shout from behind. "Breed!"

Koenig chases after me, a Mark 23 in his hand. Behind him, Takigawa and Ballard. Ballard is running barefoot, his camouflage shirt open. He's forgotten to put on his glasses.

Focus on the fleeing figure. There's no traffic on the border road. It's separated from the airstrip by a two-foot-high fence of metal pipe six inches in diameter. Lights are embedded in the tarmac at fixed intervals to mark the runway.

A C-5 Galaxy accelerates for takeoff. The roar of its engines is deafening. The figure turns and fires at me again. This time, I refuse to hit the dirt. He's running hard. The odds of him hitting anything offhand are slim to none.

The figure crosses the road, hurdles the fence. The C-5 hits V1, pitches nose-high, and lifts into the air. A quarter mile to our right, a Globemaster pulls onto the runway, bathing us in its taxi lights.

I'm gaining on him.

The figure dashes onto the runway. Turns and fires. Again, the ridiculous pop of the tiny nine-millimeter rounds. With one mighty effort, I hurl myself forward and tackle him. My arms close around his waist. He stumbles with the impact and goes down, the gun flying from his hand.

Bathed in the Globemaster's blinding lights, we grapple. I want the son of a bitch alive, but he's strong. A bodybuilder or powerlifter. I try to get a wrist lock on him. He twists out of it, throws me on my back, lurches to his feet. I twist on my side and draw my knee back to kick. The man reaches into his boot and draws a six-inch Gerber. Razor-sharp, double-edged. Hurls himself at me.

Two sharp cracks, a double-tap. The heavy-caliber rounds drill the man in the chest, damn near the same hole. He crumples to the tarmac. I get to my feet, step on his wrist, and twist the knife from his grasp. He stares at me, coughs blood all over his wool balaclava.

With one jerk, I tear the ski mask from his head.

Lopez.

The medic's face is ghastly silver in the airplane's head-lights. A rope of blood hangs from the corner of his mouth. The sight fades from his eyes.

Koenig is holding his Mark 23 in a perfect isosceles stance. "Are you okay?" he asks.

I could have disarmed Lopez, but feel like I owe Koenig. "Yes, thanks."

Koenig snorts. "What the hell was he doing?"

I look from Koenig to Ballard and back. "Trainor was right all along," I say. "He killed Grissom."

"And tried to kill her," Ballard says.

Sirens are whooping. Military Police and ambulances. I sprint back to the women's quarters. The hut is ablaze with lights. I find the back door open. Inside, a small bache-lorette kitchen, a mirror of ours. The communal showers and toilets are on the right. A single corridor, and six barrack rooms, three on either side. Designed for two soldiers apiece. With the force reductions, they have become private rooms.

A sturdy woman with cropped red hair squats at the door of the room on the left. Looks inside. The room must be Robyn's. "Who are you?" she asks. Her accent is Australian.

"Breed," I say. "I'm with Sergeant Trainor's team. How is she?"

"She's not breathing."

I poke my head into the room.

Robyn is lying on the floor, dressed in a t-shirt and white cotton underwear. She's face-up, but her eyes are closed. A middle-aged Latina woman with dark hair is kneeling over her. The Latina is dressed in camouflage pants. Barefoot, a pink sweater pulled over a white t-shirt.

"What's wrong with her?" I ask.

"All the signs of a morphine overdose," the Latina says. She's bent over Robyn, giving the girl mouth-to-mouth resuscitation. "Breathe, baby. Breathe."

My eyes scan the room. Robyn fought for her life. She was dragged off the bed. Or tried to hang onto her attacker while he tried to escape. The other women rushed to the room to help. The intruder was stronger. He either held them off physically, or threatened them with a weapon. Then he walked out the back door. A cool operator, calculating the angles.

There, in a corner, next to one of the metal bedposts—a glass syringe. The plunger has been depressed, but there remains a quarter inch of clear fluid in the barrel. I show it to the nurses. "What is this?"

"Probably morphine," the Australian nurse says. "He's given her enough to drop a bloody horse."

The Latina speaks with a New York accent. She turns to the Aussie. "Go meet the medics. Make sure they bring naloxone."

The Aussie runs to the front of the hut.

"Damn," the Latina curses. "She's not responding."

"Do something."

The woman clenches her right hand into a fist and

punches her middle knuckle into Robyn's chest. "Come on, hon. Wake *up*."

Robyn grunts.

The woman grinds her knuckle into Robyn's breast-bone. Hard enough to hurt. Robyn grimaces, tries to push the woman's hand away.

Relieved, I allow myself to breathe.

"Help me," the nurse says. "Walk her around."

I grab one of Robyn's arms. The nurse takes the other. Together, we haul Robyn to her feet.

This nurse is used to giving orders. "Let's get her outside."

"Come on, Robyn," I say. "Walk."

Robyn tries to walk, but the effort is a lousy imitation. She's hanging off us, shuffling and dragging her feet. She slumps. Her chin drops to her chest.

"Wake the fuck *up*." The Latina twists her fist in Robyn's hair and jerks the girl's head back.

"Stop it," Robyn howls. "You're hurting me."

"That's better, hon." The woman gives me a triumphant look. "Every day above ground is a good day."

GENERAL ANTHONY STANDS at the foot of Robyn's hospital bed. Stares at her with a mixture of relief and frustration. Koenig and I stand on either side. Her doctor, an Air Force colonel, stands on my side, at the head of the bed. Robyn is conscious, but wan and quiet.

"Our flight to DC leaves in five hours," the general explains. "Surely she is stable enough to travel."

The colonel studies Robyn's chart and makes a note. "I can't support that, General."

"Why not? She's recovered from the overdose."

"The good news is the tox screen is positive for morphine. That means we've given her the correct treatment. But—she's not stable. We gave her two doses of naloxone. An opioid antagonist. Its effects are temporary. When it wears off, she could slip into another morphine coma. In my opinion, she needs to remain under professional medical observation for a minimum of twelve hours."

The general looks ready to explode. Stein's management gave him a schedule. A deadline by which to get Robyn to Washington. For his part, the doctor looks prepared to stand his ground.

"Colonel," General Anthony says, "I can order you to release this woman."

"I can refuse to obey, General. You can court-martial me and find another doctor. I'll take my chances."

The two men are glaring at each other. This will not end well.

I have to find an off-ramp. "May I suggest something."

"What is it, Breed?" the general snaps.

"I think the doctor would agree risk declines with the passage of time. I suggest we push the flight to noon tomorrow. The rotation of the earth will work in our favor. We'll arrive in DC with time to spare. For the doctor's part, perhaps a trained nurse or doctor could accompany Sergeant Trainor on the flight. With the appropriate medication and equipment."

The general and the doctor stare at me.

"This is a matter of grave national importance," I say. "Sergeant Trainor's health is paramount. We can find a way to make this work."

"I can live with that," the doctor says. "I'll select the medical staff for the flight."

"I don't like it," Anthony snorts. "But I *will* live with it."

The general turns on his heel to leave. "Breed, I want to see you and Captain Koenig outside. Right now."

I watch Anthony and Koenig leave the room. Turn to the doctor and smile. "You got your twelve hours, Doctor. And more."

"I thought he would try to split the difference," the doctor says.

"No. It'll be alright."

Robyn stares at me. Her complexion is ashen, and there are dark circles under her eyes. "It was Lopez all the time," she says.

"Yes. And it wasn't the first time he tried to kill you."

Robyn looks shocked.

"Think about it," I tell her. "It will all come clear. Now, I need to speak with the general. I'll be back."

The general and Koenig are standing in a waiting room. Standing by a row of vending machines.

"What's going on, Breed? Lopez was one of ours, and he tried to kill our principal."

"Yes, Sir. What's more, he was busy at it the whole time."

"What are you talking about?"

"I can point to four incidents." I tick them off on my fingers. "The first was when Takigawa and I rescued Colonel Grissom at the village. We were making our escape, climbing the stairs. Lopez and Captain Koenig were providing cover from the terrace above. In the firefight, it was easy for Lopez to take aim and shoot Colonel Grissom. Head shots are no sure thing. Miss by a couple of inches and you get a grazing hit. That's what Lopez scored. Grissom was injured, but not killed."

Koenig protests. "I saw nothing."

"Not a surprise. We all know NODs restrict your vision. You were focused on your own targets. You couldn't be expected to watch Lopez."

"Dear God," the general breathes.

"It gets better, Sir. Second, Lopez pushed Colonel Grissom off the cliff. Lopez was the medic, he was the man we expected to safeguard the colonel. Instead, when the colonel stumbled onto the promontory, Lopez helped him over the side. Sergeant Trainor suspected the whole time. But—none of us were sure what we saw.

"Third, during the ambush at the village, someone shot Sergeant Trainor in the back. Her rear plate saved her life. I remember at the time, thinking it was either a great shot, or dumb luck. Lopez was rear guard at the time. From Lopez's position, it was an easy shot. Like the one he took at Colonel Grissom. Grissom was coming straight at him, Trainor moving away. In both cases—zero deflection.

"Finally, tonight. Trainor is on her way to DC, and this is Lopez's last chance to kill her. He doesn't want to get caught. He doesn't want to use a gun or a knife. He wants to slip her something that will give him plenty of time to get away. Be somewhere else before she is found dead. Morphine is tricky. People react differently to it depending on their height, weight, and overall constitution. To use one nurse's words, he gave her enough to drop a horse. He hoped to leave unnoticed. Trainor would be found dead in bed the next morning."

Koenig protests. "But everyone would know it was a murder."

I shrug. "Sure, as they would had he used a gun or a knife. He needed an alibi. To be somewhere else at the time she died. The effects of an overdose are so variable, she would go into a coma and die hours later. It suited his purposes perfectly."

"Except," Koenig says, "people would suspect a medic. Someone with familiarity and access to drugs."

"This is a combat zone," I say. "Morphine is the easiest drug to get around here. Yes, he has extensive experience with morphine. In fact, that is a perfect argument for his innocence. An experienced battlefield medic knows how much morphine it takes to OD a five-foot-seven, one hundred and thirty-five-pound woman. He wouldn't load her with enough to tranquilize a horse."

"Why?" General Anthony asks. "I cannot believe anyone would commit murder to derail a peace deal."

"That is one question." My voice is soft. "The other question is—who was Lopez working for? Lopez is not a big fish. Whoever wants Trainor dead may try again."

"Shahzad wants to restart talks," the general says. "When we get back to DC, some hard decisions need to be made."

I hate the duplicity Stein has drawn me into. "Above my pay grade, General."

"You two." The general sounds tired. "Return to quarters and get some sleep."

"With your permission, General, I'll sleep here," I tell them. "I think it best Sergeant Trainor not leave my sight."

33

THE SURVIVORS' CLUB

Bagram
Saturday, 0200

I'm sitting in a visitor's chair next to Robyn. There's a knock on the door. Under an open copy of *Newsweek*, I hold the Mark 23 on my lap.

Takigawa and Ballard enter.

"Mind if we join you guys?" Takigawa says.

"You can put the iron away, Breed." Ballard is carrying a shorty... an HK416 with a ten-inch barrel. He wears a chest rig with spare mags. Takigawa carries a Mark 23 in a hip holster. Bulges in the pockets of his field jacket look like hand grenades.

"We thought you might be a bit paranoid," Takigawa says, "so we came together. Here we are, the brothers and sister of the Kagur Valley survivors club."

Ballard sits in a visitor's chair on the other side of Robyn's bed. Rests the carbine across his knees. "To feel unsafe, you'd have to believe all three of us… Lopez, Takigawa and me… are dirty."

"There was a time I wondered." Robyn's face darkens.

"You'll leave here alive," Takigawa says. "Then you'll know."

"Where's Koenig?" I ask.

Takigawa grins. "Back at the barracks, sleeping like a baby."

"We figured you guys would have to sleep sometime." Ballard adjusts his glasses. "Anyone wants a crack will have to get through us."

"You guys are great," Robyn says. "I appreciate it, really."

"What happened to you?" Takigawa asks Robyn.

"I was asleep. The guy came in, held me down, and stuck a needle in my arm. I fought him off. One of the ladies came in to see what the noise was all about. After that, you know more about it than I do."

Ballard shakes his head. "Robyn, you were right about Lopez all along. I'm sorry."

Robyn shrugs.

"I don't understand why Lopez would go bad like that," Takigawa says.

"It had to be money," I tell him. "That picture of a Shelby on his bedroom wall? I think that's his car. A replica sells in the six figures. Originals sell for seven."

"He never bragged about it," Ballard says.

"He wouldn't. And he keeps it under wraps back home. Had a photo blown up and made into a poster. To remind himself what he was working for."

Takigawa blinks. "I can't believe any of us would kill an American soldier for money."

"Think again," Ballard tells him. "The special opera-

tions community has grown in the last fifteen years. Bound
to be bad apples in the box."

"How many times have we bullshitted about how easy
it would be to rob a bank? With our capability, nobody
could stop us." I meet each soldier's eyes in turn. "With the
drawdown, operators are being discharged into the population. Lopez may have been thinking ahead to retirement."

I close the *Newsweek*, set it on a side table. "Guys,
excuse me. I have to make a phone call."

Ballard smiles, pats his rifle. "No sweat."

I STICK the pistol in my waistband and tug my shirt over it.
Take my phone and go into the hospital waiting room. I
collapse into an armchair, stretch my legs, and hit Stein's
speed dial.

"You've been busy," Stein says.

"Stein, if you know anything more, you have to
tell me."

"I don't know anything more."

"Lopez shot Grissom, then gave him the push. Shot
Robyn in the back, then tried to OD her. This doesn't end
with him. They're going to try again."

"Since when is it Robyn?"

"Don't deflect. These people are serious about killing
her. This last attempt was clumsy and desperate. Anything
can happen."

"Get her to DC and I'll have enhanced security. Until
then, you're on your own."

"There's a Delta detail in her room right now. God help
anyone who surprises them. I've got a nerd with birth
control glasses and an HK416 pointed at the door. A crazy
samurai with a .45, and hand grenades in his pockets. Now

I'm worried some Tali with a Stinger will take a shot at our plane."

"Got something to worry about there."

"We aren't thinking about this the right way."

"You mean *I'm* not thinking about this the right way."

"I'm being nice."

"Be yourself."

"Who stands to gain if the peace deal with Zarek collapses?"

"Shahzad, Al Qaeda, whoever was running Lopez."

"Who can project power?"

"Al Qaeda." Stein hesitates. "You're not serious."

"Think we're the only ones who can go to war as a coalition? Whoever wants Robyn dead can partner with Al Qaeda. America's borders are porous. They have sleeper cells."

"You *are* serious."

"If you want Robyn to meet *the highest authority*, think outside the box."

34

SAFE HOUSE

Falls Church
Saturday, 1730

The rotation of the Earth can be your enemy or your friend.

Ask any sniper who has to deal with the Coriolis effect. Over long ranges, your position relative to that of your target makes a difference. Once the bullet leaves the muzzle, the Earth revolves west to east beneath the projectile. Your target moves.

In this case, the rotation of the Earth has been our friend. Following a fifteen-hour flight from Bagram to Washington, and a nine-and-a-half-hour time zone difference, we taxi to a halt at 1730 hours local time.

Apart from Robyn, there are five military passengers on the Globemaster. General Anthony, Colonel Tristan, Captain Larsen, Captain Koenig, and Captain Noelle Santiago. The last is the tough, no-nonsense nurse who saved

Robyn's life last night. They all wear digital camouflage. The general's party carry their dress blues in garment bags. Stein requested Robyn's measurements. Dress blues will be waiting for the sergeant upon arrival.

Robyn and I sat together the whole flight. I would have preferred to sleep in the cargo bay, but we rated seats in first class. The upper deck. I didn't expect trouble on the plane, but we took turns sleeping.

We deplane and I step onto the tarmac. Guide Robyn with gentle pressure on her elbow. Three black army limousines meet the general's entourage. The one in the middle has red plates above the grille, stenciled with three white stars.

The army limos are matched by three black uparmored Suburban SUVs. Stein stands next to the one in the middle. A slender figure, dressed in a tailored black business suit. Her brown hair hangs past her shoulders.

"Let's stay with the general," I say.

We step to the general's side. Stein strides toward us. Hard guys get out of the Suburbans. They're dressed in dark business suits, cut to conceal weapons.

"Here comes trouble," General Anthony mutters.

Stein offers her hand. "Good afternoon, General."

"Good afternoon, Ms Stein."

"State will take care of Sergeant Trainor this evening," Stein says. "We'll convene tomorrow afternoon at the White House."

"Where will you be staying?"

Stein smiles. "You know better than that, General. Sergeant Trainor's location tonight is classified."

"Ms Stein, I would feel better if Breed went with you. Technically, he is a civilian."

"I think we can accommodate one more." Stein's response is smooth as butter.

"Lead the way, ma'am," I say.

"Wait." Robyn turns to Noelle Santiago, shakes her hand. "Thanks for saving my life."

Stein leads us to the Suburbans. I count five men in the security detail. Two in the first and third Suburbans, a driver in the second. Stein climbs into the front passenger seat next to the driver, Robyn and I climb into the back. The security men slam our doors shut and return to their vehicles.

I notice the driver has an H&K MP5 submachinegun with a fixed stock sandwiched between his leg and the door. Stein has a folding-stock MP5 on her lap. I can see why she likes the weapon. It's sexy, stylish, easy for a woman to control. But it's a nine millimeter, an oversized pistol. Useless against body armor.

"Black Widow," a radio crackles. "This is Spider One."

Stein raises the walkie-talkie and keys the mike. "This is Black Widow. Go ahead, One."

"We are ready to roll."

"Alright, One. Let's go."

"Spider One, out."

The general's motorcade pulls out and races to the Andrews main gate. Stein's little convoy follows at a respectable distance.

Four motorcycle policemen wait outside the base.

"Motorcycle escort." I nod with approval. "Stein, I am impressed."

At the gate, an air policeman salutes the general. Another stands in front of our lead Suburban and motions for us to halt. The first two motorcycle cops race off, sirens wailing. The general's motorcade slides in behind them. The two remaining motorcycle cops follow behind.

Gray exhaust fumes drift in the air as the general's limos and their escort disappear in the distance. Robyn catches my eye and smiles.

The air policeman standing in front of our lead vehicle lowers his hand. Steps aside smartly and waves us through by slashing his forearm across his chest, palm bladed. Our convoy leaves the base and pulls into the traffic.

Little more than a month ago, I'd been in a similar convoy. Protecting a food company executive and his daughter.

"Where are we spending the night?" I ask Stein.

"A house outside Falls Church."

"Who knows about it?'

"Nobody."

"Your management?"

"Yes."

"That isn't nobody." I look out the window at the DC suburbs sweeping past us. Once you share an operational detail with a bureaucrat, consider it public. "Pass the word. Let's all take the SIMs out of our phones. Now."

"Breed, you're paranoid."

"I'm alive." I take my phone from my pocket. Extract the SIM. "You know how we found and killed Al Qaeda leaders."

"That's because we have that equipment."

"Think maybe Lopez's masters have that equipment?"

Stein keys her mike. "This is Black Widow. Pull over. Everyone take the SIMs out of your phones. No exceptions."

We stop on the shoulder. In five minutes we are on our way, one security risk eliminated.

Only one.

The miles roll beneath our wheels. My unease swells like a tide. I am drowning in it. I find myself checking the windows of vehicles that overtake us. My hand goes to the Mark 23 in my waistband. Robyn glances at me sideways. I wrestle my anxiety to the floor, but I cannot hold it down. Something is very wrong.

DC suburbs give way to the rolling Virginia countryside.

I crane my neck to stare at the sky. Fuck it. I won't be able to tell our drones from theirs. Whoever *they* are.

Stein should be over-communicating with her team.

Stop it, Breed. This is Stein's show, not yours.

Rolling hills. Farmland, horses. Fences of long, split rails. On the left, a gate opening to a narrow road. The road winds its way among wooded hills. The seclusion provides the illusion of security. I'd much rather hold Robyn in a seedy hotel room off skid row. Two Deltas with her in the room. Three or four strategically placed through the building and elevated positions outside.

I can't turn it off.

"What's the police response time?" I ask.

"Thirty minutes," Stein says.

"Do you have a QRF on standby?"

"Yes. Quantico."

That's something. "What's *their* response time?"

"Twenty minutes by air."

"Comms?"

"Landline, and a mobile phone dedicated to the property. Line-of-sight FM band radios. Another high frequency set like your ManPacks, but not as lightweight or compact."

"Assuming they don't disable all our comms, we have to hold for twenty minutes."

Stein looks at me over her shoulder. "Do you want me to arrange artillery support?"

THE WOODS ARE THICKER than I expected. Deep and dark, mystic hollows and shadows. The road covers flat terrain. Everywhere, the wooded hills overlook the road. Elevated positions from which to mount ambushes.

At last, a clearing. There, at the end of the road, a large, two-story ranch house. Four-car garage, broad picture windows, a wide porch. Outbuildings. A woodshed. Cords of firewood piled high. An axe, its blade buried in a chopping block.

My God, a swimming pool. No weird amoebic shapes. This one's rectangular, thirty yards long by twelve wide. It's got lanes. The owner had it built for workouts. Attached to the main house, yet separate, a pool house. I'm guessing more of an oversize maintenance shed. The driveway is wide and paved.

On three sides, the house is set back from the woods. Especially the front, where the land has been cleared to make way for the road and the drive.

The side with the pool—sucks. A wooded hill overlooks the house. I'll have to look at the interior to see which rooms are exposed to fire.

"Stein," I say. "We don't have the men to cover this place."

"We have a force multiplier—Technology."

The sun is going down. I want to take Robyn someplace six men can secure. No good. We're here, and it's Stein's show.

We pile out of the Suburbans. Five CIA contract security. Five suits. They sling MP5s across their chests. Reach into the vehicles, cram spare magazines into their jacket pockets. They look impressive. The MP5 has served law enforcement and commando units well for decades. But it remains an oversized, selective-fire pistol.

Stein introduces the men. Adcox, Jimenez, Nellis, Orcel, Franz.

"Adcox is the detail lead," she says.

I face Adcox. "You guys been here before?"

"This morning."

"What do you think?"

"We're thin on the ground, but the security system is solid."

He hasn't challenged Stein. Not good.

"You have any long guns?"

"No. MP5s and SIG P226s."

"NODs?"

Adcox shakes his head.

The driver looks Hispanic. "You Jimenez?"

The man straightens. "Yes, Sir."

I point to the hill overlooking the pool. "Hold that elevated position. Right now. Check in every ten minutes."

Adcox looks to Stein. *Should they accept my authority?* She nods.

"Jimenez," I say.

The man faces me.

"If anyone comes tonight, that hill is the first piece of real estate they'll want. Stay sharp."

Jimenez nods, strides across the pool deck, and climbs the hill.

I turn to Adcox. "That hill is outside the effective range of your weapons. From there, one man with a long gun can cut you to pieces."

Adcox looks uncomfortable, says nothing. He leans into

our SUV, pops the dash. He finds a walkie-talkie, turns it on, and hands it to me. "Spider One radio check," he says into his mike.

My radio crackles to life.

"Alright," I say. "Let's see this technology."

The living room and library are open-plan. They extend the width of the house, and half the length. The décor is modern, with comfortable bean bags scattered on the floor, some pulled around the fireplace. A pile of logs on a shiny metal support. A metal bucket of tongs and pokers. The back wall of the room is lined with bookshelves, a huge study table, and a sophisticated sound system with speakers hanging from the ceiling.

"Not much," Stein says, "but it's comfortable."

I wonder how much this pad set the Agency back.

Wide picture windows grace the front of the room. Smaller windows on either side. Adcox sits behind three laptops arranged on the library table. Next to the laptops sits a high-frequency radio built for desk or vehicular installation. It's a nice piece of equipment. At 400 Watts, way over-powered for this application. This piece has a range of at least three thousand miles.

"Here's technology," Stein says.

"Comms, you know about." Adcox lifts a mobile phone lying next to the radio. Points to the three laptops. "The first two laptops here are Wifi'd to cameras that cover the access road and 360 degrees outside the house. The split-screens are labeled by camera unit. We can adjust camera angle from the keyboard. The third laptop is Wifi'd to motion sensors that ring the property. Trigger height is set to two feet. We don't want small animals to set off false alarms."

I squint. One screen, displayed in the center of a nine-screen montage, shows the junction of the main road and the access lane to the property. Cars are passing in both directions. Should one of them turn towards the house, the operator on duty will see it.

"Where do you plan to post the men?"

"Two six-hour shifts, I reckon. Three men on, three off. The three men off serve as a reserve. One man on the hill, one in front by the vehicles, and one in back at the tennis courts."

"Tennis courts."

"It's a plush pad."

"Okay. I'll lend a hand."

There is a wide opening in the back wall next to the library. Stein leads us through. The kitchen on the left is as big as the library, with a large table in the middle that can be used to prepare food, or for casual dining. On the other side of the house is the formal dining room. It doesn't look like it gets much use, but the table, the silver, and the place settings are impeccable. Between the kitchen and the dining room is the stairwell leading to the second floor.

The kitchen is the point of vulnerability. There is a door at the back that leads into the pool house. Another door leads onto the pool deck. It's dark outside. Stein and Robyn stand by the center table, looking out at the pool. I reach for the switch and turn off the lights in the kitchen.

"Keep the interior lights turned off," I say. "Stay away from the windows."

For the first time, Stein looks at the hill that overlooks the pool. She cannot see Jimenez.

I raise my radio and key the mike. "Spider Two, this is Black Widow. Are you there?"

Jimenez responds, "Spider Two, copy."

"Can you see us?"

"Like fish in a bowl a minute ago. You're fine now."

I shake my head. "Not if you had night vision. Black Widow out." I turn to Stein. "Hope you don't mind my borrowing your call sign. Can you get more light onto the pool?"

"Some."

Stein flicks more switches, adjusts a rheostat. Powerful floodlamps bathe the pool and deck in a brilliant glare.

"That's good," I say. "The contrast between the lighted pool area and the darkness inside the kitchen will defeat night vision. If they have thermal, we're out of luck. Don't take chances. Stay away from the windows."

Robyn folds her arms over her chest. "Do you think they'll try anything?"

"We don't know who *they* are," I tell her. "We may be worrying about nothing, but it's best to be safe. It's only a few more hours before we take you to the White House."

Stein puts her arm around Robyn's shoulders. "Breed, I'm going to take Robyn upstairs. She can have a shower, and I'll show her the dress blues she'll wear tomorrow. She's got a room to herself and some nightclothes."

"Alright," I say. "But she doesn't have a room to herself. She isn't to leave your sight. Keep that MP5 handy."

"Yes, Sir." Stein gives me a sidelong look, takes Robyn by the hand.

A thought hits me.

"Stein."

"Yes!"

"Which side of the house is Robyn's room on?"

Silence. I know the answer—the pool side. On a level with the top of the hill.

I call to Stein. "Move her to the side away from the hill. Keep the curtains closed and the lights off."

"Breed." Stein's voice echoes from the top of the stairs. "I sense this control thing is an issue for you."

Robyn's whisper carries down the stairs. "How long have you two known each other?"

35

PUZZLES

Falls Church
Saturday, 2300

I climb the stairs and call out. "Man on the floor."

"We're in here, Breed."

The second floor is dark. Stein took my warning seriously. I look left and see a bedroom overlooking the pool. As I expected, the hilltop looks straight into the bedroom's windows. To the right is another bedroom. The door is open. The floor is lit by a dim nightlight.

Inside, I find Stein and Robyn sitting on the floor, their backs to the wall. Stein has taken off her suit jacket, exposing a SIG P226 Legion in a hip holster. The MP5 rests on the floor by her right hand.

Robyn is barefoot, wearing her digital camouflage pants, and a white t-shirt.

"Here you go." I hand them each a cup of coffee.

"Thanks," Stein says. "What about you?"

"Had some. Adcox ran through the comms with me again."

Robyn looks exhausted. She has not recovered from her overdose. "You never stop moving, do you, Breed."

"In this business, people who sit still get killed."

I sit on the floor across from the women. Lean against the bed.

"What did they have on Lopez?" Stein fumes. "Are we to believe that the Taliban and Al Qaeda had him on their payroll the whole time? If that's true, he was working for them long before Grissom's operation went live."

"Yes. If that's the case, what was he *doing* for them all that time?"

"After our last conversation, I checked everyone on the team." Stein ticks them off on her fingers. "I know you don't like each other, but Koenig is clean. A solid performer. Not the best at anything, but a solid, middle-of-the-road kind of guy. Competent at direct action."

"The general wouldn't tolerate incompetence."

"Lopez had nothing in his record other than the usual bar fights and drunk and disorderly charges. He was another solid performer, albeit something of a blunt instrument."

"That," I say, "makes him the perfect person to task to kill people."

"And our government did. Many times. Before Captain Koenig punched his ticket, Lopez scored an impressive number of notches on his gun. All enemy combatants. He has a long list of decorations."

"Earned for doing the kind of stupid things society considers brave."

"You have your share," Stein says. "Which we won't get

into. Ballard is odd. He's as you described him. A nerd who built his own radios and rocket ships in school. Joined the army, where his skills were enhanced. So he could do things bigger and better, all the while killing our enemies. None of which bothered him in the least. His fitness reports are good, but he's something of a sociopath. He looks at everything as a game, dissociates from real-world consequences."

"I get that feeling around him." The room is cozy. I can see Robyn's eyelids drooping. She's ready to fall asleep.

"Takigawa is the most interesting of the lot. He is a loose cannon. Spent time in the stockade for assaulting civilians. Seems he was in a bar in Fayetteville and some good old boys made racist remarks. He says one of them tried to brain him with a whisky bottle, then attacked him with a knife. Takigawa broke the man's arm, then assaulted the man's four friends, put three of them in the hospital. Claimed he was defending himself."

"I'm sure he was."

"So am I. His stripes need Velcro, they've been on and off his sleeves many times. He has problems with authority and was quietly asked to leave Delta. But—he continued to operate in Special Forces. Well regarded by everyone he's served with. Except for a handful of officers."

"The perfect Tier 1 operator."

"The point is," Stein says, "the men General Anthony sent on that mission were elite operators, every man a patriot. That leaves us with conspiracy theories. Neoconservative warmongers. The military-industrial complex."

I shake my head. "Doesn't sell, does it?"

Stein closes her eyes. Rests the back of her head against the wall. "No. I couldn't sell it to myself drunk."

Robyn is fully awake again. I turn to her. "Robyn, something Zarek said has bothered me."

"What's that?"

"At the campfire. He claimed the US was attacking his caravans three times more often than Shahzad's. What's the story?"

"Zarek's caravans have been shredded the whole time I was there. One of Zarek's lieutenants, Dagar, told us what happened to caravans he led. On the way south, the ANA ambushed them. He lost a quarter of the guns and explosives he was carrying. Had to disperse his men and reassemble in Kandahar. On the way home, he carried opium. Gunships attacked him north of Wanat and destroyed a third of his load. Killed many good men."

"Was that a regular occurrence?"

"I think so. A few months later, another good guy, Adim Fazili, was wounded leading a guns caravan south."

I find it jarring to hear Robyn speak of drug runners as "good guys."

"I checked on that," Stein says. "Pulled every piece of intel from CIA, State, and the Pentagon. There is no data to substantiate Zarek's claim. Islamic leaders are notorious for hyperbole. Zarek is no exception."

"I believe him."

"So do I," Robyn says.

"What if it is true?" Stein frowns. "It might be due to some operational difference between Zarek and Shahzad."

"My head hurts." I get to my feet. "I'm going for a coffee."

36

ON THE X

**Falls Church
Saturday, 2345**

I go down the stairs and look into the kitchen. The garish light from the pool deck floods the space and casts long shadows across the walls. I turn left, go into the library.

Adcox sits at the library table, cleaning his SIG P226. His MP5 lies next to the laptops. Franz sits in the living room, reading a magazine. His submachinegun rests on his lap. The curtains are drawn across the picture windows, and the lights have been dimmed.

"Anything going on," I ask.

"All quiet," Adcox says.

I stand behind him briefly, look at the monitoring screens. The cameras show no unusual activity. A pickup truck drives past the camera positioned at the main road. The motion sensor oscilloscopes show flat lines.

The house is quiet. I walk into the living room.

Standing to one side of the picture windows, I part the curtains and peep outside. The SUVs are parked in a line across the front of the house. In a firefight, their armor will afford the house some protection. They also make it impossible for an attacker to ram a vehicle through the front door. Nellis paces between the vehicles and house.

I let the curtain fall back and return to Adcox's side. Scan the displays again.

Something's wrong.

A pickup truck drives past the camera monitoring the road.

Again.

The same truck, in the same direction, at the same speed.

"Shit."

"What's wrong?" Adcox straightens.

I point to the video of the truck. Passing, over and over. "They've hacked the system. It's playing the last minute on a loop."

Radio to my ear, I key the mike. "Spider Two, this is Black Widow."

Jimenez does not respond.

I reach for the house mobile phone. Clench it in my fist.

A splintering crash shakes me—Hard as a physical blow.

Struck by a battering ram, the front door bursts open. Three men wearing balaclavas and Kevlar vests force their way into the living room. They carry suppressed H&K MP7 submachineguns. Small caliber, high-velocity weapons specifically designed to penetrate body armor. On a proportional basis, the tiny 4.6 mm cartridges pack as much propellant as an assault rifle. High penetrative ability, extremely high cyclic rate of fire. Each burst slaps three or four rounds through the same hole to get the kill.

The men navigate the living room like they know where we are. They must have killed Nellis and Orcel. Used thermal imaging to ascertain our locations before breaching the door. The first man through fires two bursts in quick succession. Franz dies where he sits.

I dive for the kitchen doorway. Hear the MP7s firing. Forty-round mags, high burst rates. The suppressors can't mask the sonic booms of the high-velocity slugs. Crashing behind me, bullets shatter laptop screens and riddle Adcox.

Through the doorway. I crouch and flatten myself against the wall.

Hold my breath. The killers drop their mags and reload. I hear the metallic clack of bolts slamming home.

An MP7 is fired through the wood, scattering splinters and bits of drywall over me. Had I been standing, I'd have been shredded.

The shooter rushes through the doorway, leads with his weapon.

That's a mistake. I grab the muzzle of the gun with my right hand, force it away from me. The man fires, and the bullets splinter the bottom step. I slash my left hand over the top of the gun, club him across the throat. With one blow, I smash his larynx. Cartilage and soft tissue collapse. Cervical vertebrae crack. The gunman drops like a stone.

I twist the MP7 from his hands, scramble for safety.

"Breed, get down."

Stein's voice. I throw myself flat against the stairs.

There's a short burst of popping sounds. Stein's small-caliber MP5 on full auto. I look back. The burst caught the second attacker in the chest, knocked him down.

"Go," Stein urges.

I get to my feet, make it to the landing. The man Stein shot gets to his feet, charges the stairs again. His armor saved him. He fires and I flatten myself on the floor.

Stein learns. Empties the MP5 at the attacker's legs, riddles his thighs and knees. He screams and falls.

I shove the MP7 and mobile phone into Stein's hands.

"Take Robyn," I say. "Call for help."

Stein hits a speed dial. The QRF out of Quantico. The clock starts ticking. Twenty minutes before any hope of rescue.

I draw the Mark 23 from my waistband and turn.

The third attacker at the bottom of the stairs drags his wounded buddy out of the way. Raises his MP7 and unloads on me. The high-velocity bullets splinter the wall above the landing.

I look through the bedroom door. It's a fifteen-foot drop from the second floor. Stein helps Robyn out the window, uses the MP7's sling to lower the girl a couple extra feet so she can jump.

Stein calls to me. "Breed."

"Go," I tell her. The attacker downstairs is changing out his mags. I fire two quick rounds, trying for head shots. He ducks back into the library, charges his weapon, and attacks.

The man unloads on me again, climbs the stairs as he fires.

I duck into the bedroom. Filmy curtains blow in the wind. Stein and Robyn are gone. I slam the door shut, lock it. The man kicks at the door. I raise the Mark 23, fire through the wood at face height. *Miss.*

There is a sound like tearing cloth as the MP7 cuts loose. The door splinters and I hit the floor as armor-piercing rounds thrash the air over my head. I fire back through the holes in the door. No effect. I'm pounding lead into armor. The gunman turns his weapon on the lock.

I swing a foot out the open window, go through it as the lock is shot away. The man crashes through the door. I jump.

In the air, falling. Fifteen feet. Equivalent to a fully loaded combat landing. I hit the lawn, crumple and roll. The world whirls around me.

The gunman leans out the window, looks for an angle.

On my back, I stare at him. The MP7 is pointed straight at me.

I'm dead.

A burst of fire. Stein's captured MP7 is a great equalizer. Armor-piercing rounds shred the man's Kevlar. In less than a second, Stein pumps a dozen bullets into his chest. He jerks like a puppet, drops his weapon, and falls back into the room.

Another gunman, MP7 raised, rushes around the side of the house.

Robyn stands flattened against the outer wall. In her two hands, the axe. With all her strength, she brings the blade down on the gunman's head.

Whack.

The sound of the axe slamming into a solid object. The gunman collapses face-down on the lawn. Robyn plants a foot between his shoulder blades, hauls with all her strength. The curved blade, buried in the meat of the killer's brain, catches on his shattered skull.

Robyn works the axe handle forward and back. Grinding, crunching sounds. A mighty tug, and the axe head comes free. Blood, pulp, and fragments of bone spatter the girl's arms and face.

I get to my feet, stuff the Mark 23 into my waistband,

and take the dead man's MP7. Loot his vest for spare 4.6 mm mags. He has six. I stuff three in my pockets, hand three to Stein.

"That's twice you've saved my life," I tell her.

We're standing at the side of the house. The pool and hill are on the opposite side. Tennis courts are to our right, the front of the house to our left. There are woods on this side, about fifteen feet away.

At least six attackers. Three inside the house. Two dead, one wounded... assuming Stein did not hit his femoral artery. One more dead outside, his head hacked in two. They must have killed Jimenez. I assume one more shooter on the hill with a long gun. Another in their vehicle, operating the ECM they used to disable Stein's technology.

I wave to Robyn. "Let's go. Into the woods."

Inside the tree line, we sit in a huddle of three. Stein and I sit back-to-back. Robyn sits with her back to both of us. She clutches the axe to her chest, shaking.

"Is Quantico on the way?" I ask.

Stein holds the MP7 in one hand, mobile phone in the other. "Yes. ETA ten minutes."

"Okay, we sit tight. If anything moves, kill it."

TWO BLACK HAWKS carrying two dozen armed men descend on the property. The QRF clear the house and dispatch hunter-killer teams onto the hill and into the woods. They find Adcox and all his men dead. Jimenez, Nellis and Orcel were killed with silenced subsonic pistols.

At the house, the QRF finds three dead assassins and one wounded. They call for medevac.

Robyn sits in the living room, surrounded by burly operators carrying M4s. Stein and I go into the kitchen, the space at the foot of the steps. The officer in command of the QRF is standing over the bodies of two attackers. He nods to us.

I bend and pull the mask off the man I killed. Viscous threads of blood spill from his nose and mouth—my blow tore his trachea, burst the pharyngeal artery, separated his spine. He's swarthy, distinctly Middle Eastern in appearance.

"Run a check on him," I say. "You'll find he's Al Qaeda. A sleeper."

Stein stares at the man she shot in the legs. He's bleeding from half a dozen wounds, including two shattered knees. Bloody chips of bone are visible through the torn fabric of his pants. He's staring at the ceiling, avoiding our eyes. Miraculously, she missed his femoral arteries. She gathers wool in her fingers and yanks off his mask.

Koenig.

I might have guessed. "Captain. Who else was in on it?"

A shake of the head.

"Captain Koenig," Stein says. "You are going to be charged with the murder of five men in my security detail. Quite possibly, as an accessory in the murder of Colonel Grissom. You can help yourself. Tell us what you know."

"Fuck you."

I look sideways at the QRF commander. "I think you should get some air."

"Good idea." The man walks into the living room.

"The captain is a tough monkey," I tell Stein. "He'll go to Leavenworth before he says a word. Let's save the taxpayers the expense."

I chop Koenig under his rib cage. The air leaves his

lungs with a painful grunt. I cover his nose and mouth with my right hand, slam his head back against the floor.

Squeeze.

Koenig struggles. His left hand grabs my wrist, his right reaches for my face. His eyes lose focus.

Before Koenig passes out, I let go. He sucks breath with greedy gulps.

"Tragic," I say to Stein. "The shock, the blood loss. He didn't make it."

I'm not sure Stein believes I'll kill him. Koenig knows me well enough to know I will.

"Okay," he says. "I'll tell you. Everything."

37

WEST WING

White House Sunday, 1400

We stayed in the house all night. Twenty operators on the premises provided security. In the morning, an advance team from State joined us. They closeted themselves with Stein and Robyn for hours. I was left to sit in the living room, to drink coffee, and raid the fridge.

We are driven to the White House in an armored convoy.

I wear a sharply creased black suit Stein prepared for me. I wonder if Stein's sense of fashion admits any color but black. In her dress blue uniform and black beret, Robyn cuts an attractive figure.

Stein leads us to the West Wing.

I'm under no illusions I'm going to meet the President of the United States. Stein went over the morning's agenda with me. We pass the White House Chief of Staff's office, and follow a corridor that looks as functional as any

working office in the Western world. Discreet Secret
Service personnel are everywhere.

Stein leads us to a conference room. Inside, seated at
the table, are General Anthony and two Under Secretaries
of State. The Under Secretary of State for Political Affairs
and the Under Secretary of State for International Security.
Stein introduces us, and we take seats.

We don't have long to wait.

The door opens, and a distinguished man enters. "We're
ready for you now," he tells Stein. "General Anthony,
please wait here with Mr Breed."

The general looks surprised, and a little unhappy. Stein,
Robyn, and the Under Secretaries file out of the room. The
door closes behind them.

I settle back in my chair and look around the plain,
functional space. A conference table with seats for twelve.
Star phone in the middle. Screens for projection briefings.
Wires for laptop connectivity and microphones snake out of
little holes cut into the tabletop.

"It's been a long time since you sent me through those
valleys into Tajikistan, General."

The general looks at me. Tries to gauge whether this is
small talk, or something more serious. "Yes," he says.
"It is."

"Those missions gathered a lot of intel. You told me to
write you the book on smuggling in those mountains. I did.
Chapter and verse. Every player, every route."

"You were characteristically thorough."

"I always wondered what you used the intel for."

"I told you at the time. We used it to interdict opium
and weapons caravans."

"Those of Zarek Najibullah," I say. "Three times more
frequently than those of Abdul-Ali Shahzad."

"This again." Anthony snorts, stiffens in his chair. "I told you, Breed. I don't know that's true. We bomb them where we find them."

I take out a small digital recorder, Stein's, and set it on the table. Press a button. Koenig's voice sounds loud in the quiet room.

It was General Anthony's operation. Shahzad paid him to hit Najibullah's caravans. Air strikes to the north. Gunship attacks and ambushes further south. In some cases, we sold captured opium to the Taliban.

Stein's voice cuts in. "Who else was involved, Koenig?"

I don't know everyone. Not many. The general's adjutant, Colonel Tristan. Myself and Lopez. Tristan was the book-keeper. He handled accounts and logistics. Lopez and I were assigned reconnaissance missions. Sometimes we went in with ground forces to supervise ambushes. The general didn't want too many mouths to feed.

The general has gone white. My stomach is hollow. This man was my commanding officer most of my career. A Tier 1 operator himself, he taught me much of what I know. Right to the end, my hunting and shooting partner.

"It's over, General." I sit ramrod straight in my chair. Look the great man in the eye. "Koenig told us everything. You never wanted peace. The deal with Shahzad was hollow, he was never going to put Al Qaeda in a box. That's why State couldn't accept it. Such a deal would never permit America to withdraw. That's the kind of deal you wanted. You didn't want the gravy train to stop."

"Koenig's lying." The general musters the voice of command. Hard, chiseled, confident. "Lying to save his own skin."

"No, Sir. Stein's team has been busy. Colonel Tristan has been taken into custody. His laptop and phone have been confiscated. No one can function today without an electronic trail. We've found yours. Traced scores of transactions. All linked to accounts the Taliban and Al Qaeda use to launder drug money and pay for arms."

"You can't tie me to anything," the general says. "Because I'm not involved."

"You and Shahzad stonewalled the kind of deal America wanted. When you found out Stein and Grissom had created a back channel to Najibullah, you freaked out. You knew the details of Grissom and Trainor's exfil, leaked them to Shahzad. You wanted Shahzad to kill them, but he got too cute. He decided to keep them alive and use them as bait to lure Najibullah into an ambush.

"The problem was that Stein and Washington demanded action. They wanted a rescue operation. You wanted the rescue to fail, but you had to make it look good. You brought me in, as Stein knew you would. You passed the first test. After all these years, I'm the only one you could get who knows those mountains.

"You couldn't leak the rescue attempt to Shahzad. That would be far too vulgar, and it wouldn't work. If Shahzad knew we were coming, he would move Grissom and Trainor, lay an ambush, and wipe us out. You'd be relieved for the fuckup, and Stein would try another rescue."

"Clearly, Captain Koenig has a talent for fairy tales."

"No, Sir. Every word rings true. Your best course of action was to put Koenig and Lopez on the rescue mission. Their instructions were to eliminate Colonel Grissom. They weren't too happy about it. They joined your scam for easy money, not to kill American officers. But they went along.

"Koenig's initial plan had him and Lopez performing the breach and rescue. Once inside that house, they could get away with anything. But it made more sense for me and Takigawa to go in for the hostages. So Koenig and Lopez had to make their move outside. They exposed the operation by firing on sentries on the upper terraces. Then, in the confusion of our withdrawal, Lopez shot the Colonel. Bad luck—he missed by a couple of inches. Grissom survived.

"Luck washes out. You were lucky Shahzad had SAMs and drove the exfil helos away. He knocked down an Apache, which gave you the perfect excuse to leave us hanging out to dry. Three days and nights on those mountains. Lopez finished the job, pushed Grissom off a cliff.

"But—Grissom and Zarek were careful men. They had a plan. Before he died, Grissom told Koenig that if anything should happen, he had to get Trainor back. Because Trainor *was* the deal. That was the big secret. To this moment, General, you don't know why that girl is the whole shooting match. But Koenig and Lopez knew it wasn't enough to kill Grissom. They had to kill Trainor, too.

"You helped, General. Shahzad couldn't have known our team split up at Lanat. He should have sent his main body after Koenig and Takigawa. I always wondered why he turned his force around and headed back to the village. You tipped him off by radio. That's why Shahzad arranged an ambush to keep us off Shafkat. That's why he rushed his main body back. He thought he could take, or kill, Robyn —before Zarek showed up.

"Lopez suspected. That's why he was extraordinarily careful as we passed the village. He knew he was bottom man on your totem pole. You weren't above sacrificing him to kill us all. The money made the attempt worth the risk, so Lopez tried to kill Trainor at the village. He failed."

Lieutenant General Anthony straightens his tie. "Breed, you are a fantasist."

"It gets better, Sir. When we got back to Bagram, Koenig and Lopez reported to you. Time was running out, so you instructed Lopez to try again. That was a desperate, clumsy effort. When it went bad, Koenig covered your tracks by killing Lopez. I don't think you planned to kill Lopez, but you didn't shed any tears. He wasn't as discreet as the rest of you. Koenig told you Lopez hung a poster of his seven-figure Shelby on the wall. Must have driven you crazy."

The general's unblinking stare tells me everything I need to know.

"I should have suspected Koenig. But he was humping over Lanat while most of the action was going on. You had two killers on that mountain, separated by fluke.

"You were almost out of time. Trainor would be brought back to Washington and kept under CIA protection. You played one last roll of the dice. Shahzad and the Taliban put you in touch with Al Qaeda sleepers in the continental US. You learned through military intelligence where Stein planned to hold Trainor. You sent Koenig's hit squad to take her out."

"Breed, you cannot prove any of this. In the end, it will be my word against those of Colonel Tristan and Captain Koenig. They may have been up to no good, but I knew nothing of their activities."

"That will be up to the court-martial to determine, Sir. Way above my pay grade. Stein has turned over all her evidence to the Provost Marshal General and CID."

The general refuses to break. I search his eyes, listen for a quiver in his voice. Nothing. Only the faintest darkening of his tanned features.

"Another battle," General Anthony says. "I'll kick their ass in court. A jury of my peers won't convict me. Why did they send you in here?"

"I told them you'd do the honorable thing."

"What's that, Breed?"

"Confess. The Judge Advocate General will cut a deal."

"Not a chance. How about a different kind of deal, Breed?"

"I don't know what you mean."

"I didn't expect you to get Grissom and Trainor out of those mountains." General Anthony's gaze is hypnotic. "But you always had to be the nastiest shark swimming through the guts."

"Sorry to disappoint, General."

"Not at all—you have affirmed my judgement. It was you, after all, who wrote the book. I'll beat this at trial, and we'll rebuild. You can be my number one."

"General, no matter the result, they will never reinstate your command."

For the first time, the general looks away. We both know his career is over. The question is whether he will spend the rest of his life in prison. "I taught you the value of cut-outs. They'll never find all the money."

"I wouldn't bet against them."

"They expect you to get me to cooperate."

"It's the smart play. There are officers from the Provost Marshal and CID in the hall right now."

The general stiffens. "I think you'd better leave."

"Yes, Sir." I get to my feet and walk to the door. Hesitate, face the general. "It has been an honor to serve with you."

I step through the door and close it behind me. MPs and CID warrant officers are waiting in the corridor. I nod to the officer in charge and walk to the exit.

From the conference room, a shot rings out.

38

WATCHES & TIME

Joint Base Andrews
Six weeks later

I stand with Robyn on the tarmac at Joint Base Andrews. Robyn is dressed in civilian clothes. An army rucksack is slung over her shoulder. A small suitcase rests at her feet.

Robyn squints at me. "You were right."

"What about?"

"I killed two men, didn't feel a thing."

I search her eyes.

Robyn looks thoughtful. "I felt more shooting a deer than the Tali in that riverbed. The deer wasn't trying to kill us."

"You do what you have to do."

"Yes. Both times, I had a decision to make…"

"And there was only one correct decision?"

Robyn smiles. "You've been there."

"Yes."

"It isn't adrenaline, is it?"

I frown. "No. Too much adrenaline hurts performance. You'd be jumpy, your hands would shake. You would lose situational awareness."

"Breed. When I picked up the rifle, swung the axe—*I was in the zone*."

"In combat, that's where the best live." I set my hands on my hips. "Be careful—it's addictive."

Together, we look at Stein's caravan of Suburbans. The CIA operators who drove us to the airfield. Stein stands at an open passenger door, a squad radio to her ear. She signs off and walks toward us.

"You call your mother?" I ask Robyn.

"Yes. Mom accepts my decision."

"She doesn't mind you and Zarek?"

"It isn't her choice." Robyn shrugs. "I want to live with Zarek in the mountains. Where the sky is midnight blue. Where the air is so thin, you can see stars in daylight. I am *not* going home to some stultifying civilian job. Commuting from a tiny apartment to a tiny cubicle. Shuffling papers, drinking bad coffee."

"Zarek's a drug runner."

"He makes me feel beautiful. I love him."

I think she does.

Stein approaches, radio in hand. She addresses Robyn. "You'd better get aboard. My people will meet you at Durango."

"Thank you, Ms Stein." Robyn shakes Stein's hand. Turns to me. "Breed, 'thank you' doesn't cover it."

Before I can answer, Robyn throws her arms around me. Hugs me with such force, I feel like our bodies are going to melt together. Helpless, I return the embrace. Look over her shoulder at Stein.

When Robyn releases me, her eyes are wet. "Come visit," she says.

Jealous of Zarek, I shake my head. "You're going back to a civil war."

"Yes, and we'll win. Someday you and Zarek can hunt ibex together."

"I'd like that."

Robyn wipes her eyes. Suitcase in hand, she walks to the waiting Globemaster. She looks back once, then disappears aboard.

"You think she'll be happy in those mountains?" Stein asks.

Stein is dressed in her signature black pantsuit. Straight as a blade, hair brushed, eyes shielded by dark designer sunglasses.

"It's what she wants."

"Can't believe Robyn's mother is okay with her being second wife to a Mujahedeen warlord."

I lift an eyebrow. "Can't you? Robyn's mother was Iranian. She may have married a Christian, but I'm sure she accepts Islamic norms. Robyn didn't seem to struggle with the decision. Besides, Zarek is more than a warlord. He's leader of the faithful."

I don't like long goodbyes. I turn and start walking to Stein's caravan.

Stein falls in step beside me. "Six weeks, and my house is still a mess. Help me straighten the place?"

I should have guessed. The pool was designed for workouts. Stein probably swims two hours a day, runs cross-country in the hills. "Are you rich?"

"Yes."

"How rich are you?"

"My grandfather gave the Stein Center to Harvard."

Another piece of data for the file.

"I'll help if you have food in the fridge."

"Done." Stein looks back at the C-17 taxiing to the runway. "Robyn and Zarek better stay together long enough to lock in the deal."

I lift an eyebrow at the darkness in Stein's tone.

"The Mujahedeen have a saying," I tell her.

"Oh yeah?"

"You have the watches, we have the time."

The End

ACKNOWLEDGMENTS

This novel would not have been possible without the support, encouragement, and guidance of my agent, Ivan Mulcahy, of MMB Creative.

I would also like to thank my publishers, Brian Lynch and Garret Ryan of Inkubator Books for seeing the novel's potential, and taking a chance.

Thanks also go to Jodi Compton for her editorial efforts, and Claire Milto of Inkubator Books for her support in the novel's launch.

Not the least, I wish to thank members of my writing group, beta readers, and listeners, who support my obsession with reading every word of a novel out loud in pursuit of that undefinable quality called voice.

If you could spend a moment to write an honest review on Amazon, no matter how short, I would be extremely grateful. They really do help readers discover my books.

Feel free to contact me at cameron.curtis545@gmail.com. I'd love to hear from you.

ALSO BY CAMERON CURTIS

DANGER CLOSE

(Breed Book #1)

OPEN SEASON

(Breed Book #2)

TARGET DECK

(Breed Book #3)

CLOSE QUARTERS

(Breed Book #4)

BROKEN ARROW

(Breed Book #5)

WHITE SPIDER

(Breed Book #6)

BLACK SUN

(Breed Book #7)

Published by Inkubator Books
www.inkubatorbooks.com

Printed in Great Britain
by Amazon

36127294R00189